SOMETHING LEFT UNDONE

VICKI KINZIE

Something Left Undone

Vicki Kinzie

Published by RavenTricks, Longmont, CO

Project Management and Book Design: Davis Creative, LLC / CreativePublishingPartners.com

Publisher's Cataloging-in-Publication
Names: Kinzie, Vicki, author.

Title: Something left undone / Vicki Kinzie.

Description: Longmont, CO : RavenTricks, [2025]

Identifiers: LCCN: 2025923541 | ISBN: 9798987720523 (paperback) | 9798987720530 (ebook)

Subjects: LCSH: Detectives--England--Cornwall (County)--Fiction. | Murder--Investigation--England--Cornwall (County)--Fiction. | Women physicians--England--Cornwall (County)--Fiction. | Ghosts--England--Cornwall (County)--Fiction. | Storms--England--Cornwall (County)--Fiction. | Nightmares--Fiction. | LCGFT: Detective and mystery fiction. | Historical fiction. | BISAC: FICTION / Mystery & Detective / Historical. | FICTION /Ghost. | FICTION / Mystery & Detective / Supernatural.

Classification: LCC: PS3611.I669 S66 2025 | DDC: 813/.6--dc232025

The Unquiet House

The unquiet house creaks
Demands for attention.
Something has been left undone
That leaves unquiet ghosts
Who haunt through doors and walls
With chills and
Moans and spectral mists.
Burrowing-in, creating
Terrifying dreams that are
Furious cries for
Justice.

Vicki Kinzie

Chapter One

Jory Moon stood on the sea wall looking from the bay back to Woodcomb. He felt an ominous shadow dropping round his village not totally explained by the gathering black clouds. He'd been prowling, mindful of everything from top to bottom. He could smell the coming rain and felt the heavy air, but there seemed to be something more in the air. He walked the seawall, watching the tide fight its way into the bay. A north wind drove across the moor and down through the village and harbor, swept out over the bay, pushing against the powerful incoming tide. The battle formed choppy waves large enough to crest. Some vague threat crawled at the edge of his mind. He searched all of the small, crescent-shaped village he could see from the sea wall, as it stepped down the steep hillside, stopped only by the edge of the bay, each house and business properly facing the sea, which fed the lot of them. Dark clouds chased the dusk into a premature night and menaced the early risen moon.

Jory had watched fishermen worrying their dock lines, double-checking everything before heading home. Walking back, he stopped beside his Uncle Denzel, a skipper of one of the fishing boats, the last man still on the quay who mumbled to Jory, "Glad I'm home and done." His lined leathery face cracked into a smile for his favorite nephew. They both silently, automatically named each boat reassuring themselves that all Woodcomb's fishermen were home safe tonight. The two men watched the chop build out in the bay for a couple more minutes before his uncle said, "Think this one's gonna blow up a real hooligan."

Jory nodded agreement, and his uncle slapped him on the back and left him alone on the seawall. Reckoning the weather can mean life or death here. For centuries men had sailed out and fished in their unique Cornish luggers with their distinctive red sails. Now the fleet had engines, but the men still worked night and day hauling nets and lines. Being wet and cold meant nothing. To feed their families they stayed out in pretty rough weather. Jory knew the hardships personally. He had been sent to learn the trade with his uncle at fourteen. Enduring four years fishing convinced him to become a policeman instead. Tall, lanky and quick witted, although just past thirty, Jory had become the detective constable of his little village, as well as protecting the south coast of Cornwall during the Great War, after his boss passed away. Jory was very young to have such a position. Others fought on battlefields leaving him this responsibility.

A warm yellow light shone briefly from the Badger, the pub on the quay, as Uncle Denzel entered, and a well-dressed man stepped out with a hearty greeting, nearly knocking into Denzel as he passed. The lord of the manor, a man gone to flab in his early sixties, had a thick thatch of grey hair, and a perpetually red face from a lifetime of drinking. Oddly, he wore his riding outfit and expensive black boots at this hour. He climbed onto his magnificent Arabian gelding named Asif. Spotting Jory returning from the seawall, he nodded briefly with a sheepish smile before riding up the street— away from the manor house, Jory noted. Jory had been assured by Ham's sister, Merryn, who knew everything about the place, that some still found the randy old goat to be attractive. Apparently being squire of the manor improved his charm. DC Moon continued to prowl, unable to rid himself of his itchy uneasiness.

At Tredwen Manor, Lady Edra, Sir Vinson's daughter, sat engrossed in another delicious novel involving romance and tragedy, unaware and uncon-cerned about the weather. Twenty-nine, tall and thin, her long gold colored hair fell forward as she read, curled up in a huge wing chair, reading by the firelight before her father returned. He disapproved of her novels, saying she lived in a fantasy world. Wrapped up in the adventures of a wretched heroine in need of her pirate, she remained ignorant that outside the stone walls of the manor a rising wind blew a deep blackness across the sky. Her peaceful quiet exploded with sudden, frenzied high-pitched barking and frantic howling of the dogs outside. Fear gripped her. A horrible memory of the same eerie, unnatural sound from the dogs flashed. The book fell from her lap as she bounded from her chair.

"My God, he hunts here again," Lady Edra thought listening for the dogs as she ran. Completely forgetting she wore no shoes, her feet pounded on the oak floorboards down the long corridor and into the conservatory. As she burst through the door, the wind slammed into her. She shouted, "Sheba, come! Blue, here boy! Oscar!"

She knew the dogs would attempt their escape at the gate near the stream. The last time the fiend drowned Lucie, poor besotted hound. Lady Edra tried to blank out that memory and concentrate on saving these dogs. She knew Dando had returned from hell on his fire breathing horse, followed by unsaved souls in the form of demon dogs craving blood. If Kitto left the gate unlatched again, the dogs were doomed. Rounding the ancient oak in a headlong dash, her long hair streaming behind in turbulent confusion, she shouted before they came into view. "Oscar, Blue come! Sheba, no! Come, girl! Stop!" Sheba can turn the others. They would be lost forever if the fence didn't hold them. She spotted the dogs as she cleared the end of the stone wall. Three dogs jumped desperately at the gate, or dug furiously in a mad frenzy to join the demon's wild hunt. She flailed her arms and screamed in a panic to quiet them, yet not knowing how. Grabbing Sheba's collar, she nearly strangled the beautiful pointer before she could hold its gaze. She spoke words into Sheba's ear as calmly and quietly as she could.

"No, Sheba, quiet. No. Sssh. You must listen." Sheba's eyes cleared for a moment and she whimpered, wagging her whole body apologetically. Holding Sheba's collar, Lady Edra tried kicking lightly at the other two to break the spell. The cacophony stopped. But the dogs only watched the tree line not a hundred yards away, noses sniffing. She knew Death had come galloping along the stream bank, leading his ghost hounds thirsty to drag down prey. Although she heard only the wind, the dogs heard and listened for the call. In the startling silence, she braved a glance toward the stream. Tall old willows lined both banks of the stream all the way through her land. Beyond the far bank, the full moon, not yet eclipsed by black rainclouds, bathed the field stubble in golden light. Even the darkling woods beyond, just past the edge of the property seemed a bit brightened by the moonlight. Menadue Wood. It had always scared her, and now as she held and patted Sheba, they darkened. A menacing blackness moved across the field with terrifying swiftness toward the stream. Her heart pounded. Although no one ever believed her, Lady Edra remembered the rare murderous excursions. Huge willows next to the stone bridge began to sway first, as if a terrific storm tossed their heads about. The dogs saw it. They broke and ran down the fence row that paralleled the stream, howling, barking and whining frantically, searching for a way through the fence. Sheba tore off her collar and soon led the others. Lady Edra held her breath, watching the whirlwind move downstream exciting the next trees as the first ones calmed. A desperate mother otter clawed frantically toward the fence line, shepherding twin youngsters away from their stream home. Birds flew screeching from the willows. Something would die tonight, ripped apart in a gory feast. Last time it struck down her beautiful pointer, Lucie. They found the dog's body the next morning dashed against the rocks at the bottom of the cliff. The strong, cold wind of death slammed into her. Its brutal atmosphere overwhelmed her, filling her mind with its bloodlust. She had sworn to be brave this time, but stopping the dogs now was hopeless. They had been summoned and would go if they found a way. She fled terrified toward the safety of the house, chased by the menace whispering in the wind. As she climbed the conservatory steps, a terrifyingly cold blast caught her, knocking her down, smashing her head against the rock wall. Her hair and dress blew straight up, furious to join the whirlwind. Just as suddenly, the air quieted, leaving her lying still on the stone steps dripping blood from her head.

Jory's endless patrol had led him back to the quayside. He held his hat on against the cold breath of the sudden angry windstorm hurtling down each street, blowing past him out to sea. The rain started at the same instant he spotted Keyan, the odd little gypsy lad, always in inappropriate places at inappropriate times, turn down the street and run in his direction. Why wasn't he home with his grandmother having his dinner like all the other children? The lad collapsed in front of the Badger. Jory ran to him and found him having another one of his fits. Gathering the lad in his arms, he pulled open the door and stepped into the warmth of the pub. The murmur of voices stopped as he carefully laid the lad on a table. Men picked up their ale and closed in to watch, but none got too close, and none offered to help.

"That's the cursed one, that is."

"Them gypsies'll curse you, they will."

Jory said, "Bring the lad some water, someone."

Only the bartender, Ham, moved and brought a glass of water. He said to Jory, "Maybe a touch of brandy?"

The boy sat up suddenly, staring wide-eyed at nothing. "Evil rules this night," he said in a deep, guttural, unnatural voice. "The Green Man is butchered in a terrible battle by the stream. The Great Horned One and his hell hounds lap up the blood." Then he slumped back on the table breathing easily, asleep.

The men pushed back from the lad. One of them said, "Get him out of here, Jory! He's cursed and sees the devil's visions."

"God give him fits for all to see he's cursed," another man said.

Knowing looks passed between Jory and Ham. The same age and friends since childhood, both men found the village superstitions exasperating.

Jory said, "You all sound like a bunch of old ladies..."

"Fire!" A man burst in screaming. "Abe Court's place is burning!"

Chairs scraped when men jumped up shrugging on coats, and boots thumped on the pub's plank floorboards as men ran to help, shouting questions while they pushed through the door, followed by Ham and Jory. The boy and his visions, curses and the devil were all abandoned to help a neighbor.

A couple of minutes later, Keyan awoke, and found himself alone in the silent pub. Barely curious after reawakening once again in strange circumstances after a seizure, he got up, scooted off the plank table, searched in vain for any change dropped, and drank everything left behind, before heading back outside. His young life had been a series of blank periods followed by people being frightened and repelled by him. Other children avoided him or tortured him with laughter and taunts. A story so familiar, he spent no time wondering why he found himself alone in a pub. The wind tore the door out of his hands, and it slammed against the wall. He struggled to latch it before leaving. He turned toward the sound of shouting men and the insistent clamor of the fire engine bell, and watched flames jutting out windows turn the rain to steam while the wind howled round them all. He dreaded crowds and just wanted to get away from the village, and struggled against the wind and rain toward home, across the bridge out of Woodcomb, where no one called him names or feared him.

Geran clutched his suit coat closer as the storm intensified. *Why is no one coming this way who could give me a ride? Because of my bloody bad luck, that's why. Why didn't I wait for morning to start walking? Because I don't have two shillings to rub together. I'd be sleeping somewhere this side of Saltash under a dripping tree getting soaked anyway. And besides, this bloody storm materialized out of nowhere. I'm not a mile from home now and then safe and dry.*

But the closer Geran got to Woodcomb, the night itself seemed to take on a heaviness full of rejection and hatred directed at him. It seemed the whole countryside knew his business and shunned him. The feeling had grown as he neared Tredwen land. Each dark farmhouse recognized him and seemed to turn a cold shoulder, protecting its own, radiating animosity towards him, whispering, laughing, confident that such a foolish plan as his would fail. Each house seemed more sinister. He remembered past humiliations from some of them. He tried to shake off his dejection and anxiety. "I swore never to return—but I have to. Once done—I'm gone. But I will tell them what I know now to be true, and shove it in their dim-witted faces." No light shone from any window in any house. No warmth. He pictured the superstitious clods clutching each other, quaking, hoping evil passed them by this night. He knew their ways on nights such as this. He grew up knowing the same superstitions. He told himself that explained these ridiculous feelings. That and the fact that the feelings came from being bone tired and wet and cold.

The fierceness of the storm abated suddenly, and he stopped, puzzled by the near silence. He heard only raindrops dripping from trees. He shuddered as he realized he stood in the middle of Menadue Wood, a terrifying place every child learned about from spooky tales about ghosts or the devil or witches kidnapping children, tales never fully outgrown. Ancient trees formed a canopy creating a sinister tunnel across the road. Heart pounding, Geran picked up his pace hurrying through the bower.

Forty yards ahead, the other side of the wood, a clap of thunder and a jolt of lightening briefly revealed the black outline of a figure clutching a pitchfork, holding tines upright in its right hand, awaiting him. A vision of the devil. Geran gasped. Straining to see again, he saw nothing. "Of course, it's nothing, you pratt." Yet he felt a chill, a nearly overpowering dread. No one expected him. Seven years ago, he ceased to exist around here. The fury of the storm hit him again as he left the thick wood, and he pushed against the fierce wind, his body at an angle.

There. Someone standing just the other side of the bridge—not Satan with a pitch fork. A hooded figure held something. It waited, watching the road. The figure radiated malevolence. Geran shook off such nonsense, yet he halted twenty feet away, with only a small, stone bridge marking the corner of Tredwen Manor itself, separating them. The shadow person stood its ground waiting. A sentinel forbidding entry onto the manor. An irrational notion flashed to him that a sacrifice was needed, and he had been chosen. Bone deep, old ways resurfaced, even after all his years away from this godforsaken place. A shiver, not entirely a result of the cold, ran through him as he forced himself to walk across the bridge. He got close enough to see no apparition had appeared from hell. He squinted at someone cloaked in a raincoat with the hood pulled up, leaving only a blackness instead of a face. Geran attempted a weak smile, but the person's face became a horrid grimace of pure hatred. The monster strode toward Geran raising a spade. Heart pounding, Geran jumped into the ditch hoping to escape, but the attacker jumped down directly in front of him and raised the shovel, slamming it down, slicing through Geran's arm and knocking him to the ground. He had to get up. Another blow sent searing pain across his back. The murderer kicked him over onto his back and stood legs apart at his head and raised the shovel high overhead. Geran's scream pierced the rising cacophony of the storm as he watched the blade drop towards his face. The blade ripped into his brain, ending the nightmare before he could even wonder why. Yet the fury continued, and the shovel fell again and again before the hatred was spent.

Chapter Two

John Ferguson was developing a headache from the sheer nearness to his fellow policeman on this interminable train ride to Cornwall. Dickie hardly deigned to speak to Ferguson, a man he considered a mere peasant. The silence was just fine by John. The smug self-satisfied attitude galled him. Inspector Richard Geever, or Dickie to everyone at Scotland Yard behind his back, had become the lead detective of this murder case. Ferguson's rapidly rising star at Scotland Yard had slowed and dimmed due to his absence battling the Hun during the Great War.

The war to end all wars nearly ended Ferguson, spitting him out close to catatonic at an English mental hospital for wounded soldiers, where he fought valiantly to regain his sanity. He battled shellshock flashbacks to wartime horrors unimagined by most. Released after six months, he had gone home to Scotland where the unwavering support of the village of Ayr, most notably his stalwart mother and his kind father, had fortified him and aided in his recovery. Refusing to surrender, he asserted a claim on the mundane of everyday, the calmness, the quiet of a Scottish town, and he recovered enough for an attempt to resume his old life in London. His return to Scotland Yard had been granted provisionally, and that owing to the support of his influential mentor, Detective Superintendent Alistair Howell. Some pushed back against his return. Lots of men returned from the war with no job. Healthy men who were eager for a chance to become a detective. Howell knew Ferguson had ability, if he could overcome his skittishness, his jumpiness. The higher ups pressured Howell to get Ferguson doing actual detecting or give the job to someone who could. John's mental health improved slowly. Due to pressure from above for a show of real competence, Howell thrust him out onto an important murder investigation in York. He had to either succeed and prove that Howell's faith in him had been justified—or be fired. He succeeded in discovering the murderer, and more importantly, he worked through the mental block causing his flashbacks. After York, he still occasionally fought potent assaults from his damaged nerves, yet he no longer fled reality unexpectedly.

During his absence, Ferguson's office had been given to Dickie. John's return meant the two men now shared the office. Howell's mistake in this case had been dropping by their office instead of calling Ferguson to his own office. Howell needed a very good detective on this strange case and assigned it to Ferguson. However, at the mention of Cornwall, Dickie's birthplace and ancestral home, things became complicated. Dickie, the second son of Lord Geever, Earl of Truro, would inherit nothing from his family's estate. Traditionally some other path must be found for second sons, and apparently Dickie thought being a Scotland Yard detective sounded thrilling. Therefore, he became one. But murder being such a messy business, it came to pass that the earl's second son spent most of his time safely ensconced behind his desk looking at the side of Ferguson's head and chattering about perceived ills and little affronts and gossip. Thus, he became the bane of John Ferguson's life whenever he must be in the office. Thankfully, for the most part Ferguson was dispatched on actual crimes.

Upon hearing of the case in Cornwall, Dickie had whined, cajoled and finally threatened to call daddy if not given the lead in this investigation. While John had Alistair Howell, famous detective, as a powerful mentor, Dickie had the ear of Brigadier General William Horwood, Commissioner of the Metropolitan Police—the head of Scotland Yard. It is good to be the second son of an earl. When Dickie finished throwing his pedigree around, Ferguson ended up the subordinate, even though Dickie had never completed a murder investigation—had never solved a murder on his own.

Privately Howell explained to John, "I need you on this, John. The *Daily News* already reported this morning a sensational account of the murdered man giving it supernatural elements, of all things. Such rot is going to get publicity. The public will love it. If not solved, it will become one of those legendary tales with a life of its own, and Scotland Yard will become a laughing stock." Howell assigned John as second instead of sending a sergeant, since he still needed Ferguson to actually solve the murder.

John was thirty, Geever was thirty-two. John was tall and muscular, Geever though nearly as tall was a touch paunchy. John had thick unruly blondish hair, which he tended to comb back with his fingers. Geever had glossy black hair, oiled and combed back to a stylish perfection. John had a thick mustache, a style from his infantry days as captain in the Royal Scots Fusiliers. Geever had a pencil thin mustache, adopted lately in the style of rich young men who frequented cabarets.

The next morning as they boarded the 10 am train bound for Cornwall, John bought a copy of the *Daily News* and found a small article about the murder on page three.

Demon Ride Leaves Murder Victim

A grizzly murder Sunday night near a small village in Cornwall is being claimed by the locals to be the fiendish work of the Great Horned One. An ancient god known throughout Northern Europe since the dark ages by many names, yet no matter his name, the entity's image emerges amazingly consistent throughout time. Announced by the baying of his hounds and the blast of a hunting horn above the cacophony of a gale, a wild rider on a black horse haunts the sky with his hounds. His ride is considered a forecast of misfortune, and he is said to stop either at places where someone has been or shall be murdered. Seen most often in autumn and winter, it was once customary to leave the last sheaf of grain out in the fields to feed his horse. Apparently the Woodcomb villagers failed last night to properly placate this fiend as an unidentified body was found brutally hacked to death near Menadue Wood, known to be where witches of old held unholy Sabbaths.

John shook his head at such fiction and fantasy passing for news. The only facts were that a man had been murdered in Cornwall, and he remained unidentified.

Hours later they passed into Cornwall and John soon delighted in what Geever had identified as Bodmin Moor, a unique and fascinating view flowing by his window. It looked to be fairly flat with undulating dry hills to the horizon dotted with tors, large contorted granite outcroppings. The tors, John thought, looked uncannily like stone sentinels keeping watch over the unique landscape including watching the horses and some grazing black-faced sheep. Cornwall, the land of the ancient King Arthur. He had read that a hundred years ago, along the coasts, wreckers lured ships, in violent storms with beacon fires, to be smashed upon the rocks, so the villagers could reap whatever spoils they recovered from the holds, often leaving sailors to drown, leaving no witnesses to their crimes. This colorful past strewn with legends of a mythical king and pirate exploits found its way into novels. Apparently three nights ago, in a small village on the south coast of Cornwall, a legend came to life and murdered a man. It reminded John when, as a lad, he listened to his mother tell a Scottish version of Cornwall's deadly night rider. Late at night by the light of the fireplace, her somber quiet voice always heightened the thrill of her ghost stories. The midnight flying fiends in her stories were called the Sluagh, a host of unforgiven dead and the most formidable and violent of the Highland faerie people, who would fly low over some lonely crofter's home or small village hidden deep within a glen. Near midnight they could be heard fighting each other and were known to slaughter cats, dogs or sheep with their poisoned darts.

Whitsand Bay lay to the left of them. The closer they got the more Geever got animated about his Cornwall. He explained the tall brick structures seen from the windows on the other side of the train. "They are beam houses and stacks from tin and coal mines—many now abandoned." He became silent. "Only the knockers left, eh?" Geever observed wistfully.

"The knockers?"

Geever explained, "A superstition of ignorant miners—and foolish little lads. Men on our estate believe that knockers are troublemakers in mines, causing injury and catastrophe when not properly placated. They can be heard knocking through the rock. Food is left for them at night. When a mine is played out, only the knockers remain."

His wistful tone left John wondering if, maybe, the earl's son had been one of the foolish little lads frightened by the story, perhaps told maliciously to terrify the rich man's son by men poorly paid, slogging away in dangerous mines owned by the earl. Or did the men really believe the superstitions?

John thought of the men who had been forced to move their families elsewhere to find work, and had left a lonely cluster of empty, white-washed shacks and huge dinosaur skeletons of rusting mining equipment to slowly collapse. Maybe Geever also thought about them. John watched harvested fields of farmland pass their view, and men harvesting grain, driving huge wagons pulled by strong teams of horses, probably to load on trains. They passed harvested fields with an occasional single shock of grain left near a farmhouse. He wondered if any of them had been left to feed the devil's horse.

"There's Woodcomb." A man sitting across the aisle pointed out the village as they neared their destination. A river emptied its burden of water beside the village that sat crescent-shaped where the bay met the land. Arms of land continued either side of the village, exposing ever higher granite cliffs, until the land turned back either side of the bay. This afternoon the vibrant blue, glittering bay reflected the clear, fall afternoon sky. The pastoral scene seemed perfect, as it often did, belying the horrors that brought strange men in to probe people's secret lives.

Their journey finally over, they left the train with six others. John scanned the crowd hoping a policeman had been sent to pick them up, while Geever fussed with the porter about his three matching cordovan leather bags. A tall young man with light brown hair, wearing a suit, spotted the Scotland Yard men as the only single men not met by friends or family, and approached them. Extending his hand, he introduced himself. "Detective Constable Jory Moon," he said.

"Detective Inspector John Fer..."

Upon hearing this, Geever had whirled around interrupting John with, "Detective Inspector Richard Geever, lead investigator, at your service, and this is my colleague, John Ferguson."

John clenched his jaw, picturing Geever mentally trying out subordinate, fellow worker, assistant and acquaintance before settling on colleague as John's description.

After shaking hands with the two men, Jory Moon said, "Well, let's get going." Ferguson grabbed the murder bag first. Each murder bag Scotland Yard sent contained equipment they might need on an investigation. It included a kit to fingerprint suspects. It also held evidence bags, rubber gloves, tweezers, a magnifying glass, two electric torches and a pair of handcuffs. Next, he picked up his lone cheap, scuffed duffel bag. Geever turned to attempt to pick up his own three bags. Seeing him fumble with them, Moon turned to help him. Geever grabbed the smallest, leaving the constable the two larger ones. Jory Moon piled their luggage in the boot of the police car and asked, "Why did Scotland Yard assume jurisdiction of this case?" as they drove the short distance to the police station.

Ferguson knew it often stepped on toes and rankled when Scotland Yard usurped local authority. He explained, "It's the supernatural implications making headlines in London. My bosses would prefer no lingering, mysterious, unsolved case. It makes us look like there are things we mere policemen can't solve. Bad for you as well. We've merely been sent to help. Your force has the local knowledge and familiarity."

"Woodcomb is a small village, gentlemen, and no one knew this man."

Geever said, "Probably a vagrant then, of no account."

"That seems unlikely. He was well dressed in a nice three-piece wool suit. And the thing is the way he …I mean the savagery of…well, it seems personal. You'll see what I mean."

Ferguson asked from the back seat, "Was he also robbed?"

"We found nothing in his pockets except a train ticket stub from London to Plymouth. He apparently walked from there. He wore a strange medallion round his neck—nothing very valuable. No one saw or spoke to a stranger in or around Woodcomb fitting his description. We're assuming he was on his way here or one of the close villages."

Maneuvering through streets, they passed a building partially devastated by fire. Splintered, blackened timbers reached upward helplessly where much of the roof and most of the upper floor should have been. Tarps covered what remained of the roof. The Crown Inn sign above the double entry, and much of the ground floor remained untouched. "The inn caught fire during the storm Sunday night. Lightening broke a limb off a tree in back, which broke a window tipping over a lantern. Then the wind took it. Thought we were gonna lose the whole place for a while, but well, you see." They turned down an alley and stopped. Officer Moon jumped from the automobile and started for the back door, opened it and waited for them.

"Shouldn't we bring our luggage inside," Geever fussed, looking up and down the alleyway.

"I'm sure it'll be fine for a few minutes, Sir."

Geever reluctantly followed the other two men inside. A lone jail cell sat on the right side of the narrow passage they were following to the front of the office, and what turned out to be the side of DC Moon's office took up the left side. The entire front opened to an open office reception area, with a uniformed man about sixty sitting behind a desk. He nodded politely while Moon offhandedly introduced them, at the same time as he unbuttoned his coat and opened the door to his office.

"This is Constable Piran Crocker," he said entering his office. And over his shoulder, "Detective Inspectors Geever and Ferguson."

They both smiled and nodded briefly to the man, who nodded, and followed the constable into his small office. Moon sat behind his desk. Two straight-backed chairs were pointed to for them to sit in. The overstuffed, small office held several file cabinets, and boxes cluttered the floor. He shouted, "Piran, tea." Then, down to business.

"The body is at the mortuary. I thought I'd take you there first. Then out to view the location where we found the body." He looked at each inspector waiting for comment.

The sergeant brought mugs of tea on a tray with a pint bottle of milk and a box of sugar cubes with its lid ripped off. And one spoon. Geever grabbed the spoon pouring milk into his mug. While he attempted to corral two cubes of sugar from the box onto the spoon, the other two men watched.

Ferguson asked, "Has an autopsy been done?"

Moon tore his attention from Geever's fumbling. "Ah, no. It's pretty obvious how he died."

Successful at last, Geever stirred his tea, set the sugar and spoon back on the tray, and Moon picked up two cubes with his fingers and brushed his hands over his cup. After John added sugar, also with his fingers, and they shared the spoon and stirred their tea, the three men sipped their tea. John noted mementos and a photo of a rugged-faced man in his sixties, wearing the detective inspector insignia on his uniform, smiling and standing next to Moon in a constable uniform.

Moon noticed and said, "I became a constable at twenty-one—minimum age. It's a hell of a lot easier than being a fisherman. That's Samuel Pascoe, a good man and a very good copper. He took to me, and I guess Woodcomb did too. He was a detective inspector, much respected by Truro's chief constable who assigned him the south coast of Cornwall to police during the war. He chose me as his second in command. There's a lot of small villages with constables, but the war brought all kinds of bigger crimes like smuggling, murders, spies. We were in charge of all the major crimes. Lots of excitement. He died four years ago in the middle of it all, and Samuel had recommended me to continue with his duties. He'd made sure I took all my tests and became a detective constable by the time he died. Jory Moon looked between the two men at the constable sitting out front, but the unasked question of why the older man hadn't succeeded his boss remained unanswered.

"Pascoe always called me Jory. I'd been hanging around even before I was old enough to join up. I became a runner for him even at sixteen, following up on things he needed. Everyone in the villages, even the village constables, call me by my first name. I actually prefer Jory, if you wouldn't mind. Everybody calls me that." He looked at the two Scotland Yard men who simply nodded.

Gulping his tea, he said, "Well, if you are ready." They stood and left through the same back door, out the other end of the alley, walking a couple of blocks to the mortuary. As they passed the car bearing the men's luggage, Jory said, "Your things will be fine. The inn is obviously not taking guests at the moment, and I'll take you to where you'll be staying shortly."

At Pengilley Mortuary they were led by a small florid-faced man, introduced to them as Orville Pengilley, to the embalming room behind the public parlor and office building. The body had already been laid out on a steel gurney in the middle of the room. Mr. Pengilley explained, "Jory, I got the body ready cause I reckoned you'd bring the detectives here soon after the train arrived."

He pulled back the sheet revealing a naked, slender man with several crescent-shaped wounds nearly obliterating his face, and more down his chest, some deep, some mere bruises where the weapon hadn't penetrated his suit, and a deep bruise on his right arm. His ribs had a nearly circular bruise. Geever tried to disguise his small gasp by coughing.

Ferguson said, "He appears to be about twenty-five to thirty years old," and looked up to see Jory nod agreement and Geever avert his eyes. "Could we turn him over, please?"

Pengilley pushed the body onto its side, where another crescent-shaped wound had penetrated his left shoulder to the bone. Ferguson asked, "Do you suppose these wounds were caused by a spade? One of the bruises, possibly the one on the arm was probably the first blow knocking him down. Then the spade repeatedly slashed him as he lay prone."

Both Jory and Pengilley nodded. Jory said, "That's what I figure. But virtually every man owns a spade so it doesn't help much."

They gently turned the body and laid it once more on its back. "His skull seems split open here. That could be the fatal blow," Ferguson said. "And this deep bruise on his shoulder looks like a horseshoe print. Possibly a horse trampled him. Either two men were there, or one man with a spade and a horse. It does seem personal. There are way too many wounds to merely stop someone." Ferguson stepped back pondering the hatred involved. "I still would like an autopsy performed. Does Woodcomb have a physician?"

Both men beamed with pride, and Jory said, "We most certainly do, for over a year now, and you will meet her shortly when we go up to the manor."

Pengilley said, "Doc Abby's moving this morning to the dower house since her office nearly burned up in the fire. Already followed up there by some patients."

Jory added, "She lived and worked out of the Crown Inn, and Lady Edra is fixing up the old dower house for her. She's hoping the doc will use it permanently as her surgery and her home."

This surprised Geever. "Your doctor is a woman?"

Pengilley said defensively, "And we are very grateful to have her. She does a great job." He glared at Geever defying him to disagree.

Geever turned away and asked Jory, "Where are the man's personal effects?"

Pengilley brought a pile of clothes from a drawer and set them on a desk. The clothes were bloody and ripped, but nicely folded, and Geever started to examine them. "Not bad tweed—if an unfortunate garish shade of green. Obviously, the man was not a vagrant," he announced, ignoring the fact that Jory earlier came to the same conclusion.

Pengilley set the personal items next to the clothes. They included a used crumpled handkerchief and a train ticket from London to Plymouth, as well as a small medallion on a silver chain, with curious lettering circling a five-point star in the center. The reverse had the same lettering surrounding an eye in the center.

Jory said, "We found the ticket balled up with the handkerchief."

Ferguson said, "It seems the murderer didn't want the man identified, emptied his pockets, but didn't want to touch a handkerchief that had been used. And failed to search thoroughly enough to discover the necklace. Somebody in Woodcomb knows his identity. Perhaps showing people the medallion could help identify him. Does this writing mean anything to you?" He looked to both local men as they shook their heads.

Pengilley said, "Occult something."

Jory said, "What are you talking about, Orville?"

"A pentagram—the devil's symbol. That's what the star is. And the other side is some evil-eye object. Queer hex letters. That there is some kinda magic charm." Pengilley spoke with conviction.

"Oh, you know all about it do you?" Jory asked unconvinced.

"Well, it sure looks that way to me," Pengilley nodded.

But Jory exploded, "What the hell are you talking about?"

"Now, Jory," Pengilley said, "you know that storm was fierce strange. The Crown being set afire, then that gypsy boy—and your own self heard him say in one of his trances that the Green Man was going to kill Dando. Or did he say the other way round?"

Jory looked incredulous, "You're telling me Dando is the dead man?"

Ferguson asked, "Who's Dando?"

Pengilley ignored John. "Well, it was a strange storm, coming from the north and all the rest of it. That's all I'm saying."

"Who's Dando?" John repeated.

"Our dead man wore a green suit. Maybe Dando killed the Green Man," Geever added, causing the three men from Cornwall to stop and look at each other.

"Who's Dando?" John asked again.

Pengilley nodded toward Geever, looking convinced. "Strange isn't it."

Jory shook his head in disgust, "Discounting a couple of myths fighting to the death, Piran and I spent all day Monday and Tuesday asking around—even out to the farms and such. Nobody knows anything. Nobody knows about anybody fighting over anything that they came to blows over. And nobody knows anybody missing. And, the medallion meant nothing to anybody either."

Ferguson then dropped the necklace into his pocket, "We'll keep asking about this." Jory nodded.

John gave up on Dando for the moment. "How did the story get to London so quickly? The murder occurred Sunday night. A London paper printed an article, describing this as supernatural, Monday evening. News travels fast, but not usually that fast."

"I have no idea. Very little news from Woodcomb makes the London papers." Jory said looking towards Pengilley.

"I certainly don't know," Pengilley said indignantly.

Jory turned to Ferguson and said, "Dando is a nonsense superstitious tale! Now can we please get on with this investigation of the death of a very real man, gentlemen?" He turned and walked out of the mortuary. They returned to the car in silence, Jory fuming. He asked, "How did the London paper describe it?"

Geever answered, "That the villagers believe the Great Horned One and his devil dogs were either drawn to an impending murder, or they killed the man during their bloody hunt. Oh yes, this took place in a haunted wood."

"Of course," Jory said as if he expected nothing less. "London writes us up as all a bunch of clods to be laughed at for our ignorance." Then more to himself he said, "A haunted wood, huh?"

Ferguson asked, "How did they get this story? Did your paper run information on Monday about the Sunday night murder? By Monday evening, this fanciful story appeared in print."

"Our news gets printed once a week and doesn't come out until Friday. It's all about births, deaths, who's visiting relatives." Jory shook his head. He had no idea how the story reached the London papers so quickly.

"Now, I'll take you to see where we found his body."

Chapter Three

They drove in silence east across an old stone two-arched bridge at the southeast edge of the village over the river rushing into the bay. Out the right, rear car window, Ferguson saw the east arm of the rugged grey cliff, which rose to over a hundred feet spectacularly from nothing next to the river and extended hundreds of yards before curving out of sight back east. The car took a left fork almost immediately after crossing the bridge, and John lost the cliff view. From the rear seat of the car he noticed a couple of very old stone columns marking an entrance near the right fork.

Jory said, "Straight up that way on the right is Tredwen Manor—less than a mile from the village. We'll go there next. And, Inspector Geever, the dower house is also up there—where you and your luggage will be staying. But first, I'll show you the murder site." Continuing on briefly, the car stopped, and they all got out and looked around. Directly in front of them a small stone bridge crossed a sparkling stream.

"This bridge marks the edge of the manor land, but Tredwen land continues on.

To their right a stream continued through this back edge of manor property and fed the willows growing along it. A sturdy, two-rail fence to which wire had been attached paralleled the stream and the willows. Next to the road, the fence turned the corner and joined the stone fence marking the boundary along the road.

Ahead of the men, the road continued through a sprawling thick wooded area with tall trees on both sides forming a bower. Jory saw them peering at it and said, "That's Menadue Wood."

"That's it! The paper said the man had been murdered near a witch's something or other called Menadue Wood." Geever smiled.

Ferguson glanced at Jory, who shook his head, but said nothing. He asked, "Does the Wood belong to the Bandrys?"

Jory answered, "Probably. It seems to belong to the village. But there is more Tredwen land and farms up that way past the Wood."

The men turned around facing back down the road. "Tredwen land all along on our left?" Ferguson asked him.

"And on the right back to the village." He let them look for a moment.

On their left lay the manor land. A stone fence ran along the length of the left side of the road until the road curved back out of sight. Behind it tall trees and huge bushes blocked much beyond that. Only parts of the roof, that Ferguson assumed was the manor house, were visible from here. A prosperous farm lay directly across the road on his right. "Is that the manor farm?" Ferguson asked.

"It is. Groundskeeper and his family live there." Jory brought their attention to the reason they had stopped there. He walked to the other side of the car and stepped into the ditch next to the Tredwen stone fence. Ferguson followed by jumping into the ditch. Geever started to follow, noted mud on his shoe and stepped back onto the gravel. Jory pointed to an area where the weeds and grass had been flattened and trampled. Bits of dried blood could still be seen.

Jory said, "This is where we found the body. You're welcome to search as long as you want, but I doubt you'll find anything. We searched pretty thoroughly."

Ferguson noticed horse hooves had made impressions near the spot they examined. "Who rode a horse while you searched?" He pointed to the tracks.

"No one. I doubt any curious soul would ride over where a man had been murdered, especially since the general feeling is that something otherworldly happened."

Geever snorted, "Great! A horseman is involved. That should narrow it down to just about everyone around here."

Ferguson picked up a tiny bit of dark grey horsehair from a briar, showed it to Jory, who shrugged and shook his head. Ferguson wrapped it in his handkerchief and continued, "The circular bruise on his back might have resulted from a horse hoof and might explain how his face got so destroyed."

"Who found the body?" Geever asked. Ferguson thought that a surprisingly good question from the self-absorbed man.

"A lad. Lives down there." Jory pointed to a thatch-roofed, dilapidated house on the same side of the road as the well-tended groundskeeper's farm but closer to the village. "He's nine. Keyan. Lives with his grandmother."

"The gypsy boy of whom the mortician spoke?" Geever asked as if this would explain a lot.

"His mother was half gypsy. Mary Inch, the boy's grandmother, married a fisherman from an old Woodcomb family probably forty years ago. Her husband drowned with two other fishermen in a terrible storm, fishing years ago. She's considered a valued friend and neighbor, until something like this happens. Now Mary and Keyan are berated as gypsies. Keyan has spells. Sometimes he just faints, sometimes he mumbles stuff."

Ferguson could tell Jory thought the boy badly treated. "Does he have friends?" he asked.

Jory shook his head. "Kids his age make fun of him. He won't go to school. He goes over to the manor most days, and Lady Edra teaches him."

"A lady would, you know. Take pity on those of such low station in life." Geever's viewpoint.

Jory shook his head. "I don't know. They have a special bond." He climbed out of the ditch, followed by Ferguson who felt they had nothing left to see here.

Standing on the road, Ferguson looked again at how close the lad's home sat to the crime scene. "Explain the incident Pengilley talked about. This is the boy who said something about a murder, which occurred very near where he lives?"

"Sunday evening, as the storm broke, I saw Keyan fall down right in front of the Badger, a pub down on the quay. I took him inside, laid him on a table. Then he sat up and said something about how the Great Horned One would kill the Green Man tonight. Or the other way. Maybe the Great Horned One would die."

"Could he have seen the actual murder? When did the murder occur?"

"Don't know exactly. But he picks up supernatural ideas from Lady Edra. I don't think they mean much. She's been interested in all that strange nonsense for years."

"I'd like to talk to the lad about his story," Ferguson said.

"Sure, when we find him. He's always roaming around. In town or around the manor. His grandmother owns a little pasty shop near the quay and has trouble keeping up with the lad." Jory saw Ferguson looking towards the boy's house. "We can check over there if you wish, but he's probably hanging round the manor and Lady Edra." John nodded his assent, and they got back into the car. Jory turned it around and they headed for the manor.

They passed the two stone columns at the entrance to Tredwen Manor. The cliffs John had noticed earlier paralleled the road briefly as they climbed, engine whining. He saw from his limited back seat view, a pasture fence hug the cliff edge, disappearing around the edge of the cliff as it turned to parallel the English Channel. Watching cows graze near the fence, oblivious to the precipice so near, he wondered if animals were so stupid they would graze themselves right off a cliff, dashing their bodies onto the rocks without man's thoughtful fencing. He concluded they were probably smarter than that as the car crested the hill presenting a rambling, tall, two-story, gray stone edifice perfectly framed by the automobile's windshield. The manor house had been situated to impress guests upon their first glimpse. Two large gables, one at each end, appeared seventeenth century to John. They balanced the indented front entry of the building. Lichen spotted the slate roof, and numerous tall chimneys from three hundred years ago spoke to the apparent age of the building. Large trees grew either side of the road, further focusing one on the manor house. A manicured, broad, green lawn, bordered by intense purple lavender, lay along the drive, which dropped visitors directly in front of the entrance. The drive continued on around and led to impressive barns and stables. Impressive enough for a baron, but the manor lacked being palatial enough for a lord. In fact, it would be embarrassing, if compared to Culzean Castle where John spent much of his youth. Ferguson's father had been ghillie and gamekeeper for the Kennedys, an ancient Scottish family, as his father before him. As John would have become had not Lord Charles, taken an interest in him and given him an education. But most grand homes suffered in comparison to Culzean.

They stopped, and Jory used the iron, lion's head knocker, answered by the snobby looking butler to allow them in. "Morning, Lander. Could we speak with Sir Vinson?"

"I'll see if he's available, Officer Moon," he answered imperiously, disappearing soundlessly into the tomb-quiet building.

As they waited in the front hall, only a clock could be heard quietly ticking. Then a boisterous, red-faced man of sixty, dressed in a three-piece tweed suit, appeared. "So terribly sorry, gentlemen. I hope I haven't inconvenienced you in any way," he said as he approached.

"Quite alright. No problem. I am Detective Inspector Richard Geever, and this is John Ferguson." Another slight, implying Ferguson's subordinate status. John merely shook his head—inwardly.

"Geever? Are you perhaps related to the earl of Truro?"

"Yes. I'm his son."

"Of course you are! I recognize you now. The earl's younger son. Quite the dressage man! Amazing coincidence! I'll be seeing your father this weekend."

"How nice." Geever glanced at John. "Sir Vinson, we have been sent from Scotland Yard."

"Oh, quite. We couldn't help but know of your impending arrival. Such frightful business. In our quiet little village too. Do come in gentlemen. How can I help you?" He led them into a large, bright conservatory filled with plants both exotic and common overlooking a splendid garden on the south side of the property. As subordinate, John enjoyed the freedom to observe the room, the lord of the manor, and the view out the back.

"Lander, coffee please," Sir Vinson spoke offhandedly to the butler as they passed the man, unobtrusively standing against the wall.

Glass enclosed three walls of the conservatory down to knee level, with French windows opening onto a curved stone terrace, leading gracefully down along a stone wall, visually pulling one into the gardens. Many different kinds of trees, arranged to appear natural, were grouped at the far sides. The central garden, charming and rather formal, encompassed well-tended slate pathways, flowers and box hedges, and it seemed designed around one magnificent, ancient oak tree radiant with its scarlet autumn leaves . Obviously, the groundskeeper did an excellent job. The estate terraced down to a livestock fence at the east end of the formal garden. The stream, banked by willows Ferguson had noticed from the murder scene, cut entirely through the property, dropping out of view precipitously off the far cliff creating a distinctly abrupt conclusion to the manor property.

While the two men blathered on about the superb estate, the tasteful room, fox hunting, dressage competitions, and the marvelous coffee once it arrived, Ferguson watched Sir Vinson who seemed a bit nervous, glancing at him while he talked to Geever. Did he spot sweat? Ferguson interrupted, "Sir Vinson, do you have any idea who the murdered man might be?" He liked to see how people reacted to abrupt questions.

A blustery, "Why of course not. That's preposterous. I told Jory, Officer Moon, so yesterday when he insisted I view the disgusting remains. It quite upset me."

"Of course. Such a tiresome request." Geever soothed the man. "However, it couldn't be avoided, I suppose. It is an unfortunate fact that he had to die on your property."

Ferguson gladly allowed Geever to somewhat soothe the man. "But, how can you be so sure you didn't slightly know the man from the village or maybe he was one of your tenants?"

"No one from around here is missing, Mr. Ferguson."

"Inspector Ferguson," John corrected.

"He was a vagrant. We get them occasionally."

"He had on a suit, sir. And a fairly nice if inexpensive tweed. Hardly a vagrant, I think." Geever once again claimed Jory's initial observation. But when that led to more discomfort, Geever again came to Sir Vinson's aid.

"Ferguson, vagrants occasionally get perfectly nice clothes donated by their betters in charity shops or pick them up at jumbles for next to nothing." The two gentlemen nodded slightly to each other.

"Who else lives with you, Sir Vinson?" Ferguson asked.

Visibly relaxing at the new turn in the questions, he replied, "My daughter, and my mother-in-law."

"Could I speak to one of them now, please?"

Geever agreed immediately not wanting to appear second chair. "Yes, Ferguson is right. If not too inconvenient, Sir Vinson?"

"My daughter is not at home at present, but Lady Steren is." He turned, and the properly invisible butler magically appeared immediately and left, dispatched with barely a word. He returned with a request that she meet them in the blue drawing room. The three policemen left Sir Vinson in the conservatory sniffing an orchid.

Lady Steren rose from her chair and greeted them leaning on a silver-handled cane and asked that they be seated. Probably near seventy, John estimated, with grey hair coifed into an elaborate bun, she wore an emerald, floor length dress complete with white lace trim and cameo at her throat. She did not seem in the best of health.

After Jory's introductions, she asked, "How can I help you, gentlemen?" She had a soft, wispy voice.

Ferguson asked, "What do you know of the murder, Lady Steren?"

"I know it was a vicious and terrible act committed by some brute with a hateful and personal vengeance."

"Vengeance? That implies the man was known to someone round here. What makes you think that?"

"From what I know, they found him hacked to pieces. Hardly something a robber would bother doing to a stranger, do you think, Inspector?"

Ferguson nodded, impressed. "Do you have any idea who might have done such a thing or who the victim might be?"

She shook her head, "No, I do not. But I hope you find the fiend who did it and bring him to justice."

Geever jumped into the conversation. "What makes you think this was done by only one man—or indeed—by a man at all?" He looked very pleased with himself.

She furrowed her brow. "From what I know, the bludgeoning eliminates a woman. And it is doubtful two men hated this one man enough to so brutally kill him."

At this stage, John tended to agree with her.

"I'm sorry gentlemen that I can't be of more help." She seemed drained by their brief exchange. "If there is anything I can do, please don't hesitate to ask." Then "Geever, are you . . ."

"Yes, I'm the earl's younger son."

Ferguson asked, "Where is your granddaughter this morning, Madam?"

"Edra? Why she's down in the dower house, I'm sure. You'd never know she'd been rendered unconscious only three nights ago by that horrible storm."

"Rendered unconscious? Did she get caught out in it?" Geever asked.

"She ran out into the storm that had upset her dogs. She adores all the animals. Somehow, she got knocked out. I think Lander, or more probably Marrak, the footman, found her actually bleeding lying against the stone wall in the back garden. She remained unconscious for several hours. We had sent for Doc Abby by the time she came round. When they reached the doctor, they found poor Doc Abby's surgery and apartment had been destroyed by the fire. So, she spent the night with us. All of that seems to be working out. My granddaughter seems fine today. Busy fixing the doctor a place to work as well as live. Sad memories down there. Maybe all the excitement will cheer up the old dower house. I won't be down to see it." She looked at Jory as if he would understand. He nodded to her as Lander reappeared and escorted them out.

"What sad memories?" John asked Jory as they headed for the car.

"Lady Edra had a baby—murdered. Six years ago. Nothing to do with this."

A sharp right turn onto a circular drive about fifty yards from the manor house brought them abruptly in front of the dower house. Unfolding from the rear seat, John chided himself on missing the house entirely while musing about animal-cliff danger. A rather neglected, brick, three-story house faced them. Some sort of ivy enveloped the major part of the ground floor windows, its arms reaching toward the upper windows nearly blinding the ground floor. Parked in front sat two horse-drawn wagons and one odd looking motor vehicle. It had been created by securing a wooden wagon bed behind two enclosed front seats from an automobile. This improbable truck was filled with tools and iron pipes. Standing in front of the dower, Ferguson looked down at the village of Woodcomb. He could see how the village sat at the bottom of the two arms rising either side of it to become cliffs. The arms created a protected bay, and a red-sailed fishing boat could be seen out near the mouth of the channel. Other fishing boats motored into and out of Woodcomb this afternoon. The sun nearly touched the top of the west cliff opposite them.

A powerfully built man with a shock of extremely blond hair stood in the weeds, hacking at the tendons of the huge overgrown hedge engulfing the large bay window to the right of the dower house front door. Dropping the hedge clippers, the man picked up a small axe and glared silently at the policemen before turning back to his work. With a mighty whack he slashed a large arm off of the hedge, which cracked with a scream as it crashed to the ground. Oblivious to the workman, Geever opened the heavy front door, and they were blasted by a surprising amount of noise and activity. They dropped their luggage at the door and looked around. Workmen in heavy boots strode across the English oak floor of the two-story front hall, and two workmen continued up a beautiful stairway to their left that had been carved of the same oak. Paintings of old noble Bandrys, male and female, hung on the wall, each stepping up the staircase. Men worked on the gas lamps either side of a fireplace in a parlor which opened directly to their left, and men hammered and sawed from an open doorway newly cut into the right side of the hall, straight ahead near the end of the hall. The hall ended with a closed swinging door which probably led to the kitchen. A pretty, young woman who looked to be not 20, with red hair curling around her shoulders, came round the corner of the larger room to their right, holding a piece of paper and smiling when she spotted them.

"May I help you?" she asked, seating herself at her small desk perched at the entrance to the room. John thought the people waiting in chairs against the window, where the hedge had just fallen outside, seemed amazingly calm and cheerful, considering the clamor surrounding them.

"We are…" Ferguson started to say.

"Oh, my, but you must be the Scotland Yard policemen, aren't you?" She popped back up and came beaming to shake their hands.

"Doc Abby will be out in a moment. Everything is at sixes and sevens, I'm afraid. They are trying for plumbing at the moment. Indoors. Flush toilet, even a bathtub with heated water. And water in the kitchen turned on by a valve." She seemed less than convinced the attempt would have a favorable outcome.

"I'm the doc's assistant, Sally. Right this way, gentlemen."

She led back into the room she had just emerged from. John thought the room dark and oppressive. The low beamed ceiling that seemed to barely clear the tops of the men's heads added to the general gloominess and feeling of closeness. Through the impressive bay window, behind the people staring at them, more green branches shuddered briefly then disappeared before the axe, yet the light didn't quite dispel the corner shadows or brighten the gloomy room much. Men in overalls hammered, measured and discussed all around them. The people sat meekly cowed and seemed to have been shoved to the edge of the work area in front of the window out of the workmen's way. John assumed they were the doctor's patients and couldn't decide if he thought they found the commotion interesting or mildly annoying. Either way, the policemen presented one more distraction while they awaited the doctor. Geever recoiled as a feverish looking man coughed. He veered to the opposite side of John and quickly pulled out his handkerchief covering his mouth.

A door at the back of the room opened and a striking woman emerged, giving instructions about a small blue bottle of medicine as she handed it to a mother holding her toddler. Looking around she spied the two men and came towards them.

"These here are the Scotland Yard men Jory…Officer Moon, I mean, brought, Doc Abby," the assistant announced.

Geever pushed past Ferguson and the assistant and oozed, "How do you do, Doctor? I'm Inspector Richard Geever and this is John Ferguson," he said dropping his voice when he mumbled John's name.

Pushing a wisp of mahogany curls from her face, which had escaped the coil into which her hair had been twisted, she extended her hand and smiled. "Welcome, gentlemen." Ushering them into her examining room, she closed out a lot of the chaos as she shut the door.

Tall and handsome was John's first impression. She had a confident air as she spoke, "I thought we should meet since we will be sharing the dower house as long as it takes. I hope you can solve this murder." She included Jory, the local man, in her statement which impressed Ferguson.

He glanced around a good-sized room approximately the same size as the parlor on the other side of the central hallway. A small portion of the room had newly built walls to divide it. Ferguson figured it would become her office off the examining room when finished. The larger room looked nearly devoid of furniture. A wall of books against the far wall suggested that very recently this had been the dower library. In her examining room, an old chair had been pushed up to a beautiful ornate desk, and on the opposite wall sat a tall nearly black wardrobe. John thought the furniture probably had been recovered from an attic for the doctor's use. Perhaps the wardrobe had been salvaged from her examining room in the Crown since the open doors revealed shelves half filled with medical needs. Trunks sat on the floor next to the wardrobe. A glance into one revealed more medical supplies. An examining table, obviously also from her office, had been placed in the center of the room with its head against the wall. Another straight-backed chair near the examining table was the only other furniture.

"Yes, we will give it our best professional effort to solve this baffling case." This from Geever.

Ferguson asked, "Have you inspected the body at all, Doctor…?" He felt funny calling her Doctor Abby.

She smiled, "It's officially Doctor Gobnait Maguire. My first name has always been shortened for some reason to Abby, but Doc Abby is just fine with me. And no, I haven't seen the poor man."

"I would like for you to perform an autopsy on the body—today if possible," Ferguson said.

She looked perplexed. "Surely, it's obvious what killed him. Hadn't he been hacked to death?"

"Yes," Ferguson continued, "but we might find other valuable information about him."

She nodded and seemed convinced. "I've never performed an autopsy before, but I suppose I can gauge his last meal, and if he had a heart condition—that sort of thing."

Geever answered, "That's right. The sort of thing we need."

"It's getting late. I promise the autopsy will happen first thing tomorrow. You can see I still have several patients. Walked out here. Putting up with the mess and the noise." As if on cue, a loud bang brought plaster bits about a foot above the floor right behind where the men were standing. Everyone turned to see a hand-auger bore through the wall, then wind back to the other side.

Ignoring the commotion, she said, "Good gracious, Pengilly hasn't embalmed him, has he?"

Jory said, "No, I asked him to hold off, but the body is only getting riper."

"Of course. I will see to it. Tell him I'm coming, Jory, if you get a chance."

Jory nodded to her then held his arm out toward the door for the other two. "We'll leave the doc to it." He ushered them back to the small desk right inside the front hall and asked, "Sally, where might we find Lady Edra?"

"In the kitchen, last I knew, directing this whole mess," she answered cheerfully, looking past the stairs toward the back of the house. A small rush of cold air from the stairwell caused the men to glance upward, and Ferguson noticed Geever nod and smile politely, as if to someone who stood on the stairs. John couldn't see whoever Geever smiled at.

Abby watched Jory and the two detectives a moment longer before resuming her work. The two men from London were the same approximate height and weight. The man who purported to be in charge seemed polished and adept, yet the other man filled the space with something more. Tall and strong, he gave the impression and bearing of command. He dominated the space. She felt immediately drawn to him and his unruly mop of sandy hair and his full officer's mustache. She had seen many British officers during the war, who all seemed to sport the same style. He pushed back his hair as she watched. When they met, his amazing blue eyes had assessed her entire consulting room as well as appraising her. She sensed his evaluation of her had been a bit more than professional. She smiled.

The men squeezed past three workmen building walls to form a little room opposite the stairs. Ferguson looked in, curious as to what the room might become. A plumber stared into a hole which had been made in the floor, while another man stood on a ladder, sawing a round hole in the ceiling. Noticing John's interest, the plumber announced smiling, "It's a toilet room. It'll take a bit of jiggery pokery to fit in a flush toilet and a sink—including a sink on the other side for Doc." He pointed to the hole the policemen had watched being made in her office. An iron pipe thrust up through the hole in the floor, and the plumber turned back to his work. Jory pushed open the swinging door at the far end of the hallway into the kitchen. A man's legs stuck out of a cabinet under the sink, more plumbing. A table with four chairs sat to their left. A floor to ceiling cabinet held the dishes, crockery, silver and such needed for the household. Next to it came the back door. A gas stove, centered in the arch of what had been a huge walk-in fireplace, took up one whole wall across from the table. The kitchen contained only the man under the sink. Through a second swinging door to their left, an empty dining room smelling of freshly waxed furniture led into the front parlor still cloaked in sheets. They passed the men examining the gas lights either side of the fireplace, and watched as two others packed up tools and a set of sawhorses. This completed the policemen's fruitless circuit back into the front hallway.

"I saw an attractive young woman going upstairs as we went to the kitchen—with long black hair. Lady Edra perhaps?" Geever asked Jory.

He shook his head and shrugged. "Lady Edra doesn't have dark hair."

"We might as well bring up your luggage," Jory suggested.

Geever felt a shiver run up his spine, recalling something shadowy, unpleasant about the dark-haired woman he saw earlier.

Carrying his duffel, Ferguson led them up the stairs that were lit from above by a beautiful stained-glass Palladian window. Geever followed carrying one of his bags, then Jory with Geever's last two. Ferguson came eyeball to eyeball with a striking, hunting hound who watched them intently. The dog sat quietly beside a young woman who stood in the doorway directly to the left at the top of the stairs. She faced into the room talking to others and had yet to notice them. The dog, whose body was ticked liver and white, examined them from golden eyes set in her dark brown head.

"But ma'am, we can't all sleep here," a female voice came from inside the room.

The woman in riding clothes and dark blond hair pulled back and tied with a black bow answered, "But the wall will separate you. It will be fine." The dog decided to wag her tail at the strangers. The woman noticed and turned toward them, smiling when she saw Jory.

"Lady Edra," Jory scrunched Ferguson and Geever against the Palladian window, stepping onto the landing, "these are the policemen."

"Oh welcome, gentlemen." She started to extend her hand, then noticing they carried luggage, she dropped it. "Please, this way." She indicated the hallway round the other side of the Palladian window. John noted two women and one man in the small room dressed in servants' attire that she had been talking to as he passed their doorway. Opposite that room, and directly above where an addition of running water was being added in the kitchen, a full bath was being added upstairs. A glance inside revealed only a black hole where the ceiling should be. Two carpenters on ladders heaved a square of wood up and nailed it into place, partially enclosing the ceiling over the sink. A plumber knelt, squeezed into the other corner, and wrestled with a gleaming claw-foot porcelain tub. A toilet squatted in the hallway awaiting its turn to be placed in the new water closet.

"Now gentlemen, I'm Lady Edra Bandry" She shook both their hands.

"Detective Inspector Richard Geever."

"And, I'm DI John Ferguson."

"Geever? Are you related…oh Richard, I didn't recognize you. I haven't seen you for ages. Still involved with dressage?"

Geever fairly purred when she mentioned dressage. He smiled ducking his head in modesty. "No. I've no time for that. I'm a Detective Inspector now at Scotland Yard, and I've been charged with getting to the bottom of this terrible murder."

"Of course. Impressive. Remember we used to call you Dickie?" She held her hand to her mouth pretending to hide a smile. Geever nodded and grinned, embarrassed. She added, "Probably felt a Cornwall man presented the best choice for such a horrible crime right here."

Ferguson sighed.

Lady Edra led the way past the noisy workmen, came to two doors side by side, and opened both of them.

"A room for each of you."

"I shall take the room at the front of the house, if that is satisfactory," Geever said, stepping into that room and dropping his bag. Jory placed the two bags he carried up next to Geever's. John then placed his bag in the back bedroom. Small and made smaller by a new wall taking a few feet from this room for the water closet, His room had two windows and a striking small fireplace with a deep green tile surround. A warm soft muzzle touched his hand, and he stroked the brown velvet head.

Indicating the room next to the one Geever chose, which also faced the front of the house, Lady Edra said in a wistful tone, "This was my room years ago, and I've put Doc Abby in it." Geever stood in the doorway to his room, and she looked past him, remembering something about that room, but she silently turned from it. "I'm hoping to keep her here in the dower house for good. That's why all the noise and bother. Changes I'm making which will become her new surgery and residence. The phone line will come in a couple of weeks. Then she'll have a phone, so patients can call and make appointments. I am rather busy at the moment, so if you'll excuse me."

"Of course, Lady Edra, we understand," Geever assured her. "I did wonder about the suitability of servants on the same floor with…with others in the house."

"The room at the top of the stairs where I spoke to the servants, had been a servant's room when I lived here before. We needed a nurse close to the babies. The new water closet used to be the stairway up to the servants' quarters when we last used the dower. I decided the room on this floor will be quite suitable for servants now, and I needed to use that corner so there will be a water closet including tub on this floor."

That explained the hole in the ceiling. It had been a staircase. Ferguson said, "When you get a moment, I'd like to ask you a few questions about the storm and fire Sunday night."

"Downstairs then, in the parlor, in a moment." She turned and went back to the servants' room at the top of the stairs.

As she entered, the dispute resumed. "It simply won't do. Alan needs his own room."

"It just ain't right him in here with us."

"But the wall…" Lady Edra began.

"He should be upstairs like before—above that water room."

Then a male voice, "I'll stay in my room up to the manor house. It ain't more than a few yards' walk."

The policemen overheard no more as they descended the stairs and stood in the front hall, just outside the parlor and watched the workmen finish packing their tools and leave. The dog chose to stay near John. Through the door across from them, the last remaining patient was being ushered into Doc Abby's surgery by Sally. Quietly coming down the stairs, a plain woman about twenty-five, in a black, long-sleeved dress with white collar, gave the men a half curtsey and shy smile as she entered the parlor, followed by a red-haired man about thirty, wearing a suit. Jory mumbled, "Sukie. Alan." They mumbled back and removed the sheets covering the furniture, folding each one carefully. Sukie turned up the newly serviced gas lamps, and Alan lit a fire previously set in the fireplace. The two slipped wordlessly by them toward the kitchen. A prim-looking, plump woman about forty, wearing a dark skirt and white blouse, came down, eyes averted, lips pursed, and strode away from them into the kitchen. The front door opened, and a lad who appeared to be about nine or ten, with dark curly hair and piercing blue eyes, appeared and looked around tentatively.

"Keyan," Jory said. "Just the young man we've been looking for." The boy turned and bolted. Jory ran out the front door after him.

Reaching the last step, Lady Edra asked, "Did I just see Keyan run off? Why on earth is Jory chasing him? He'll be back." She turned to the policemen, "Now gentlemen, how can I help you?" and directed them into the parlor. They sat on the newly revealed chairs.

"Could you tell us, Lady Edra, about the storm and your injury? Weren't you knocked unconscious? What were you doing out in the storm?" asked Geever.

"I needed to check on the dogs." She noticed her dog sitting next to John while he stroked the dog's ears. "Sheba, come." The dog obediently went to Edra and sat next to her. "I'm sorry she bothered you."

"No problem. I love dogs, and Sheba is a striking animal and so well-mannered."

"Thank you." She rubbed the dog's head while Sheba eyed John.

Geever asked, "Why did you need to check your dogs? Don't your grooms or someone look after the dogs? They are hunting dogs, are they not?"

"They are hunting dogs or could be trained to be. They're German Shorthair Pointers. They have fabulous noses and will sniff out birds and point them, so the hunter can flush and shoot them. These dogs will then retrieve the birds and drop them at the hunter's feet, but my dogs haven't been trained for that. We don't hunt anymore since I became mistress of Tredwen. At least there are no fox hunts here. My father occasionally joins a hunt. Last Sunday night, I heard my dogs start howling and barking. The storm upset them terribly. I didn't want them to be lured by…to be hurt. By anything."

Geever asked, "Did you stop them from being hurt?"

"Well, the dogs are all fine. Only because the gate and the fence held. I tried to force them back, or force them to calm down. They weren't listening. They didn't respond." Repeating the story troubled her. "I couldn't stand the storm any longer. Once the wind became so fierce, I simply ran for the house. They were saved, but not by me. The gate held. The wind blew so furiously, it blew me down, and I smashed my head into the wall by the steps, leading out to the garden from the conservatory. I have a terrible lump on the back of my head." She unconsciously fiddled with the bruise.

Geever scolded her, "Well perhaps your grooms should be given a good talking to. It is outrageous that the lady of the house is injured because they can't see to the dogs' well-being."

In the hallway the last patient and Sally were putting on coats, and Doc Abby quietly spoke to them, apparently saying goodbye, since Sally left with the man. Ferguson assumed Sally caught a ride back to the village. The open door let in no light. Night had fallen. Doc Abby felt drawn to their conversation. Lady Edra noticed her, smiled and motioned her into the room. She patted the couch next to her, and Abby came and sat next to her folding one foot under her.

Ferguson noted two things as she spoke. Lady Edra was mistress of the manor—not her father. And she said something lured her dogs into danger. "Tredwen Manor then belongs to you?" he asked her.

"Yes. The Bandry family has held the baronetcy here for hundreds of years. When my grandfather, the baron, died, my mother, an only child, became Baroness Sarah. When she married my father, he agreed to take the family name. When she died about twelve years ago, I inherited the land and the title—not my father." John knew both she and her mother were lucky to inherit. Many families would leave property to some distant male relative before leaving it to daughters. Geever had a look that said he disapproved of such an arrangement, even though as second son he had been excluded from inheriting any part of his own father's property or title.

Ferguson moved on. "And you have fine hunting dogs, but you don't hunt?"

"No. I hate fox hunting. I always root for the fox. My dogs simply accompany me when I go riding or just walking. They're companions and wonderful dogs." She looked down petting Sheba.

"What were you afraid might lure your dogs to danger?" John asked.

She looked intently at each man, apparently deciding to tell them something she thought they may not like. She directed her answer to Geever the Cornwall man. "It was Dando."

There was Dando again, Ferguson thought. Geever raised an eyebrow.

She sighed then decided to continue. Solemnly she said, "Dando came hunting Sunday night. He's ridden down the stream through the willows before on his hellish hunt." Her voice trembled a bit as she spoke. "He calls to the dogs. Lures them to join in the bloodlust. They smell it and are afraid, but they can't resist his call. Last time Lucie, one of my dogs, got through the fence. I was too scared to try and stop her. Next day we found her. Poor dog had been thrown off the cliff, dashed to pieces in the surf." She looked distressed remembering. She stroked Sheba's head. Ferguson looked at Geever who seemed surprisingly upset by her story.

"What or who is Dando?" Ferguson demanded raising his voice. He turned to see the last four workmen, who had been trying to leave, quietly stop and stare at him wide-eyed. Without a word they left shutting the door silently.

Geever said, "Lady Edra, let me try to explain. Ferguson, Dando is merely Cornwall's version of the ancient horned god of the forest. According to legend Dando had been a corrupt priest who cared for nothing but sensual pleasures and hunting. He even hunted on Sunday—very frowned upon back then. One Sunday his entourage found themselves out of wine after a hunt, and the priest Dando went into a rage. "If no wine can be found on earth, I will go to hell for it! The devil, disguised as a stranger, materialized suddenly and offered the hunting party wine. He actually told them the wine came from hell. Only Dando laughed and greedily drank. A great storm arose suddenly and as the others watched, the stranger, along with Dando and his horse disappeared into hell in a great burst of flame. Since then, Dando sometimes returns from hell, riding his fire breathing horse on his bloody, murderous hunt across the land." The two women sat enthralled, and John had to admit Geever told the tale well.

Ferguson blurted, "Surely you don't actually believe that this Dando threatened your dogs?"

Looking at him, Lady Edra said quietly, "There is real evil, you know, Detective. I would have thought your chosen occupation convinced you of that. And some stormy nights it runs past here. Sunday, that evil killed the poor man."

The front door flew open and Jory pushed Keyan in ahead. "Keyan! What in the world?" Lady Edra said jumping up from the couch. "You ran from Mr. Moon?"

Jory said, "We've been sitting on the step having a chat. Keyan, tell these policemen about the night of the storm."

"I didn't see nothing," he said defiantly.

"But you had a spell at the Badger. You said quite clearly the Green Man would die, remember?"

"No." He looked around at them uncomfortable and unsure.

Doc Abby said, "I don't think he does remember anything he says when he's having a seizure. It's just random bits and pieces from his brain."

Keyan stared at Lady Edra. "I think Dando killed the man," he announced to her.

Doc Abby began, "Now Keyan…" The embarrassed boy bolted, charging up the stairs.

Abby stopped Lady Edra from following. "Leave him. He always wants to please you, and I embarrassed him by disagreeing."

Ferguson asked Jory, "Did you ask him if he actually saw anyone get killed? Perhaps he saw the body—a man in a green suit gruesomely covered in blood—who became the Green Man?"

"Yes, and he denied seeing anything Sunday night. He said he went straight home after leaving the pub. He found the man next morning on his way over here."

"With no autopsy, we don't have any idea when the murder took place," Ferguson reminded them.

Abby said, "And an autopsy at this stage certainly won't give us a time of death."

Lady Edra said, "I should get on…" A blood curdling scream from upstairs stopped her. "Keyan!" She darted up followed by the others.

The terrified boy stood backed up tight against the now dark Palladian window at the top of the stairs, sweat covering his face, eyes wide, shaking his head slightly, staring down the hallway. Lady Edra asked, "Keyan, are you alright?" She looked back down the stairs at Doc Abby for her opinion about what Keyan had experienced. Abby just shook her head and shrugged. Ferguson stepped around them, looking toward where the boy seemed to stare and saw only a dim hallway lit by one gas lamp at each end. He asked the boy, "What scared you? What did you see?"

"Something. Black." He gulped air with each word. "A black ghost. It wanted me." His trembling voice rose, "It reached out…it tried to touch me." He shuddered and turned his face into Lady Edra's shoulder, and she held him.

She said to him, "There's nothing here that can harm you. Let's go back downstairs. I think it's time for us all to go home." She led them down. Halfway down he glanced back up. John saw his eyes still wide with fear and knew he wasn't faking for Lady Edra's sake. Keyan's face had gone ash white, and he still shook. Something terrified him. Searching the three bedrooms, the servants' room and the burgeoning bathroom, the three policemen found only undisturbed silence.

Reassembling at the bottom of the stairs, Jory decided the time to leave had come and promised to pick up the Inspectors Ferguson and Geever first thing. He said, I'll drive Lady Edra to the manor house and give Keyan a lift home. That way I can make sure his grandmother is home before I leave him." Keyan still looked shaken.

As the front door closed, John turned to see the three shocked servants at the other end of the hall peering around the kitchen door. Alan asked, "Everything all right, sir?"

Geever said, "The lad just had a fright, that's all. Nothing to worry about. I wouldn't have been telling spooky stories if I'd known the boy listened. He ran upstairs alone and saw shadows." They seemed skeptical yet somewhat relieved and retreated into the kitchen, disappearing as the door swung shut behind them. Geever then remembered, "The lad hadn't been here when I told the Dando tale."

Ferguson said to Geever and Doc Abby, "Don't you think it's a familiar story any nine-year-old boy would have heard?" Neither answered.

The older servant appeared, forcing a smile, "Your dinner's ready anytime you are." Before they could wonder how, only a short time ago, an empty kitchen produced their meal, she added, "Sukie and Alan brought it down from the manor house. Came round the back, proper like, you see."

"I could certainly eat now," Geever declared patting his stomach. "Didn't eat much from the dreadful dining car." He looked to the others who both nodded indifferently. Eating seemed such an abrupt change. John welcomed Abby's suggestion to go to their rooms and freshen up before dinner. He washed his face and hands using the filled pitcher and basin in his room and sat down on his bed to think about the people they had met. He hung up his clothes in the mahogany wardrobe from his duffle and set the murder bag in there. A moment later, he heard the doctor and Geever in the hall and joined them. He noted the formal way dinner was served. Alan served the dinner in the dining room wearing white gloves, while Sukie, also gloved, aided Alan. She never served them directly. Had she served them, it would have been embarrassingly gauche. He wondered if Geever would have been offended, or if his life in London had changed him enough to overlook such things. Both servants stood motionless against the wall, only moving in anticipation of serving more drink or food. As they ate, Geever prattled on about the train ride, tales of his luggage's adventure today and an explanation about his suit choice, while John considered the dower house itself. Dower houses usually came about in order to get the old master's widow out from underfoot of the new mistress when the son inherited the title and the manor. This dower had been well built with quality workmanship, including brass gas lamps. Each fireplace had a marble surround, and the floors were all polished English oak. The furnishings were expensive, a fine mahogany dining table with six matching chairs and vivid Oriental rugs. Heavy draperies hung at each window, and the parlor had plush chairs and a couch upholstered in expensive tweed wool. They had eaten on fine china with silver utensils. This seemed a fine home for one rich old lady and her servants. It would do nicely for Doc Abby as her surgery and residence. Lady Edra must appreciate her very much.

Geever's chronicle seemed about finished, and John turned their attention to the doctor, "Where in Ireland are you from, Doctor?"

Her brogue gave away her heritage, and she smiled at him over her glass of wine, "County Armagh. And from where in Scotland do you hail, Inspector?"

"Ayrshire, south of Glasgow." His accent also gave him away.

She had been observing John as he scrutinized his surroundings while Geever spoke. She saw a man alert to everything around him at all times. A serious man, she felt, who would discover who murdered that poor man. Geever asked her, "Why the interest in medicine? Seems odd for a lovely young woman to pursue such a profession. Surely some man will sweep you off your feet, and you'll be having babies and taking care of him." Then another thought occurred to him. "An Irish woman studying medicine in England?" Geever had only blurted out the obvious. Any Irish person, male or especially female, would have a hard time getting into a British university.

"I studied medicine at Trinity College in Dublin, which incidentally became the first of the ancient universities to admit women as full members." It impressed John that the tactless question had not angered or upset her. "My education was possible because my father, Inspector Geever, is a viscount." John turned to watch Geever become suddenly more interested in the Irish woman, as he suspected Dickie would. Her pedigree intrigued his snobbish side.

She continued, "He married a commoner, a local beauty, over his family's objections. My father adores her still, even though he discovered he had married a 'wise woman', a psychic." She stopped to see their reaction. Neither seemed shocked or particularly amused, so she continued. "People from all round use her knowledge of folk medicine, even while some are skeptical or fearful of her psychic ability. She might be a witch, you see. I suppose that explains why I pursued conventional medicine and then psychiatry.

"I thought science might explain Mother's abilities. I wanted to finish my medical degree, then study psychiatry at the University of Zurich with Carl Jung. Have you heard of him? He's becoming quite famous." Both men shook their heads no, and she waited for the question which she knew would follow.

Geever obliged her, "And what branch of medicine is that exactly?"

There it was. Abby found that few people knew much about psychiatry and fewer still had heard of Jung. "It is studying human behavior and mental states. The doctors treat various kinds of emotional distress like anxiety or depression."

"Ah, hysteria," Geever stated. "My mother has been treated for that for years. She keeps smelling salts near at all times. And her physician prescribes periodic water massage treatments to calm her."

Abby smiled discreetly at that. Doctors prescribed water massage to anxious women of a certain class. A jet of water caressed the woman's genitals until they achieved a high point of physical excitement, thus generating a more relaxed and contented person. Husbands, who never wanted to know anything about their wives' physical being, had no idea of the secret of water massage.

She noticed that Ferguson appeared to be lost in his own thoughts, head down, as she spoke. The information had a different effect on him than on Geever. He knew something about psychiatrists. The war. "Perhaps another topic," she suggested.

Ferguson looked up and quietly said, "No, please. I'd like to know more."

"These doctors try to discover the root of a patient's problem through talking to their patient. Often the patient has buried some trauma or swallowed unhappiness and it doesn't just magically disappear. It becomes some sort of physical ailment."

She saw Geever glance uncomfortably at Ferguson. Geever turned and smiled at her. She deduced John Ferguson, detective inspector, must have suffered some trauma which Geever knows about. She believed the conversation over until John said, "And this doctor you studied with, was he good at what he does? How does he do it?"

"Dr. Jung is quite good. He tries to understand a person's problem through talking, but often it's buried, so he explores their dreams using what he learned in art, mythology, religion and philosophy to understand. His work is exciting, and I was eager to learn from him. I thought maybe he could understand what it meant to be psychic. They drafted him as an army doctor. Swiss neutrality obliged them to intern soldiers from either side of the conflict who crossed their frontier to evade capture. Yung became the commandant of an internment camp for British soldiers and tried to deal with the shellshock that many of those soldiers exhibited as well as the physical wounds we saw." She hurried on without looking at Ferguson. "I went there to learn from him, and the Swiss nurses and I had to work together, so they taught me some German, and I taught them some English. Jung, however, is phenomenal with languages. He speaks numerous ones. Besides most modern western European languages, he can read several ancient ones, including Sanskrit. We dealt with some terrible physical injuries, of course. Mostly, men fled to Switzerland because they could no longer take the war." She saw the faces of both men. They were tired of discussing war. "But enough about me and about Carl Jung, what about you two?"

Geever began, "Actually my story is not nearly as interesting as yours. After university, I became a policem…" Ferguson interrupted, "I'd much rather hear the doctor's story…Inspector Geever. Tell us, Doctor, how you came to Woodcomb." Alan and Sukie silently removed plates and served coffee.

"After the war, my father fell ill, so I returned to Ireland. He recovered, but I couldn't find any place that would hire me as a physician. Many people seem to have trouble accepting a woman as a doctor, Inspector Geever." Geever shook his head, embarrassed to be challenged about his prejudices and mumbled a weak protest.

"I worked as a hospital administrator and a research scientist for a bit, always advertising my services in newspapers, hoping some village would rather hire me than have no doctor. I caught Lady Edra's attention with my psychiatric training. She brought me here to study Keyan's illness. It must be some mild form of epilepsy but very unusual and has many psycho-logical aspects."

John asked, "Are his trances real then?"

"Quite genuine, I'm sure. I don't believe he remembers what he sees or says. However, I have never known him to speak as clearly as he apparently did in the Badger the other night. It is usually only mumbling, and maybe a few distinguishable words."

"And his terror a couple of hours ago?"

"He does much to impress Lady Edra. If she wishes him to believe something supernatural happened during the storm, he will. She became enthralled with the supernatural several years ago after the murder of her son." She reflected a moment then, "However, poor Keyan seemed genu-inely panicked when he went upstairs." Ferguson nodded his agreement remembering the boy's face.

Alan inserted into the silence, "Excuse me, but you might wish to retire to the parlor. Perhaps some brandy?"

Glancing at both policemen who each nodded, Abby said, "Thank you, Alan, that would be nice. We won't be needing you further this evening."

He brought their brandy and glasses and said, "I'll lock up as I leave then, Doc. Dobbs and Sukie'll go on upstairs then when they are ready."

"Fine," she smiled at him. The three moved into the parlor and spent the rest of the evening cozy around the fire, sipping a fine brandy and discussing other topics. Geever explained the extent of his knowledge concerning London nightclubs, fashion, fast cars, great horses and society. John told about growing up a ghillie's son on one of Britain's grandest and most ancient estates, mentioning Lord Charles' interest in his education, and how Alistair Howell mentored his early years with Scotland Yard. He answered her question about the war, simply, without looking at her. "I joined the Royal Scot Fusiliers, spent time in Belgium and France." There was more to his war experience, but for now she accepted his simple, modest statement.

Abby felt drawn to him and his controlled strength. She said, "I'm glad you came back alive and are here now."

Her voice displayed a tenderness without pity that touched John. She had experienced close up what war did to men. How a man's soul, who had seen the horror, could be shredded. Her experience in the Swiss internment camp had given her deep insight into the human condition, as well as forcing her to use all her medical abilities.

He said, "You must have seen a lot being with an internment camp?"

"I found it difficult to watch what war did to men."

Geever became bored as the conversation centered on the war—where he had never been and said, "Well, today's been rather tiring, so if you'll excuse me, I think I'll retire for the night."

John became self-conscious alone with Abby. If he stayed much longer, he would be telling her more about his experiences, and he didn't want that. They soon turned in for the evening, also. Upstairs, he watched her go to her room. She turned and smiled at him before silently closing her door. As John closed the door to his bedroom, he remembered the mention of Lady Edra's son and made a mental note to find out more about it in the morning. A small boy murdered a few years ago. John found coincidences hard to believe in, even ones separated by years. He discovered how tired he was when his head hit the pillow. His last thought was of the lovely doctor.

However, each person sleeping in the dower house found the night anything but quiet and restful.

Chapter Four

With little moonlight to guide her, Abby heard the baby's terrified sobs once more as she ran through deep woods. She stopped, holding her breath, to listen. At first, she heard only her pounding heartbeat, then came menacing snorting and growling. The monster crashed through the underbrush close enough that she could hear it snuffle, smell its rotting breath. Trying to find the child's scent. Or hers. Holding her breath in fear of being discovered, she heard rustling behind her. The baby screamed! Whirling toward the sound, she caught sight of the back of the hideous beast standing on two legs, covered with long, black fur hunching over the toddler. As the beast touched the child with its dagger-like claws, Abby screamed and awoke in a strange room. It took a second before she understood she was in Lady Edra's dower house. Sadness overwhelmed her. She nearly cried. She had failed to save the child. She understood caring so deeply about the child in her dream seemed ridiculous, and the monster impossible, still evil seemed palpable all around, waiting to pounce. Scanning the impenetrable black corners of her room, Abby lay still a long time trying to convince herself the fear was irrational. Just as she finally dozed off, she heard one heartbreaking child's sob.

Sukie lay perfectly still, feeling such hatred all around her, prowling. She knew it searched the darkness for her. The rancid smell grew more sickening. She hadn't noticed it earlier when they moved back into the dower and brought their things up. The smell became so overpowering, she brought her hand up to cover her mouth and nose hoping the movement didn't alert the murderous, searching thing. The stench radiated everywhere. She heard a sound, very small as if the smell crawled through the walls. It searched for her. Couldn't Dobbs smell that? Sukie heard the woman's snoring and guessed it didn't trouble her. The hatred seemed to want only her and not Dobbs. She squeezed her eyes shut and thought to herself, it's not real. I got to get some sleep, else I'll be worthless tomorrow. I just got to concentrate on Dobbs' snoring and nothing else. Maybe that'll do it.

A pitiless rain poured from an ink black sky as Ferguson slogged through mud and dead men's body parts, in what remained of their bombed-out trench. He searched frantically, nearly unable to see anything through the downpour. Where were his men? Was he the only man alive?

A deafening bang, then two metallic clangs startled him awake, and the dream evaporated. Had the noise been part of the dream, some battle once fought? Silence. Moonlight dimly lit the serene room. A second earsplitting, bass-drum sound banged, then two clangs sounding like lead pipes banging together, then no sound. What would make such sounds? Something involving the new plumbing? Absolutely not. A thunderous bang brought him out of bed as the two metallic clangs followed. Opening his door, he saw the doctor's door open a crack and light flicker. Upon seeing him, Abby stepped out wide-eyed, barefoot and wearing only her nightgown, holding her lamp.

"Good. You heard it too. What on earth could it be?" she asked him.

"I've no idea. Where does the sound seem to come from?"

"Not my room. It's out here." She pointed down the hall toward the black opening of the new bathroom.

Wishing he had unpacked his torch, he walked down the hall into the tiny room under construction, followed by Abby holding her lamp. A thunderous bang made him jump back into her. He took her light as two more clanks resonated. Shining the light into all the corners revealed only the sparkling porcelain sink and tub reflected by the weak light. Tense and expectant, they waited in silence in the chilly bathroom for the next sound. Abby glanced up into a square, black void where the new ceiling hadn't been finished, and Ferguson held up the lamp, illuminating only the blackness of what had been the servants' quarters. Ferguson shivered leaning against the sink, looking down into the black open mouth in the floor the plumber had stared into earlier. They both felt rather self-conscious after a couple minutes of silence.

Ferguson said, "Apparently it's over—at least for a while."

"What could that have possibly been?"

"I've no idea. It sounded rather like pipes clanging. Perhaps the plumbers…" he trailed off knowing of nothing plumbers could have created that might raise such a series of sounds. Especially not hours after they left.

"Well, I guess we should try and get some sleep." She smiled a little, noticing his scant attire, made her clutch her own gown. As she left with the lamp, the back of her gown faded into darkness, and he heard her door softly close. Standing in the darkness of the burgeoning water closet, he imagined how laughable he must have seemed to the doctor, standing in his undershirt and shorts leaning rakishly on the lavatory, legs crossed at the ankles. As he stepped to the doorway, he saw the candlelit faces of the frightened maid and cook peering through their barely open door.

"What in the world made that sound, sir?" Sukie whispered.

"I've no idea, Sukie, but I'm sure it's something to do with the new plumbing," he lied.

Both faces relaxed. "Oh, fine then," the cook said. "Then there's nothing to worry about. I told you so, didn't I, Sukie? Back to bed then." The two faces and the candle disappeared, and the door quietly closed.

Ferguson started toward his room, the hallway lit only by a little moonlight filtering in through the Palladian window. The gas lamps had been turned down for the night. A person had to have made those noises. He didn't know why or how, but knew he would search them out. He checked the doors before they came up to bed. Alan definitely locked them. He wondered if the person would be returning to scare people? Who else has keys? He glanced at Geever's closed door, which seemed odd. Why hadn't the pounding awakened him? Ferguson quietly cracked the door and peered into blackness created by Geever's tightly closed drapes, but Geever's even breathing could be heard, so Ferguson closed the door and went back to his own bed and eventually back to sleep.

A rumbling, deep-throated animal-growl next to his head startled Geever awake. He scrambled away from the animal, heart pounding, wondering how a dog got into his room. Even a little moonlight kept him from sleep, and closing the drapes had certainly succeeded in creating darkness. He remembered the lamp on the bedside stand next to where the growl came from. Silence. He wished he had unpacked his torch before going to bed. Slowly he stretched his arm, trying not to alert the beast, until he nearly tipped over the lamp. Steadying the lamp, he snatched the matches, struck one and glanced around. Nothing. He lit the lamp. Shadows not driven away by the pale-yellow flame remained in every corner. He ventured out of bed and took the lamp to each corner, shone it under the bed, into the wardrobe and found no dog and nothing unusual. Then came a scratching at the window behind the curtains. Could the sound have come from outside? He shivered, remembering it so near his head. Yet nothing hid in here. Stepping beside the window, Geever could hear it whining and snorting as it tried to scratch its way into his room. He couldn't bring himself to look. No animal could possibly stand outside the upper story window, which he remembered from when he unpacked his bags. It had no balcony nor any ledge. Gathering his courage, he whipped the draperies aside revealing only moonlight. All remained quiet and peaceful on the circular drive below. He heart slowly returned to normal, and he went back to bed wondering, could he have possibly dreamt the growl? He must have. Yet it had seemed so real. And so near. He blew out the lamp leaving the drapes open. Now the moonlight streaming into the room soothed him enough to eventually allow him to fall back to sleep.

Keyan awoke to the familiar sounds of his grandmother preparing to leave for the pasty shop. Barely light, he huddled under his covers against the chill of morning.

From the other room he heard the familiar, "Keyan, go to school today!"

"Yes, Baba."

"I mean it. Get up and go. It is the law. Do you want the school police after us?"

"Yes. I mean no. I will go today." His heavy quilts muffled his sad answer. He always pulled them over his head whenever she brought up school. She sighed. He wouldn't go. She knew it. Her heart nearly broke every time she thought of the cruelty this sweet little boy suffered because he had a sickness.

But she must leave him alone. Their money came mostly from the shop. A lot of her customers picked up their lunch pasties on their way to work, and she needed to get them baked.

"I love you, Sweetheart. Be good."

"I love you too, Baba."

She closed the door of the house softly with her usual prayer for his safety. She walked up the gravel path toward the road, stopping to squint up into the dark limbs of the pine trees next to the path, until she could make out the hunched crow sentinels who dismissed her presence as harmless, a morning ritual for both her and the crows. "Watch over him, Good Crows." A few of the crows shuffled a bit on their limb at the familiar sound of her voice. This assured her that they would guard the boy, and she walked on toward her little pasty shop on the quay at the edge of the village. The crows brought good luck, and God knew they needed all the good luck they could get. It was hard providing for herself and her grandson, the only two left of their family.

Keyan had pulled himself up to his window, dragging his blankets which were tented, over his head for warmth, to make sure his grandmother didn't forget her daily delegating of the crows as his protectors. Satisfied, he plopped back down planning his day. He would need to avoid Tommy and Claire Penrose on their way to school. Especially Tommy, the class bully, and the principal reason Keyan rarely made it to school. Picturing Tommy's red face laughing so hard he doubled up after Keyan skinned his knees tripping over the rope positioned especially by Tommy to trip him, brought Keyan abruptly out of bed. He must dress quickly, eat the breakfast Baba prepared and be gone before they walked past his house toward school in Woodcomb.

Keyan slammed the door as he rushed out. He carried his finished homework as well as two carrots for the horses. He stopped in front of the crows' tree making sure they saw him before asking politely, "I beseech thee, Good Crows, please peck out Tommy Penrose's eyes today, if you're not too busy." It was an old plea. He knew crows couldn't do such a thing—or wouldn't. It just made him feel good to ask, and he scurried up the lane smiling.

The dawn sky glowed resplendent in pink and gold as Keyan cut across the road and climbed over the stone fence at Tredwen Manor and spoke to the horses. "Good morning beautiful *grast!*" He knew only a few Romani words. Baba taught him that horses were some of the best luck of all. "And, the Tredwen Arabian *grast* are the finest of all," she would add. He liked Lady Edra's mare best. A beautiful red chestnut named Sadeem, which he knew meant "gentle breeze." Keyan's mare, which really had been Lady Edra's mum's horse, they called Naazir. The protector. He was learning to ride and secretly considered Naazir to be his own. Both Sadeem and Naazir came to the fence to get their carrot from him. Sir Vinson's white gelding stayed on the other side of the pasture as usual this morning, but Asif dipped his head and stamped one foot in greeting, and Keyan waved. "Arabian" he pronounced carefully as he walked around the back of the dower house being fixed up for Doc Abby and the policemen. He began spelling the word Lady Edra had taught him because spelling was very important to her. "A-R-A-B" he began, but a dark impression of the hideous visage he saw in the house yesterday drifted unbidden, intruding on his thoughts. He glanced over at the dower, but the dark windows seemed to watch him. Spooked by the impression, he ran on to the road leading to the manor house.

Morning at the dower found them all subdued at breakfast which included omelets and sausage. They ate quietly. Abby neither mentioned their scantily clad rendezvous, nor the eerie thundering booms. Jory's cheerful patter seemed to grate when he arrived. Grabbing a piece of toast, he asked, "I hope you all slept well?" He looked around, and no one answered. Glancing at Ferguson, Abby excused herself and went to her surgery to gather up her medical bag in preparation for going with Jory to autopsy the body.

Ferguson said to Jory, "I have a job for you." He went to his room and retrieved the murder bag. He pulled out two electric torches, one for him, the other for Geever and laid them aside. He found the finger printing kit and took it to Jory. "I need you to fingerprint the body and get the prints on the train back to the Fingerprint Branch at the Yard." He doubted the man had ever been fingerprinted, but their files grew yearly. Maybe the dead man had been in trouble with the law. "Do you have a camera?" Jory nodded. "Take photographs of the man. Up close."

Jory nodded again. "Yes. I've done this before. We have a fingerprint print kit and a camera. We actually did this a lot during the war while we policed the whole southwest coast."

As Jory and Abby left, a thought occurred to Ferguson. "Geever, don't you think we might learn something if we check with the telegraph office. I probably should handle that…"

Geever quickly interjected, "No, Ferguson, I believe I should handle that. While I do that you should …"

While Geever considered, Ferguson said, "I should stay here and interview the servants, don't you think?"

Geever seemed dubious that the three servants might know anything, so gladly answered, "Right. Of course, you do that."

Ferguson instructed him, "Get over to the train station and telegraph the Liskeard police and ask them to question railway employees to see if anyone from the train noticed the murder victim on Sunday, or if they can help us with any information. Also, ask about any telegrams that were sent to or from Woodcomb in the few days leading up through Sunday. Perhaps our victim sent a telegram announcing his visit to someone here." Geever finished up his breakfast and left Ferguson alone at the table. He picked up the last piece of toast and had another cup of tea before launching into his first task which led him into the kitchen to have a chat with the servants. Ferguson found their views always illuminated his investigations.

Sukie cleared the dining room breakfast. Alan used a small plane on the back door near the knob, and Dobbs wrote in a ledger as she surveyed the contents of a cupboard. "Excuse me," Ferguson began, and each looked up from their work looking surprised.

"Sorry, sir," Dobbs closed the cupboard door, "May I help you?"

"I need to ask each of you some questions, if I may. Perhaps in the dining room," he gestured through the door he just entered. All three seemed more surprised he would take an interest in them. "But first, I'd like to know if any of you recognized this medallion found on the dead man?"

They each shook their heads, and Alan said, "Constable Crocker showed us all that necklace before."

"Then I think I'll speak to Dobbs, first."

Glancing at the others, she set her ledger on the counter, and went through the swinging door held open for her by Ferguson, and they sat at the dining room table. A neatly dressed woman of about fifty with brown hair arranged in a neat bun atop her head, she sat down folding her hands on the table waiting for his first question.

"Dobbs, are you also the cook for the manor house?"

"Oh no, sir." She thought that a strange thing to assume, but she merely waited for his next question.

"No? You have become the cook for the dower house then?"

"Heavens no. I can't cook a lick."

"Then Sukie is the cook?"

This brought a chuckle. "God help us all if Sukie were to try that!" She waited to see what outrageous thing he might say next.

"Well, then who made supper last night and breakfast this morning?"

"Mrs. Key, the cook, of course." Deciding to have mercy on him she explained, "Mrs. Key cooks for the Bandrys. Has for years. Alan trots up to the house and hauls it back. He's got a little hand cart. No trouble at all. Better'n paying two cooks for now."

"Did they have a cook when the dower opened before?"

"Oh yes, they brought Mrs. Zelly on for that couple of years."

"Your position here is officially what, then?"

"Well, I'm to be the housekeeper of the dower."

"And are you the housekeeper up at the manor house?"

"That'd be Mrs. Lander."

He decided he better write this down in his notebook—always good to keep the servants straight. It certainly worked at Culzean Castle where both his parents worked. He remembered listening to the gossiping staff as a lad below stairs, roaming at will, occasionally pilfering cookies—when the cook gave him a wink and a nod.

"Let's see. Mrs. Lander is the housekeeper, and the cook for the Bandrys is Mrs.…."

"Key," she provided helpfully and watched as he jotted it down.

"What position did you hold before the dower opened?"

"I have been personal maid to Lady Steren Bandry—that's Lady Edra's grandmother—for nearly twenty years," she said proudly.

"Won't she still require a personal maid?"

"Of course. Fern Deane has taken that position. She had been Lady Edra's maid. Now she's the maid for them both."

"Lady Edra and Lady Steran sharing a maid?" Quite unusual.

"Lady Edra doesn't require a lot from her maid. She's pretty independent. This'll work fine till we see if the dower stays open."

"Might it close back up after all this remodel?"

"Depends. Doc might not like it and move back into the village once the fire damage to the Crown is fixed. Course you might never solve this queer murder, and I guess we would all be here forever." She didn't seem to be trying for humor.

"Is housekeeper of the dower a better position for you than personal maid?"

"Course. I really enjoyed the position last time we moved into the dower. I became both Lady Steren's maid and housekeeper. Good money then, I can tell you."

"Shouldn't you rightly be called Mrs. Dobbs and not just Dobbs as either a personal maid or housekeeper?"

Dobbs smiled at that, looking impressed that he knew that. "Absolutely. Everyone knows though, I actually prefer just plain Dobbs."

"When did the dower open previously?"

"Oh, let's see. That was in 1912." Realizing she touched on private Bandry history, she closed her mouth and looked at her hands.

"Why did the dower open in 1912, Dobbs?" He tried to sound nonchalant as if he didn't notice that she didn't want to talk about it.

"I…I'm not sure. You know it's not my place to chatter on about reasons of the Bandrys."

Apparently, Lady Edra's grandmother, Lady Steran, hadn't been forced out of the manor, when her daughter Sarah inherited, and mother and daughter must have been fine living in the big manor house together. So why open up the dower nine years ago, Ferguson wondered.

"When did Lady Edra's mother die? Is that why it opened?" That could have caused a shift in domestic power.

A shake of the head. Dobbs had finished telling him about that. Ferguson wondered about the fact that Lady Steren, Lady Edra's grandmother, shared her maid instead of sending the newer maid or hiring someone until they were sure the dower would stay open. Dobbs apparently had been assigned to be her spy. Why did she need one? He made a note to find out about the dower being opened in 1912 and switched to his immediate concern. "Do you have any idea who the murder victim might be?" Ferguson asked.

"No, sir."

"Have you heard anyone state an opinion why the man was murdered?"

"None, sir."

"That will be all for now. Thank you for your help, Dobbs. Please ask Alan to come in here."

She nodded, rose from the table and left. Only moments later Alan appeared through the kitchen swinging door and took the seat at the dining room table that Ferguson pointed toward.

"Alan, please tell me your full name."

"James Alan, sir."

"Oh, and I forgot to ask Dobbs' first name."

"Uh…oh yeah, it's Kerra. Don't hear it much, barely remember it."

"Alan, how old are you?"

"Thirty-one, sir." A little taller than average and nice enough looking— traditionally footmen were chosen for just those reasons.

"And your job here at the dower?"

"Houseman. A promotion. I am first footman up at the house." He smiled amiably at Ferguson.

He knew Alan had locked the doors last night because he checked before going to bed himself. "You locked the doors last night, Alan, correct?"

"Yes, sir. I have been given the key by Lady Steren. She said there are no other keys, and I should be very careful and not let it out of my possession." He patted his breast pocket.

"Are there other entrances? Side doors or other ways into the dower?"

"No other entrances, only the front door and the servants' entrance in the kitchen."

"You locked the front door by turning the lock from the inside and used the key to lock up when you left last night, correct? Have you used the key to unlock the front door? Do you know if it also works on it?"

Alan seemed surprised. "Don't know, sir. I only used it to let us into the kitchen door."

"Let's go try it." They walked to the front and turned the lock unlocking the door. Ferguson took the key from Alan. "Lock it please when I go out." Alan turned the knob. Ferguson inserted the key and opened the lock and stepped back inside. Alan seemed pleased. The same key unlocked the only two doors, and supposedly only one key existed. Alan held it. As much as knew of him, so far, Alan seemed unlikely to have returned last night to terrorize them, before relocking the door and returning to his bed at the manor.

They returned to the dining room. "Were you here the last time the dower opened?"

"Yes, I was. Second footman at the manor and houseman at the dower." His smile faded, and Ferguson realized he was remembering when he last worked at the dower house.

"I understand the dower opened in 1912. Why do you think they created a staff for a second household? Why would they need that?"

Alan gave him a cross look. "No idea."

"What's that you were doing to the back door?"

Alan relaxed again. "Just planing off a touch of wood. Door sticks a tad."

"Alan, do you know who the murdered man might be or have any idea why someone would kill him?"

"I haven't the faintest idea who he was or why he was killed." His answer seemed quite genuine. Becoming interested in 1912 did not solve this murder.

"That will do for now, Alan." The man pushed back from the table. Suddenly, Ferguson had a thought. "Why did the dower get shut down?"

"You need to ask the Bandrys 'bout that. I reckon you'll want Sukie next." He solemnly left the dining room.

Ferguson overheard them cajoling Sukie so she wouldn't be frightened, then they thrust her through the swinging door. She stood shoulders bent looking at the floor.

"Sukie, you're not in any trouble. Please sit down here." He pointed to a chair across from him at the table. A plain woman in her mid-twenties, Sukie had limp dark hair that fell across her face. He asked her, "Sukie, what is your last name?"

"Evans. Sukie Evans, sir."

"How long have you worked at the manor?"

"Oh ever-so-long. Since I were fourteen. That'd make it thirteen years now." She looked surprised.

"And your title would be what?"

"Cor, I ain't got no title. I'm just the kitchen maid."

"I see. And is this the first time you have been assigned to work here in the dower house?"

"Yes, sir. Except for when the dower opened last time."

"Sukie, do you have any idea why the Bandrys opened it up last time?"

"It were so Lady Edra could live with that rat of a husband of hers and raise her sweet baby in peace. Her father didn't never approve of that rascal, and he got proved right when he run off without no word nor nothin'."

That took him by surprise. "I see." Her father disapproved. "What did her mother and grandmother think about all that?"

"Her mother had died, but Lady Steren got them to fix up this dower and she even moved down with Lady Edra to help her with the baby and all."

This must be the murdered baby. "And where is the baby?"

"Murdered." Her face twisted into a grimace. "By the nursemaid, Jenna. Right in this very house. It were awful."

The other two servants burst into the dining room silencing Sukie. "You can't go getting your information from a kitchen maid. She doesn't know anything about it," Dobbs said.

"I do so know," she said as the other two hustled her away.

Ferguson's next task took him up to the manor house. Lander, the butler, explained to Ferguson that Lady Edra had estate business this morning and wished to speak with him later if possible. She would be having lessons with Keyan probably within an hour or two in the nursery. She would be back supervising the work at the dower house after that. Ferguson agreed and asked to speak to Lady Steren. Lander ushered him down a hallway into a brightly lit morning room, decorated in cheery pale yellow and beige, where he found her writing at a small, ornately inlaid desk.

Laying her fountain pen aside, she blotted the paper and turned to Ferguson. "Yes, Inspector?"

He needed to get the question of the medallion out of the way first, and she assured him she had never laid eyes on it before. Next, he asked about the key to the dower.

"Yes, I gave Alan my key."

"Are there any other keys?"

"No. Not that I know of. Why would there need to be?"

"What if that key gets lost?"

"We would need to call a locksmith, of course, wouldn't we?" She became agitated. "What is your concern, Inspector?"

Ferguson had learned that trouble in the past often somehow attached itself to people and brought them new trouble. Still, he dreaded asking Lady Edra's grandmother about the old tragedy. Quietly, he said, "Please tell me about the murder of your granddaughter's son."

This shocked her to the point of standing and glaring at him. "That, Inspector, is none of your concern! How dare you…"

"You are probably right." He remained seated. He found it hard to meet her eyes and concentrated on the small fire and the beautiful pink marble griffins guarding it. He said, "In my line of work, I find that the more I pry into the past, the more I discover about the present." Murder usually tore open people's neatly wrapped and packaged lives exposing ugly truths—most of which turned out to be not related to the case. When he again looked at the dowager, her face revealed great sadness.

"My granddaughter is the only thing in life I love dearly. Her darling little son, Caden, ran around chattering a lot. A bubbly two-year-old toddler and such a joy. For some unfathomable reason, it is supposed the baby's nurse—a girl I trusted as much as anyone—maybe more, murdered him. They found Jenna's body next morning smashed against the rocks over the cliff at the edge of our property. They never found little Caden's body."

"He was in her care. If not her, that leaves the question of why she died and who did murder the boy."

"Some in the village decided she must have killed him, maybe accidentally, then in a fit of guilt threw herself off the cliff, and Caden's body must have washed out to sea with the tide. I have always found it utterly unbelievable that Jenna did these things. She never would have left her own son, Keyan. None of it made sense, so it became quite impossible to solve."

Ferguson simply stared into the fire taking in the tragedy.

"Any other questions, Inspector? Perhaps about the stranger murdered four days ago?"

"Of course. Was anyone from the staff unaccounted for on Sunday night? Anything unusual?"

"It is quite unusual for my granddaughter to be rendered unconscious and bleeding during a storm." She said this as if even a policeman should have figured that one out.

"Tell me about that. What time did this happen Sunday night?"

"Shortly after the storm broke."

"Who discovered her?"

"It could have been Lander, but probably Wherry or Marrak. When Dobbs informed me, both Wherry and Marrak had her on the couch in the conservatory. Mrs. Lander washed the blood from her face. The whole thing terrified me." She put her hand to her throat, and her shoulders raised as she spoke, "What would I have done if she had died?"

He had no answer and only scribbled something in his small notebook. "And Sir Vinson. Where was he?"

"He hadn't arrived home yet. The doctor arrived before Vinson. Thank God, Edra had managed to regain consciousness before he arrived. Doc Abby declared Edra would be fine in a day or two. She seemed terribly distracted. The doc had been dragged away from watching her apartment and surgery go up in a blaze. We insisted she spend the night with us. She stayed here in a room down the hall from Edra, until the changes to the dower were sufficiently finished for her to work and live there. Yesterday became her first day in the dower."

"She had a number of patients already yesterday, I believe."

"The fire meant the whole area had no physician for two days. She's the doctor, not just for Woodcomb but for villages miles around here. Anything else Inspector?"

"Dobbs," he consulted the notebook, "Kerra Dobbs, is your personal maid, I understand. Why did you allow her to go to the dower house?"

She looked reluctant to answer.

Ferguson pressed, "It seems more obvious to send the newer maid."

"Dobbs knows the dower house and everything needed. Fern Deane would be more of a hindrance there. Here I can easily show her my needs until the future of the dower is settled. If there's nothing more, Inspector."

He thanked her, and she sat again at the writing desk. Lander, of course, appeared and informed him of Sir Vinson's busy schedule which would cause him to be unavailable all day. He led Ferguson below stairs to begin questioning the servants. As they descended, Ferguson wondered about Sir Vinson's being unavailable all day. Had Sir Vinson put him off because he knew something he didn't want the detective to know? Perhaps to establish his dominance in the situation. Aristocrats. Sometimes one of them decided he must choose when and where he would be questioned. Ferguson wondered if Sir Vinson's excuse made any difference. Perhaps the man was just a thoughtless, self-absorbed toff. He still found Sir Vinson's absence all day suspicious.

Lander ushered Ferguson into his own parlor, past three startled women working around the kitchen area. "This should afford you privacy for your investigation, Inspector."

"I'll have a go at you first then, shall I?" Ferguson said.

Lander nodded curtly and sat behind his desk, allowing Ferguson to sit in the comfortable rocker next to a small side table and lamp. A bookshelf stood against one wall of the small, cozy room and held a few books and mementos as well as a photograph of a man and a woman. A window beside the desk overlooked the kitchen garden and the barns and stables across the way.

"Lander, how long have you worked for the Bandrys?"

"Oh, let me see. I came as an under-footman at about fourteen. That would have been in 1886 which would be about 35 years or so!" He shook his head amazed at how much time had passed.

"Worked your way up then? Footman maybe, then valet, etc."

"That's right sir."

"Ever work for anyone else."

"Never. I have worked hard and never felt the need to seek employment elsewhere."

"Just a quick question, have you seen this medallion before," Ferguson asked, pulling it from his pocket.

"As I told Constable Crocker, I have never seen anything like that, sir."

"Thanks," he said putting it back in his pocket. He figured everyone at the manor had been shown the necklace with the odd medallion, but thought it worth a try. "Please tell me who discovered Lady Edra outside the night of the storm?"

"I believe Kitto, the stableboy, discovered her. Heard the ruckus the dogs were making and came to check, and found her unconscious lying on the conservatory steps. Ran in and found Wherry and Marrak. They were lying her on the couch in the conservatory when I came in. She was bleeding and not moving a muscle. I sent Wherry with the automobile to fetch Doc Abby." Lander spoke all this with his professional butler detachment, but Ferguson could still detect a little of the concern it had caused him.

"Kitto is the stableboy. Wherry and Marrak are…?" Ferguson asked.

"Wherry is Sir Vinson's valet and chauffeur, and Marrak is the footman."

"Lander, next morning did you go over to check out the spot where they discovered the dead man? It's just the other side of that wooden fence at the corner of the property—not more than fifty yards from this room."

"No, sir. I have no wish to look upon such a gory sight."

"How about the other servants? Did they go gawk at the gory sight?"

"I tried to prevail upon them not to—but I can't swear no one's curiosity got the better of him."

"Thank you, Lander, that will be all for now. Next, I need to talk to the housekeeper, your wife I believe. When can I question her?" There is a hierarchy in servants and the housekeeper came next. He would get to the two men who helped Lady Edra inside in due time.

"Now would be fine. I'll send for her."

She appeared a moment later. Ferguson moved around to sit at Lander's desk and indicated Mrs. Lander was to sit in the rocking chair. She had been one of the women he saw working in the kitchen area. She knew nothing about the medallion. He asked her about Lady Edra's accident.

"It chilled me right to the bone when I saw Marrak carrying her in and lying her on the couch. I had Sukie, the kitchen maid, run get my kit and a basin of water. She was breathing, thank God. I got her cleaned up a bit, but her head didn't stop bleeding until Doc Abby got here and took over."

"I'm sure everyone's so thankful you know what to do in case of an accident. You've been very helpful. Thank you, Mrs. Lander. I'll ask to see the other maids shortly, but first I would like to interview the cook. Could you please send her in." The cook always had high authority in a household, so he knew it would be proper to interview her next.

A red-haired, plump woman in her fifties came in and sat down and had no knowledge of the medallion. "Mrs. Key, have you heard about anyone coming to Woodcomb, perhaps for a visit. A rumor perhaps."

"I've no time for rumors, sir. We're a bit short staff now days. I rarely know anything about anything except this kitchen."

"No inkling of a visitor coming to see the butcher or grocer?"

"Sorry, no sir. I do hear a lot of town gossip from the delivery boys, but I'd heard nothing till all the buzz about a murder. Lots of nonsense about Dando riding on the storm though." She shook her head.

"Anything you know about Lady Edra's accident?"

"Only what Emma, er, Mrs. Lander told us next day."

"Thank you, Mrs. Key." Ferguson knew next in importance would probably be the valet, but footmen often knew more. The valet would spend most of his time with his master. Footmen usually knew the staff better and could be anywhere at any time. "Could you please send me the footman, Marrak, please?"

"Of course."

The tall footman in full livery and gloves came, introduced himself, sank into the chair and waited rather uncomfortably, Ferguson thought. He knew nothing about the medallion or who the man might be. "Tell me about the storm and Lady Edra."

"That storm came up fast and fierce. It rattled shutters. We scurried around making sure windows were shut and the like. Then Kitto burst in through the conservatory door yelling 'Help!' We rushed outside, and she lay there perfectly still. My heart stopped. Blood on the terrace." He looked appalled remembering.

"Where were you when you heard him? When you heard Kitto yelling for help?"

"I was in the blue drawing room, supervising the boy laying the fire in that room for the morning. It's fairly close."

"Go on."

"It was shocking! She lay sprawled out as if she was dead. The wind and rain was that fierce. Kitto and Wherry were just gawking stunned like. Course, you never touch a lady, but I picked her up. Someone had to carry her inside. I could see blood on her and on the steps. Landry told me to carry her into the conservatory and lay her on the couch in there. He sent Wherry to bring Doc Abby. Mrs. Landry gathered water and cloth and such to clean her and try and stop the bleeding. We were dismissed when Doc Abby took over, and everything was fine then."

"Sounds like you did some quick thinking and did a very good job of helping Lady Edra."

Marrak smiled, "Thank you, sir." He paused a moment and looked up shyly at the policeman. That look probably meant he knew something more.

"What is it?"

He shook his head unready yet to tell Ferguson more. "Thank you, Marrak. That's all for now." As Marrak left, Ferguson thought about Alan, who had been so recently promoted to houseman. Alan would have been the head footman above Joseph Marrak before they decided to open up the dower house. The large manor for now was down to one footman.

Now for the valet. The butler stood outside the door. "Lander, next I need to speak to the other man who helped bring Lady Edra inside."

"Certainly. That is Howel Wherry. He is Sir Vinson's valet and chauffeur. I'll send him in immediately."

That surprised Ferguson. Since the war, economic conditions had forced many grand old families to cut back on their number of servants, and many now doubled their duties. Having the valet also serve as the chauffeur would have been unthinkable only a few years ago. Lander called to a man passing through the kitchen carrying a pair of pants folded over his arm. Howel Wherry was a tall and dark, pleasant looking man in his mid-thirties. "Wherry, what is your position here?" The man seemed unduly edgy. That always alerted Ferguson. Maybe he knew something, was guilty of something, or maybe he was just a very nervous man.

"Uh, I'm…I'm Sir Vinson's valet, sir. I'm also the Bandrys' chauffeur."

"How long have you worked here, Wherry?" Ferguson asked a question Wherry could easily answer to calm him down.

Wherry sighed audibly. "Since aught three. I were near fourteen. The boot boy. Eventually, worked my way to be the head footman, and when Basker died of a heart attack, I got promoted to be Sir Vinson's valet. I became the chauffeur when they bought the town car."

"You had experience with cars?"

"Not when they first bought the Bentley, but I'm getting there. That car is such a dream to drive." He certainly perked up when the Bandrys' automobile was mentioned.

"When did Sir Vinson arrive home the night of the murder—and from where?"

"Probably after ten. I'm unsure exactly. We were rather in a bother, what with Lady Edra and the fire at the Crown and Doc Abby's and all."

"Where had Sir Vinson been so late?"

"I'm sure that's none of my affair, sir."

"Why are you in the kitchen at. . ." Ferguson pulled out his pocket watch, "ten in the morning? A bit past breakfast, is it not?" He smiled, knowing the man probably had been using the laundry room, but what made him so uncomfortable?

Wherry shrugged, then held out the pants for Ferguson to see, without looking at him. "Just came to iron these."

"I understand you helped Lady Edra the other night when she was injured, is that right?"

"Yes, sir."

"You reached the conservatory even before Marrak, is that correct? How did you hear about the commotion with Lady Edra? Were you down here in the kitchen where the other servants seemed to have been? But they heard nothing—or were you up in Sir Vinson's room? Still a long way from the conservatory, right?" Ferguson tried to rattle him and maybe find out what made him so nervous.

"I was passing the conservatory."

"Why? The route from an upstairs bedroom to below stairs—even by way of the main stairs—doesn't take one past the conservatory."

"I…I don't recall what brought me there, sir."

Ferguson didn't know if it related to the case, or if the man was perhaps stealing wine—or more appropriately from the conservatory—stealing rare orchids to sell. He would question him again. Now, he changed his questions. "Have you been shown the necklace the dead man wore or did you go over and look at his body?"

"I have no idea about the medallion and I absolutely did not go near the body! I don't know anything about that."

Wherry knew something he chose not to tell, and would need to be questioned again, but for now Ferguson knew he hadn't found out much in his investigation.

"Thank you, Wherry. Do you know who Lady Edra's personal maid is?"

"Of course, sir. That would be Fern Deane. She's also Lady Steran's maid, I believe."

Another example of double duty no doubt because of extreme cut backs. "Would you please tell Lander to send her in?"

"Certainly."

A few minutes later she knocked lightly, and he invited her to sit. A slight woman in her fifties or early sixties with grey curly hair escaping from its bun entered. "Mrs. Deane, you are Lady Steran's personal maid, I believe?"

"Yes. I'm also Lady Edra's personal maid."

"How did you become a personal maid to two ladies? How can you manage it? You must be worked off your feet."

She perked up at his acknowledgement of her responsibilities. "Needs must these days. It's not as much work as you would presume. I only have been Lady Edra's personal maid since her mother died. I had been her mother's personal maid since before Lady Edra was born. I've only become Lady Steran's maid since Dobbs moved to the dower house. Dobbs has always been before this. And neither lady is terribly demanding. They only change from their day clothes for dinner every night, and I use one of the house maids to help me if I get behind."

The only other question to be asked, had she seen the medallion received an answer of 'no'. She further claimed no knowledge of seeing any stranger. "Thank you for your help, Mrs. Deane."

The two kitchen maids knew nothing, and the two housemaids knew nothing. The boot boy was eager to know anything at all about Sunday night's excitement. Each of them only learned of Lady Edra's accident the next morning. Ferguson noted that there were only two kitchen maids to help the cook prepare meals for family and staff and clean the kitchen. And there were two housemaids who were responsible for cleaning this entire manor house? Parts of the house must be closed off because the two of them could never take care of such an immense house.

"Next, Lander, I need to see the stableboy who helped Lady Edra." He glanced at his notes, "Kitto. Could I speak to him?"

"He's undoubtedly at one of the barns or probably in one of the stables," Lander said glancing out his window, "but I could send someone to fetch him if you wish."

"That won't be necessary. I'll find him." Ferguson hadn't discovered much from interviewing the staff, but he didn't really think he would. Now, however, he knew more about who worked in the manor house and everybody's role. So far, he hadn't scratched the surface of how or why a man had died. Pulling the strange medallion from his pocket, he decided that, after interviewing the grooms, he would walk into town and see if any progress had been made.

Landry waited close by. Still unsure of the layout of the house, Ferguson asked to be escorted to the conservatory to see where Lady Edra had fallen.

Outside, standing on the top step, he could detect no blood where Landry pointed out Lady Edra had been found.

Barns and stables were at the far edge of the lawn to the right of where he stood. Again, he absorbed the beautiful design and meticulous grooming of the gardens and lawn. Walkways led around perfectly laid out bushes, and trees shaded ornate wrought iron benches. Ferguson chose a path leading toward the barns and found himself half way there in the shade of that ancient oak, with a diameter of five or six feet positioned in the middle of the formal gardens that he had noticed when they first met Sir Vinson. The red, gold and orange leaves rustled slightly, some of them floating to the ground around him. The tree's gigantic limbs creaked a bit overhead. Magnificent, he thought. Trees seemed always to be silently keeping watch. From ancient times, people understood oaks to be sacred. He thought oaks were probably chosen because their size gave them strength, and they were so durable, so hardy. This sentinel has watched over the Bandrys and their estate for at least a hundred years. What it could tell him. A shiver of unexplained sadness passed through him, and he had an urge to place his hand against the rough bark, but he had no time for ancient ways and continued on to the barn.

The barns included several rambling stone and heavy beam affairs, parts of which were two story and parts of which were much older than others. In a paddock behind the nearest stable, Sir Vinson sat very erect, leading a beautiful white gelding with a long, dark grey mane and tail through a series of turns. Horse and rider became one. He seemed to move not at all. He guided the horse through some high trots and turns. Apparently one of those things keeping him from being interviewed now.

An older man stood at the fence with one foot up on the railing, apparently giving Sir Vinson some instruction. The man appeared to be in his seventies. He had lined, leathery skin, and thick, curly grey hair. A young man in his twenties, with similar curly hair except brown, stood next to the older man and noticed Ferguson approach. The two men turned as Ferguson said, "I'm the detective looking into the murder." They both nodded, and the younger one said, "We saw the necklace and have no idea who he could be, sir."

"I figured as much. I'd like to ask you both some questions, if I may?" Ferguson asked, "Is Sir Vinson training the horse?"

"Sir Vinson and Asif are both training. There's a dressage competition Sunday over to Chough Hall. Why don't we go into the barn and talk?"

Both men led Ferguson, and the younger one pulled open a heavy weathered door, and they entered into a shadowy pungent atmosphere. As his eyes adjusted, Ferguson made out an area with hay stored in a loft above, and haying tools and other farm equipment on both sides of a dirt aisle down the middle with horse stalls on both sides. They moved through to a small workshop. Two other pointers, very similar to the beauty he met last night, followed them in and came over to Ferguson wagging their tails. Neither man seemed surprised by his visit.

The older man said, "Let's go into the office here, and we can have some tea." He led the way with a slightly stooped body and an odd, old man gait, to a room with a stove used for both heat and cooking. A battered metal kettle set atop the stove, which kept water perpetually hot. The man filled the teapot with hot water from the kettle and dumped in some tea. He invited Ferguson to sit at the battered table.

"I'm Mitchell Tink, Mitch to most," he introduced himself and held out his hand for Ferguson to shake. "I'm the Bandrys' groom, and this here is my grandson Kitto Tink. He's the stable hand."

While drinking their tea with Ferguson, both men disavowed any knowledge of the dead man. Kitto said, "It was a fascinating strange medallion. We never saw the likes of anything like that before. No man from around here would be wearing no necklace, and that one seemed kinda like some foreigner might wear." He noticed Ferguson petting the dogs and said, "that one's Blue, and Oscar is the bigger one. Lady Edra don't allow no fox hunting, but she sure loves her dogs. They tag along on her rides." He glanced at his granddad, who nodded at Kitto as he spoke.

Mitch said, "Lady Edra won't brook with fox hunting. She's too kind hearted. Won't even allow her father to have hunts here. He loves the fox hunts but has to go to other estates. That Arabian of his, Asif, always does him proud, whether he's hunting or competing in a dressage competition. Now Lady Edra, she loves to ride. Always has since she were younger than that lad Keyan. She likes to go on long rides onto some trails. Now, she's teaching him to ride. He's a keen learner. I reckon he just about loves horses as much as her."

Kitto said, "Keyan hangs around the stables sometimes so he can exercise Naasir with us. Calls her his horse." That made the two men smile. They had some affection for the boy.

Only when Ferguson brought up the storm and Lady Edra being knocked unconscious did either man seem reluctant to talk.

"Oh, it were a bad storm. I heard her yelling at the dogs as I closed up the stable doors," Kitto said. "I went to help and, when I got to her, she just lay there, blood on her, blood on the stone wall. I was right scared for her till we got her in the house and the doc come and all."

"She saved all the dogs from Dando," Mitch added, obviously proud of her and not the least bit embarrassed to admit he believed in the same superstition as his mistress.

Kitto, however, looked embarrassed. "It were a bad storm that night."

"Do either of you live on the estate?" Ferguson asked them.

"I had a little cottage in town, but now the wife's gone, I just usually stay in one of the rooms back here that used to be for hired hands—when we had such things," Mitch said. Then he added, "Kitto often stays in one of the rooms, too. It's kind of a long walk to his parent's farm."

Kitto nodded. "I spent the night here the night of the storm."

Ferguson thanked them for their help and the tea and decided to walk into town to see if he could discover anything there.

Chapter Five

Directly after passing the old columns at the estate entry, Ferguson stood at the fork in the road looking up the road toward the murder site. From here everything looked peaceful on another beautiful autumn day. To his left, a gravel path led to a rundown, brown shingle-sided house that had aged to nearly black in places, and soon would be hidden behind overgrown trees and bushes. Keyan and his grandmother's place. Probably no one home now. Keyan studied with Lady Edra, and his grandmother worked in Woodcomb selling pasties, the Cornish meat pies. Ferguson turned back and walked across the bridge into Woodcomb, a comfortable fifteen-minute stroll from the dower into the village. Doc Abby could readily maintain her practice from the dower. It's not a much farther walk than where her surgery had been located at the Crown Inn. Ferguson added all this information to the map he always developed in his head anywhere he went. Yesterday, in the back seat of the constable's car, his view had been so constricted that he needed to fill in most of where they had been.

The tide was nearly out, and boats sat on their keel leaning into the mud in the harbor, awaiting the rising tide to refloat them. Fishermen sat on the sea wall and the quay mending their nets and setting things right. He found Pengilley's Mortuary a block from the quay and went directly to the embalming room where he found Pengilley cleaning the room, and Abby sat speaking as Jory took notes.

"Ah, John," Doc Abby said, "we're just finishing up. I asked Constable Crocker, about whether he found rigor mortis when they found the body, and he said it seemed quite pronounced."

Orville Pengilley added, "Piran said he was stiff as a board."

"Yes," Abby agreed. "They found the man about nine Monday morning, so if what Piran believes is correct, I think he probably died between seven and eleven Sunday night. Cause of death is certainly no mystery. He was battered and hacked and finally trampled by a horse. I do think the horse came after the shovel blows. One of those shovel blows nicked his carotid artery which is what killed him." She pointed to a blackened crescent wound on his neck. The horse hooves were over several of the shovel cuts. And the horse was shod if that makes any difference. Most horses have shoes if they're being ridden, so that doesn't seem too helpful. From the body, I can only tell that his age was late twenties or early thirties. He was in good shape, strong heart and lungs, so I seriously doubt he was a vagrant or had been one very long. There was little left in his stomach, so I don't think he had eaten much that day. That's about all I can tell you."

"That's very helpful, thank you," Ferguson said. Pengilley looked quite pleased with himself so Ferguson added, "And, thank you as well, Mr. Pengilley."

Jory picked up his camera and said, "I'll get some shots of these wounds. I don't think the battered face will help much."

Ferguson said, "Get shots of that too. It might be pertinent in court, you never know."

Jory began by shooting close ups.

"Right, then," Abby said. "I'll be getting back to the dower." Ferguson walked with her as far as the police station. Wordlessly. Neither seemed to be able to think of any small talk.

"Well, I leave you here," Ferguson announced needlessly at the police station door. She merely nodded and smiled as she walked on. Ferguson watched her confident air and friendly manner as a couple of people spoke briefly to her. He felt particularly drawn to how her dark hair, which she fastened at her neck with a black ribbon, flamed red in the sunlight as it cascaded down her back. He found Sergeant Crocker sitting at his desk and asked him, "Piran, did you find any fishermen who had yet to be questioned about the pendant?"

"Some were still out on the boats when we showed it around before. But the ones this morning were no help. No one could tell me anything about it."

"Take the pendant down and show whoever is down there now. Several men are waiting for the tide to return. It might be a good time to question them. See if anyone knows someone who might have been missed before."

"Might ought to wait for Jory. He's my boss and might have better ideas for my time."

Ferguson placed the necklace back into his vest pocket as Jory came in the back door. They still needed to show it around. He found two pieces of paper, drew two circles, then sketched the front and back emblems on both and handed one to Jory saying, "Someone needs to take this sketch down to the waterfront and make sure every fisherman has indeed had a chance to look at it. Perhaps Crocker could do that?"

Jory said, "Sounds good. Why don't you head out now?" Without looking at either man, Crocker grabbed the paper silently and left.

"Did you get the fingerprints on the train to London?" Ferguson asked Jory.

"Yep. Managed to catch the morning train. You didn't tell me how to address the package. I addressed it to your boss DI Howell at Scotland Yard. Hope that works. If I'd missed that train, the next train doesn't leave until late this afternoon. Maybe now they'll get them analyzed today."

"That's perfect."

"I've been thinking," Jory said, "it's over twenty miles from Liskeard to Woodcomb. The train from London on Sunday reached Liskeard at eleven forty-five am. If our murder victim got off that train, and had to walk to Woodcomb, at a steady four miles per hour, it would take him over five hours. That would get him here about six or seven Sunday night. But, someone may have given him a ride. So, we still don't know the time of the murder."

Ferguson added, "That fits with what Abby says is the approximate time of death."

Geever came into the station and stood listening then asked, "If Woodcomb had been his destination, why didn't he get a ticket to Woodcomb? Surely, it's not that much more money."

"Probably didn't have the money. It's cheaper to come into Liskeard. People from here often get off the train at Liskeard to save money. But they always have someone to pick them up. Wherever he was bound, anyone in Cornwall expecting this man would know about the murder by now, and would have shown up to tell us about him."

Ferguson added, "Perhaps he didn't alert whoever he wanted to see because he intended to surprise someone. He apparently did succeed in surprising someone, but that someone certainly did not want him here."

"Could someone he knew have picked him up and given him a ride who doesn't want us to know about it?" Geever said.

Ferguson said, "Maybe someone passing through dropped him near his destination or even dropped him here in town. Maybe they dropped him at the Crown."

"We asked over there, but they sure had their hands full Monday. I ought to ask again."

Ferguson said, "Also, we need to question anyone else near the murder scene. I haven't spoken to the farmer across the road from the scene or Keyan or his grandmother. Doc Abbey said the man died between seven and eleven. What time did Keyan have his attack or seizure or whatever happened to him."

Jory answered, "Probably about six, six-thirty. When I saw him, he didn't seem excited or upset like you'd expect if he ran on to a bloody body—or worse watched someone murder a man."

"Probably true. So Keyan probably only found him Monday morning. What other farms are east on that road past Tredwen Manor? Maybe he spoke to someone."

"Hicca Stark owns the land just east of the manor the other side of Menadue Wood north of the road and all the land to the cliff south. Beyond him are some other farms that face the main road. Someone from that direction could have seen a man walk by. The one directly across from the murder scene is the manor farm. Arthur Penrose and his family live there, and he runs the place. Penrose is also the groundskeeper at the manor," Jory said.

Geever asked, "Ah, is he the man responsible for the lovely gardens?"

"Him and a gaggle of locals who do most of the actual farming and garden work. Most of them live in or near Woodcomb."

Ferguson turned to Geever, "How'd you do with finding out who received or sent telegrams around last Sunday?"

Jory chuckled at that, "Georgia is our telegraph person at the train station, and she won't give you that information. We'll need a court order for that. I've tried. If you need that information, Ferguson, we need to get on to Truro and find the judge."

Geever looked from Jory to Ferguson, then said, "She told me. There have been three telegrams sent to Woodcomb. Two of them were sent Sunday, and one was sent from Woodcomb to London on Monday. Of the two telegrams that arrived last Sunday, Mrs. Liza Zelly received one." He paused a second before saying, "The second one was sent to Lady Edra Bandry." Both detectives looked at Jory. He shrugged his shoulders. Geever continued, "And the one on Monday arrived at the London Daily News signed from Ruth Dahl."

"Ah, I understand the Monday morning telegram. Ruth Dahl is the editor and publisher of our local paper. I think that explains how a London paper got the sensational story about a village in Cornwall so quickly," Jory said. Then to Geever, amazed, "How in hell did you get Georgia to give you all that private information?"

Geever answered simply with a shrug, "It is good to be the second son of the earl of Truro." All three men grinned. Geever impressed Ferguson. He had accomplished something.

He felt Geever could adequately reinterview some people, and said, "I think we need to reinterview all the merchants on the High Street and make sure we reach everyone. That would be the most important task for us. Maybe our victim headed to the Crown. Now that they have settled down after cleaning up from Monday night's storm, so I…"

Taking command, Geever said decisively, "Yes, I agree, Ferguson." He grabbed the other drawing saying, "I will get on that immediately, and Jory you need to redrive the route from Liskeard asking at each farm for who might have given our victim a lift. Ferguson, you should go interview the gardener fellow, Penrose, and the boy and grandmother. Also, Jory, think about people who drive to Liskeard regularly or even occasionally and interview them."

"I talked to the constables in some of the villages on my way back from Liskeard. Nothing."

"Jory, then you and I can interview Penrose and drive on east and question the farmers along the road the victim would have passed," Ferguson said. He wanted to interview the groundskeeper himself.

Driving with Jory back across the bridge to the crossroads, Ferguson remembered he still hadn't interviewed either the boy, Keyan, or Lady Edra, but felt that could wait and be his next job after questioning those who live along the road the dead man walked Sunday night. They passed the overgrown cottage barely visible from the road where Keyan lived with his grandmother and stopped at the well-tended manor farm. The lane off the road leading to the manor farm sat almost directly across from the murder site. The farmhouse stood solid, made of stone, with a slate roof. A strip of grass and some well-tended, autumn blooming flowers bordered the house. The outbuildings, including two big, stone barns and the large granary, all in good repair, except for the hurriedly repaired damage to one corner of the granary. The grounds surrounding the farm were neatly maintained. He saw pens for geese and chickens as well as a few milk cows contentedly grazing. He saw no one and wondered if all the farm hands and groundsmen had been recruited to do the remodel work on the dower. As they approached the house, he considered whether they should approach the obviously little used front door or go on around to the kitchen door, when a woman about thirty appeared on the kitchen porch, startled to find them. She turned back immediately, and the same blond man they had seen hacking back bushes from the front of the dower yesterday stepped out. Jory said, "Arthur, this is Detective Inspector Ferguson. He has some questions.

"You are Arthur Penrose?" Ferguson asked. The man looked angry but nodded. "Can you tell me your occupation, please."

"I manage this here manor farm. I also am the groundskeeper over to the manor itself." Penrose, a tall, powerfully built man in his forties, scowled at both men. "I know why you're here and don't know nothing."

"A man lay murdered practically right across the road from your place, and I wondered if maybe…"

"Well, you'd be wrong then wouldn't you, in wondering any such thing. Don't know nothing and didn't see nor hear nothing."

"I'd like to speak to the woman I saw a moment ago and ask her…"

"That woman is my wife, and she knows nothing also."

"Nevertheless, I need to ask her myself as this is a murder investigation."

The man simply glared for a moment, then seemed to realize he would need to answer. "Fine then." And he yelled back into the kitchen, "Eva, get out here!"

Eva seemed much younger than her husband, probably in her early thirties. She slowly came onto the porch, keeping her eyes down. She had brown hair pulled out of her face by a sloppy ponytail. She had a pleasant enough face. She denied knowing anything by shaking her head at each of Ferguson's questions, glancing at Penrose to make sure her husband approved of her answers. Ferguson pulled the medallion from his pocket and held it out. The man shook his head. Ferguson noticed a slight hesitation from Eva, but she also shook her head no. Penrose said, "I saw that yesterday and have no idea what it is." Eva knew something, but Ferguson realized he needed to speak to her alone to get anywhere. Otherwise, Penrose would control all her answers. Perhaps it meant nothing, but this came as the first inkling that anyone recognized it.

"Mr. Penrose, what were you doing last Sunday night?"

"I was trying to get all of the oats out of the fields and into the granary. We had a long day, and we had trouble with a loaded truck backing into the granary as you can see." He nodded toward it. "Then the storm hit."

"Busy day. Where did your crew of men come from?"

"Several village men."

"Their names?"

Penrose looked at Jory, impatiently shaking his head. "Let's see. Trew and James Jones. I don't know. There were several."

"I'll need a complete list, Mr. Penrose. You can leave it with Constable Crocker this afternoon." Penrose was about to protest when Ferguson said, "As they left, your men were not more than twenty feet from where a dead man lay. His body barely off the road. It seems improbable that as everyone walked out of your lane and headed home, not one person noticed a body as they left."

"I can tell you now we left during that eerie storm, and we spotted the Crown fire, and every man of us rushed to help Abe. Darkness and rain and wind, as well as being tired, prevented every one of us from peering into the ditch across the road, Detective."

"Next morning, didn't these men return Monday morning to work the harvest?"

"Next morning, Lady Edra had us start working on the dower for the doc."

Ferguson thanked them for their cooperation, and both he and Jory shook the man's hand and nodded at Eva. He would return to the angry Penrose and his timid wife. They left the manor property, heading east, crossing the small stone bridge and drove through Menadue Wood. Branches converged overhead, creating a leafy canvas dappled by sunlight.

The car suddenly jerked to a stop throwing Ferguson forward. Jory had slammed on the brakes. Keyan had popped up from the trees and crossed the road in front of them. Both Keyan and Lady Edra's dog, Sheba, stood wide-eyed and frozen.

"Watch out!" Jory shouted before jumping from the car. "What are you doing, Keyan? I nearly ran over you! You have to be more careful." Jory took a deep breath, calmed his voice, then asked, "Are you all right, boy?"

Keyan mumbled, "Sorry, we're just playing."

"Well, be more careful please."

Lady Edra's two other dogs, introduced to Ferguson by the Tinks in the barn earlier, appeared, and the troop walked on across, before erupting into a run through the forest, on toward the cliff. Jory returned to the car. "Sorry about that. He plays a lot over here in these woods. Scared me." Jory chugged to a start, slowly picking up speed again. "He spends a lot of time on his own. His gran works hard. Lots of hours. He hates the kids at school. Rarely goes. Might have a seizure. I can understand how much the faces of the other kids, either of fear or of disgust or worse, just laughing would hurt a lad. Without Lady Edra, I don't know. I don't think he'd be such a brave, happy lad."

Ferguson thought about Keyan. Did he have too much freedom for a lad of nine? Would there be more to know about him? "His mother is accused of murdering a baby. Possibly mental problems he inherited." Jory's mouth fell open. "Sorry," Ferguson said. "I have a copper's brain. Always have to contemplate the worst." Ferguson watched his reaction out of the corner of his eye.

Jory shook his head slightly, then said, "Course you have to think the worst, but that's not this lad. He's not mental. He has seizures, that's all."

And his mum…did others think well of her? At least right up until she killed a child?" he asked.

"Not a shred of evidence to prove that. It was so out of character. A lot of people don't believe she did it. I know we can't explain what happened so she became the logical, the easy answer to whatever happened."

As they cleared the woods, a prosperous, well-tended, old farm appeared to their left with a large half-timbered farmhouse and several barns including a couple of ancient stone barns. The surrounding grounds were well taken care of. "Hicca Stark and his wife Anne live here." A tall man, who looked about sixty, stepped out his front door to greet them as they emerged from the car. Jory said, "Hicca, this is Detective Inspector Fergeson, and we'd like to ask you and Anne some questions about Sunday night. I've told the inspector that you both saw the medallion and didn't recognize it."

"Pleased to meet you Detective," Hicca said with a booming voice and offered a firm handshake for both men. He was tall and powerfully built, with a ruddy complexion, a shock of steel grey hair and an impressive grey mustache. He looked exactly like who he was—a prosperous, life-long farmer, dressed in a nice wool suit and tie. Ferguson could tell by the way Hicca introduced him to his wife, he was proud of her. Anne was an attractive woman ten, fifteen years younger than her husband. She had dark-brown hair pulled into a bun atop her head and had a lovely face surrounded by curls. "Annie, give these gentlemen some tea." She served them tea with thick slices of bread slathered with butter. After one bite Ferguson said, "Oh, delicious. Thank you. Are you tenants of the Bandrys?"

"No." Hicca explained. "We've been freeholders since the 1660s. One of my ancestors fought with the loyalist Bandry baron at the time in the civil war. My grandfather saved that Bandry's life and in gratitude he gave us this land." Mrs. Stark came and sat next to him, and Ferguson noticed their hands touched.

"Impressive farm, Mr. Stark. How do you and the present Bandrys get along today?"

"Just fine. We have been good neighbors for near three hundred years. We have no problems."

Ferguson glanced at Anne who smiled, nodding at that. "Would either of you care for more tea," she asked. They seemed devoted to each other. Their home gave off a well lived in, comfortable, contented feel. It passed quickly through his head that he wished they stayed here instead of the dower.

Jory added "Hicca here, is the Bandrys' estate agent, aren't you Mr. Stark?"

"For years. I do accounts for several of the big land owners here as well as some big wigs in Truro." Hicca Stark reminded Ferguson of his father. A man of strength, integrity and honesty. Even Stark's mustache and mutton-chop side burns mimicked his dad's. His father's loyalty to Lord Charles at Culzean Castle neared excessive at times. Ferguson pictured his dad's warmth, his booming voice and his roaring laughter, and smiled at the similarities.

"Did you, either of you, notice anyone walking by your farm on the road Sunday night?" Annie shook her head no. Stark answered, "Sunday night I stayed in Truro. I had business with some clients, and I just spent the night with them."

Ferguson couldn't think of any other questions. Shaking hands with the man he added, "Thanks for your time. It's been great to meet you, Mr. Stark and you, Mrs. Stark."

As they pulled away Jory teased, "You seem to care for the Starks a great deal more than the Penroses."

"Not even close. One family lives mostly in fear or rage, the other in pride and contentment. The Starks remind me of my parents. I know he could be a brutal killer…"

"But you hope not," Jory grinned. "You're right though. Everybody respects both of the Starks."

Ferguson and Jory continued on to two farms farther along the road toward Liskeard and learned nothing. They decided to return to the quay for some lunch at the pasty shop run by Keyan's grandmother, before locating Lady Edra and Keyan.

Keyan waited for Lady Edra at the bottom step of the terrace that led out of the conservatory. He inspected a small spot, convinced he spied a splash of blood on one of the stones from the wall. He thought it must have been missed when someone, probably that new girl Sukie's sister, scrubbed the terrace after Lady Edra had been chased by the evil demon. He became interested in the gardens and the huge oak safeguarding the manor. He decided to walk under its massive limbs. He stood daring himself to touch the bark of the trunk. He knew this grandfather tree protected these grounds, and although the tree always scared him a little, today he had a grievance. Something stirred in the branches, and he spotted a crow watching him. Under the obvious protection of one of his crows, he felt confident to touch the tree trunk. The bark felt rough and thick, and Keyan instantly felt a rumbling, beginning deep in the tree's center. Before he lost his nerve, he shouted up into the autumn leaves, "Why didn't you protect Lady Edra from the evil demon?" The rumbling grew to a low wail. He leaned in, hugging the tree tightly. He wouldn't let go until he had an answer. Leaves trembled, then branches pitched back and forth until they dipped to nearly slap him. He held fast and yelled, "Tell me!" His hair blew wildly. Darkness descended. A dead grey face with bulging eyes appeared from the bark. It screamed, yet Keyan heard no sound. Tree branches enveloped him. They grew tighter, suffocating him. He tried frantically to free himself or yell for help, as they closed tighter, but he had no breath to scream.

Lady Edra stood on the terrace searching for Keyan, who usually waited for her here. She spotted him standing under the oak looking so small, dwarfed by the gigantic oak, and wondered what he played at, this morning, arms wrapped around the tree. She walked over to him smiling and touched his narrow little back. Immediately, he fell to the ground limp and sweating. As she held him, he gasped and opened his eyes.

Sobbing he said, "The tree tried to kill me!" He threw his arms around her.

———————————

Jory bowed out of joining Ferguson for lunch at the pasty shop. He had his lunch at the station. The little pasty shop squatted near the water's edge, facing both the High Street as well as the inlet. As Ferguson walked toward it, he noticed on his right, the tide returning to the bay and starting to float the boats. Inside the shop, he could see some stools at a small counter and one small table. All were full. Two fishermen stood waiting to order from a little window in the side of the shop. As Ferguson looked out over the water, Geever spotted him and came up to the shop.

"Nothing new from any of the merchants, and the sluggish and uninspired Constable Crocker got no new response to the medallion from the men working down here," Geever said. "A little lunch sounds good. You discover anything?" Ferguson shook his head.

Inside the shop, they found a dark-haired slim woman, probably near sixty, red faced and perspiring a little from the heat of the oven behind the counter.

She hesitated before speaking. "Detectives, what can I do for you?" She knew everyone in town and reckoned these strangers must be the police.

The men gave her their order, and Ferguson said, "We'd like a word with you after the lunch rush." She nodded and served both men. Ferguson told Geever of his lack of progress, as they sat on the seawall, both eating bacon pasties with their tea and watching the activity with the boats in the bay. "The Bandry estate agent, Hicca Stark, impressed me. He seems interesting."

After a couple of bites, Geever said, " We need to find and question Keyan and Lady Edra." Ferguson wanted to interview them alone, but knew Geever could not be expected to team up with Constable Crocker again.

"I think it would be better if we split up this afternoon. I'll stay here and question Keyan's grandmother. It won't take but a minute for her to agree she knows nothing. Then I'll find Keyan and Lady Edra. If you would, I think you might be more successful at interviewing Sir Vinson than I would. He'll feel more at ease with you, and maybe you can find out if he knows more than he's telling us." Geever nodded his assent and left to go to the manor. Ferguson remained sitting on the wall, soaking up the lovely warm weather, while he watched Woodcomb come and go around him, until the pasty shop emptied out. When he noticed her cleaning the tables, Ferguson approached saying, "I understand you're Keyan's grandmother."

"Yes. I'm Mary Inch."

"I need to ask you some questions about your grandson, Keyan. But first, some questions about the murder just up the road from your home. Were you expecting a young man in his twenties or early thirties on Sunday?"

She shook her head.

"Did you see the body while it lay in the ditch?"

She looked shocked. "Oh, course not. I'd have told Jory."

"I've heard that Keyan roams around the Bandry estate during the day." She appeared indignant. Did he suggest the lad was not well taken care of? He asked, "Did Keyan come and tell you about discovering the body?"

"He said nothing to me at first, but he seemed very quiet. I knew something bothered him. He finally told me what he saw, and I sent him to Jory."

"I've heard he skips school a lot, and you know about that."

She sighed. "I try to get him to go to school. He has no friends. The kids are afraid of him or tease him mercilessly like that bully Tommy Penrose." This last, she practically spit out.

Ferguson told her, "He had one of his attacks on Sunday, the night of the murder, at the pub on the quay and declared that Dando would kill the Green Man. The dead man wore a green suit. Doesn't what he said seem odd?"

"Sometimes he sees or knows things that others can't see."

"I've heard you are what some here call a gypsy. Do you also have some unusual abilities?"

"I am Romani," she said indignantly. "I have no special powers. Sometimes when someone asks, I can help my neighbors with problems that seem to have no answer. Romani is my culture, just as much as the Cornish culture I've acquired in more than forty years living here. I came as a fisherman's wife and have always been treated the same as any other man's wife. I have no problems with my neighbors."

He pulled out the medallion with the strange markings and held it up. "Does this look familiar at all?"

Her face blanched, a shocked cry escaped her lips, tears nearly overflowed, and she shook and would have fallen, if Ferguson hadn't caught her and helped her to a chair.

"I gave a necklace exactly like that to my daughter Jenna and one to my son Geran to protect them from evil. Keyan also has one, but he won't wear it. I haven't seen Geran for seven years since he disappeared without a word." She sobbed, with her head in her hands. "Is the dead man my poor Geran?"

Chapter Six

Lots of people wear all kinds of talismans for luck or protection and some for protection against evil. Thinking about it though, Ferguson believed it made sense that the unique medallion might be related to the son of the woman the townspeople call the gypsy. He asked Mrs. Inch to walk over to the police station so they could talk. He locked her shop door for her.

From the quay, Officer Crocker watched Ferguson walking with an obviously upset Mary Inch, and he hurried back to the station. "What's he doing now," Crocker murmured to himself. "He shouldn't upset her. She's such a nice woman. Always been good to me. Some folks take against her. Always will. All the sadness that's been hers to bear. That nasty piece of work her son, her daughter, Jenna, killed then blamed for murder. Stuck raising her grandson, who's marked by some evil. How long would this woman need to live in Woodcomb before she's judged as just a fisherman's widow. He shook his head as he opened the door to the station and entered in a rush muttering as he closed the door behind him, "Mary doesn't know anything!"

Ferguson turned at the suddenness of his entry. "Crocker, would you get Mrs. Inch some tea?" Ferguson waited for her to calm down a little, although she still shook moments later as she accepted the cup of tea from Crocker.

"Would you be able to identify the body over at Pengilley's Mortuary, do you think?"

"What?" The realization hit Mary Inch that Ferguson believed the body might be Geran. "I don't know," she answered quietly. "I haven't seen Geran since the day he left seven years ago—a year before Jenna died."

"Jenna?" The name rang a bell for Ferguson.

"My daughter, Keyan's mother. They found her body at the bottom of the cliff at the far reach of Tredwen Manor after that poor babe disappeared." Then she started shaking, crying and becoming very angry. Her voice grew, "They blamed my Jenna for his disappearance and said she killed herself for what she done. But that's not true. She loved that little boy like she loved her own Keyan. She would never have hurt him and she never would have abandoned Keyan."

A question occurred to Ferguson. "And the little boy's body?"

Officer Crocker answered, "Never found. Some said she took him over the cliff with her, and his little body washed away with the tide." He looked sympathetically at Mrs. Inch and added, "But others say he never died. He got stolen while young Jenna visited her mum. Maybe they sold him. She felt the guilt of him disappearing on her watch and ended it over the cliff." He looked at Mary Inch sympathetically and added for her benefit, "But none with brains ever believed any of it."

"Jenna never would have left Keyan!" Mary declared and looked around defying anyone to dispute it.

Ferguson heard more about the murders from seven years ago. Did they lead to this murder? "Could Geran have had something to do with the deaths of your daughter and the boy?"

"Come back a year after he left, killed his sister and took his son?" Mrs. Inch looked at him like he must have lost his senses. "That's absurd. He had it pretty cushy married to a proper lady with a son to inherit the whole Tredwen estate eventually. That makes no sense."

Ferguson wondered why he did abandon such a life. Mrs. Inch said, "I always figured something happened to him. I had no idea he was alive. What has he been doing all these years? Why did he never write or visit?" She sounded hurt.

Ferguson wondered why he came back on Sunday. "Do you think you could look at the body?" She nodded, calming a bit. "I'll go over to Pengilley's and tell him to get the body ready for us to examine." He left her with Crocker who seemed sympathetic and more engaged than Ferguson had ever seen the man. "Crocker, walk her over in a few minutes, please."

At the mortuary Pengilley told him, "The body's as presentable as possible. I have him ready for burial. I figured very soon you'd release the body. I can put him on the embalming table again, and of course, I'll cover up the most damaged parts. Which doesn't leave much for identification."

Crocker walked Mrs. Inch over a short while later, and she saw a body shape covered by a sheet with hands, arms and feet sticking out. She hesitantly neared the shape and looked very closely at the corpse's hands and arms, then the feet. She reached out to touch his hand but recoiled at the last second by the eerie bluish white skin. His dark hair that had been washed of blood peeked out from the sheet. She ran her hand through it as tears ran down her face.

"The hair certainly looks like it could be his," she quietly said, "but there's nothing else about him that would allow me to swear he's my son."

"Did your son have any distinguishing marks?" Ferguson asked.

"What are distinguishing marks?" Mrs. Inch and Pengilley asked at the same time.

"Something like a scar or birth mark. Or even a tattoo."

"A tattoo? No, not that I know of." She thought a second. "No birthmarks. And he had no scars that I know of. If he wore that medallion you showed me, it's him. No one else would have it." She touched his hair again.

Walking back to the station, Mary still shook and slowly sobbed. Ferguson knew she needed someone to take her home and stay with her for awhile. Crocker needed to stay at the station to update Jory upon his return, and Geever remained at the manor house talking to Sir Vinson. "We'll get someone to give you a ride home and stay with you for a bit."

"I can't go home yet," she said. "I have to clean up my shop and get it ready for the morning."

Crocker said to Ferguson, "You could go ask Ham, sir. He'll know someone."

"And who and where is Ham?"

"He'll be working at the Badger, the pub. Right on the quay."

Ferguson had seen the Badger but hadn't been in it yet. Upon entering he saw one very thin old man, shoulders sagging with a scraggly beard sitting at the bar hugging a pint of beer. He didn't even look up, although Ferguson's entering had let in a blast of sunlight and a squeak from the hinges quite noticeable in the silent bar. Ferguson noticed noise coming from behind the bar, and about that time, a man stood. He was slim in his early thirties with dark hair. "I'm looking for Ham," Ferguson said.

"That's me. How can I help you, Detective? I've been shown the medallion, and I don't recognize anything about it."

"That's fine. Officer Crocker said you might know someone who could give Mary Inch a ride home and stay with her a bit. And possibly someone who could clean her pasty shop. She's had a shock and is very upset right now and could use some help."

It took Ham a second to process all that. He had a lot of questions, but realized now was not the time to ask them. He would get no answers. "Sure. Sure. Let me think. Well, I'll ask my sister, Merryn, if she could spare the time to stay with her and maybe spare the time to clean up her shop or know someone who could. It'll take a few minutes, but I'll pick Mary Inch up very shortly. "Joe, you're in charge until I get back," he yelled to the old man at the bar who nodded once, and didn't look up from his beer. Ferguson laid the key to the pasty shop on the bar. Ham picked it up, and they both left.

"Right now, she's at the police station. I'll tell her to wait and someone will give her some help."

At the station, Jory had returned and spoke with Mrs. Inch. "Excuse me. Jory, a minute, please," Ferguson said walking Jory aside.

Jory said, "Mrs. Inch says the body is definitely her son, Geran?" He made it a question.

"His age and general description fit, and it seems unlikely anyone else would be wearing the medallion that he always wore, according to his mother," Ferguson said. "I need to get back up to the manor and inform Lady Edra and Keyan.

Jory offered, "Maybe I could do that. It might be easier coming from a friend."

"No. I need to see her first reaction. I've sent Ham to find someone to take Mary Inch home and be with her. I'm more convinced this case has some bearing on the murder of Lady Edra's baby and Keyan's mother. Tell me about that investigation."

"Not much to tell," Jory began. Geran abandoned them soon after the war started. The next year the murders happened. That would have been 1915. I was second in command to DI Samuel Pascoe then, and we had the whole south of Cornwall to protect from invasion and crime. That kept us busy. Besides, we found no evidence in this case. No witnesses. The family, the Bandrys were away for the holidays. No one remained around the estate.

All the servants had been given the time off while the family were gone. Jenna, the nurse to Lady Edra's son, remained behind at the dower with both toddlers—her son and Lady Edra's. We found the house empty. Nothing disturbed. No furniture upset, nothing broken. Just Jenna's body washed up at the bottom of a cliff and a missing two-year-old boy, the heir to Tredwen Manor. Of course, the baroness' son being murdered became an immediate priority. We questioned everyone who could have known anything. Nothing."

"Could you or Crocker round up the file and get it to me?" Ferguson asked. They both looked in at Mrs. Inch who appeared bewildered sitting in Jory's office. Ferguson sighed. "By tonight?"

Jory agreed. "Since Ham's finding her a ride home, I'm going to check out some local stuff. Nothing to do with this case. It's a couple of feuding farmers. It'll take awhile to locate the file. I'll get Piran on it." They both looked toward Crocker. Mary Inch seemed lost in sorrow and shock. Crocker had moved next to her and took her hand in his. She looked toward him with a tiny smile and patted his hand.

Ham found his sister at the farmer's market packing up her baskets, two empty and one still half full of vegetables, into her wagon, when he grabbed her. "Merryn, can you drop what you're doing?"

His sister answered, "Alright, Alright! What's going on? Ham what…"

"That detective asked me if someone could give Mrs. Inch a ride home, and then clean up the pasty shop. He asked if I knew someone who might help."

"Why would I need to do that? I'm all but on my way home. School'll be out. Dinner." Amazed at the request, she waited.

"The detective said Mary Inch was too upset to do it herself. He didn't say, but I think maybe she identified the body of the murdered man." He waited a beat, then "And who would that be except Geran Inch come back from the dead?"

She nearly dropped the cups before she dropped them in the wagon. "Dear God! Can it be?"

"Come with me now, and we'll know shortly."

Opening the dower door, Ferguson met the same commotion as yesterday, including the perky receptionist, who smiled again, and the patients quietly waiting, as well as workmen clanging and hammering and the servants bustling around. But, he found no Geever or Lady Edra or Keyan. He asked the houseman Alan where they were. He needed to fill Geever in on the latest developments as soon as possible.

"I suppose they're all up at the manor," Alan responded. The other detective walked to the house, maybe half an hour ago. And I haven't seen Lady Edra or Keyan today."

Ferguson walked up to the manor and Lander let him. "Where would I find Detective Geever?"

"He's in the library with Sir Vinson," and then Lander stood silently offering no direction toward the library. "Where would the library find itself then? Lead the way, Lander—now. Please." Lander seemed offended at Ferguson's abruptness, but led the way. Ferguson stepped into the magnificent library and found floor to ceiling books, mahogany carved woodwork and a beautiful red Persian rug, under the feet of Geever and Sir Vinson, who sat in two wingback chairs facing a small fire.

"Ferguson, I've been talking with Sir Vinson."

"Yes, Detective, Geever's been asking about the night of the murder."

"And what have you told him?"

"Well, I visited with a lady I know." He made a small, knowing smile, clear in its meaning.

"And what time were you with her?"

"I'm unsure. Just after the storm broke. We chatted until eleven or somewhere there about."

"Her name?"

"That would be very indiscreet, you understand, and I'd rather not." Probably married and one of his tenants, Ferguson thought but held his tongue.

Geever said, "You know, Sir Vinson, we really do need this. It is a murder investigation, after all." Geever was being very solicitous. His tone might be perfect to secure Sir Vinson's cooperation.

"I really can't say," Vinson thrust out his chin in defiance.

Ferguson lost his patience with this. "Detective, I need to speak to you, immediately," and he started out the door. Geever excused himself, rose, and followed.

In the hallway, Ferguson explained that Keyan's grandmother identified the body as that of her son. "She knew the medallion he wore had to be his. She's very upset. We need to find Lady Edra and tell her that her missing husband has returned. Keyan also needs to know. Lander will have to show us where they are." No surprise to Ferguson, but Lander immediately appeared, as if speaking his name conjured him from thin air. He led Geever and Ferguson upstairs, down long winding hallways where the walls were progressively less grandly finished. The rich eight-inch elaborately carved baseboard, oiled and dusted, disappeared, to be replaced by plain three-inch pine baseboard. No beautiful wall paper or brass sconces decorated this hallway. Lander opened a door and led them into a classroom with a chalkboard and a huge world map on one wall. Ferguson realized he had reached the children's wing. The nursery and quarters for a nurse and a nanny would be near. Keyan sat at a desk while Lady Edra, sitting across from him, helped him with his lesson.

Ferguson abruptly stopped just inside the door. The suddenness and savageness of what he needed to disclose hit him. How could he gently express everything? He stood numbly looking from one to the other as Lady Edra and Keyan stared. Geever moved past Ferguson understanding his hesitancy, and sat in a chair facing them. In a quiet calm voice he said, "Lady Edra, we have some distressing news for you."

Lady Edra looked from one detective to the other, puzzled. "Perhaps we could chat a moment, gentlemen." She rose and took them into the hallway. "What's going on?"

Ferguson knew no way to soften the information. "I'm sorry, Lady Edra, but Mary Inch has identified the dead man as her son, Geran."

Shocked, she quietly asked, "Geran, my husband? Geran who has been missing and presumed dead for years? Alive until Sunday?" She felt weak and leaned against the wall. Geever sat her down in a nearby chair.

"Did you not see the medallion to identify?" Ferguson asked.

"Yes, of course."

"Mrs. Inch says her son always wore a medallion exactly like the one the dead man wore."

"What? He did wear some necklace, but I never really examined it. I never dreamed this could be Geran." Ferguson thought she must be a great actress, if, in reality, none of this actually shocked her, and she recognized the medallion immediately as belonging to Geran.

"I'm sorry I upset you. I also need to tell Keyan. He needs to go to his grandmother now. She needs him."

"Yes, of course." She opened the door and returned to Keyan and sat taking his hand. The two detectives remained in the doorway.

Keyan asked warily, "What's going on?"

Lady Edra said, "Do you know who your Uncle Geran was?" Keyan stared. "He was my husband. Do you remember any of that? He disappeared when you weren't quite two."

They could tell Keyan didn't understanding what she told him, but he watched Lady Edra closely, hoping she wasn't upset. She smiled and held out her hand. "Let's go see Baba."

Lady Edra and Keyan, followed by the detectives, walked down the road past the columns and turned up the road that ran by the Inch house. A horse and wagon waited next to the overgrown path to the small dark, rundown house. Keyan ran ahead and rushed through the door. They entered and found Keyan's grandmother sitting in a chair, not really looking at anything. A young woman with light brown hair, twisted into a rushed knot at the back of her head, sat next to Mrs. Inch holding a cup of tea. A teapot sat on a tray with milk and sugar in front of them. But it didn't look like Mrs. Inch had touched hers. Keyan ran into her arms. "Baba?"

Ferguson asked, "Is it okay for Keyan to stay, or should he and the young woman go?" He nodded to the young woman.

"My name is Merryn," she said quietly.

Mrs. Inch said, "Merryn, it's fine. He should know. Let him stay."

She looked first at Keyan, then at the rest of them. "Geran my son, my beautiful boy grew up loving everything *grast*. That's Romani for horse. He just seemed to understand what horses wanted. The Bandrys noticed his skill, and he worked with Sir Vincent as well as working alongside the grooms. He became a wild young man. Lady Edra, you were such a strong-willed girl. I always thought his rebel ways is what drew you to him. Unique compared to the predictable young men of your set." Lady Edra simply stared into Mrs. Inch's eyes and took her hand. Looking around at the others she continued. "Lady Edra actually married my son. He lived in the manor house, had privilege and respect. I never understood why he would leave you. They said he wanted a more exciting life." She shook her head. "But to leave his son, Caden?" Tears now streamed down Lady Edra's face.

Keyan became upset looking from Lady Edra to his Baba. "Don't cry. It'll be alright."

He asked, "Baba, the man who died was your son?"

"Yes, and he was your uncle." Puzzled how any of this affected him, he only cared that the two people he cared for more than anything were so sad.

Merryn said, "Keyan, why don't you show me around?" The boy led her outside into the late afternoon day.

They sat quietly for a few minutes with Mary Inch's sorrow then, Lady Edra asked, "Should we leave you in peace, Mrs. Inch, for now." She nodded. They filed quietly out closing the door behind them.

They stepped past Keyan and Merryn sitting on the front steps. Lady Edra said, "Keyan, dear, you stay with your Baba, all right?" He nodded. Merryn and he watched as Lady Edra and the policemen walked up to the road and disappeared behind the pines. From the steps, Keyan pointed up to the crows watching from their branch. The black hunched-shouldered birds hopped from one foot to the other and made cooing noises. "Crows are good luck. These keep an eye out for us." Merryn nodded looking up at the crows barely registering what he said. She had a lot to think about, remembering the daring, laughing Geran Inch who so beguiled her all those years ago as she sat watching the sun lower over Woodcomb.

The workmen packed up to leave as they returned to the dower. The last patient must have gone because Sally no longer sat at her desk just inside the front door. Abby emerged from her consulting room and joined Lady Edra, Ferguson and Geever as they all sat in the parlor. She noticed the subdued atmosphere and asked, "What have you discovered?"

Ferguson said, "We have identified the body as Lady Edra's husband, Geran Inch, who disappeared seven years ago." Stunned, Abby took Lady Edra's hand.

Ferguson started to ask Lady Edra, "I need you to…" Before he could finish, from somewhere deep in the quiet house, a low moaning startled them. A deep growling lament, an almost human, utterly despondent sound swelled until both the thunderous sound and the feeling of both hopelessness and hatred it produced became almost unbearable, paralyzing them. Abruptly, it stopped, and Ferguson immediately shot up following the stillness to the dark, from where the sound had emanated, across the hallway into Abby's dark waiting room. The oppressive atmosphere he briefly felt yesterday in that space now filled it. The room seemed sinister almost as if it stalked him. As if it probed him.

Abby grabbed the lamp from a nearby table and shone it ahead of her into the room. Nothing. She looked directly into Ferguson's eyes and quietly said, "It seemed sad. I know it arose from a creaky old house being changed radically and so quickly, but it seemed heartbroken. To Ferguson it felt quite different, threatening. It scared him. He shook off the feeling as being ridiculous. Abby was right. Sounds in creaky old houses are normal. He was just tired. They both stepped back into the hallway. Lady Edra, Jory and Geever stood at the edge of the room peering in. The three servants appeared from the kitchen looking astonished and puzzled.

The front door burst open, allowing in the last golden rays of sunlight, startling everyone as Jory stepped in. "Why are you all standing in the front hallway?" He wondered at their quiet stunned atmosphere. "What's going on here?" He had a questioning grin, but no one answered him. "Ferguson, here's the file you requested." Ferguson took the file without saying a word.

The group slowly retreated across the hall. Geever stopped abruptly at the staircase and looked up, astounded by the visage of a young woman. The others followed his gaze. Abby held up the lamp. Only darkness and silence. Geever turned to them and said sheepishly, "I thought I saw a young woman standing on the stairs. She had long black hair. I saw her when we first arrived." They looked at him strangely. "Must have been only a reflection off one of the portraits on the staircase wall or something. It's just all the strange things…" He drifted into silence embarrassed. The servants quietly went to the kitchen and the others moved back into the parlor and again sat mostly looking into the fire.

Abby felt the atmosphere in the room sizzle with tension as she looked around at the others. "We're all on edge," she said. Lady Edna sat rigid, hardly registering anything around her. Jory took both of Lady Edra's hands and spoke softly to her. Ferguson thought of asking Lady Edra about Geran, but she just stared. He could see questions needed to wait until tomorrow.

Jory gathered her up and quietly left with her. He had walked from the police station and quietly walked her to the front door of the manor. Before he opened it, she turned toward him and held his face with both of her hands and kissed him tenderly leaning against him. "Do you want me to stay with you tonight," he asked her. She nodded, and they went inside.

In the dower, Doc Abby and the two policemen had little to say at dinner. Nor did conversation pick up as they sat in the parlor. Geever retired to his room, then Abby left to read in her room. Ferguson sat alone gazing into the fire and heard Alan lock doors as the servants left through the back door. They chose the manor house over the dower tonight.

He thought about the strange haunting noises and, earlier the look of terror on the lad, Keyan's face. Nonsense. This case is strange enough without this ridiculous distraction. He needed to concentrate on the murder the Yard sent him to solve. Seven years ago, in 1914, the dead man, Lady Edra's husband, Geran, disappeared suddenly. The Great War had started. Maybe there is a military record of him. Maybe he disappeared to escape being called up for duty. One year later, two people die. A suicide and a murder. A few days ago, Geran returns unexpectedly and is murdered before he can reach Woodcomb. Someone did not want him back. It's looking like I need to understand the murder from six years ago to understand the why of who killed him. He noticed the slim file Jory handed him earlier that he had abandoned on a side table. It held only a few pages. The only interesting ones were statements by the stationmaster and his wife. They remembered a person board the train that Christmas morning in 1915 who remained totally covered by a heavy overcoat, with a scarf over his face and his hat pulled down. The couple thought the man odd at the time. They knew most of the people leaving or arriving at their train station. Although they found the stranger, odd enough to remark on, they didn't think anything of it until they heard of the murder and suicide. It was a lead that was impossible to follow up. There had been an easier solution. Blame the young woman found at the foot of the cliff. He'd ask Jory in the morning what he thought of this strange man leaving on the train that same day. He walked up to his room hoping for a quiet night with no nightmares—for anyone. With the servants gone, the house contained only Geever, himself and the lovely doctor.

Ferguson woke to a knocking sound from somewhere. A dull thump knocked against wood over and over. He put on his shirt and pants this time, grabbed his suit jacket, turned on his torch and went out into the hall. Abby's door stood open. He tapped softly and entered the dark room. Empty. Geever's door remained closed. The knocking continued and came from downstairs. It grew louder in the doctor's waiting room and louder still as Ferguson entered her consulting room. Moonlight fell across Abby who banged the back of her head repeatedly on the large bureau which held her medicines. She leaned at such a stiff sharp angle, he feared she might fall backwards. It appeared she remained rigid as she rose slightly and banged her head. Placing his palm between the back of her head and the cabinet door startled her awake. She gulped in air and fell back terrified, fighting until she recognized him, then embracing him tightly, sobbing. He held her until she could speak.

"John, the hideous beast I dreamt of last night caught and strangled me," she said, looking around wild-eyed as if the monster might be crawling up the walls, lurking in the shadows. "He pushed me back against the wall while tightening his grip on my neck. His claws were cutting into my throat." She rubbed her neck absently. "I wasn't strong enough to stop him. I couldn't breathe. I felt myself dying. It seemed real." Tears streamed down her face. She couldn't stop crying or shaking. He held her until she calmed down.

He didn't know what to say. The darkness of the room seemed to clot around them. The torch light feebly stabbed a small area of light around them. "This house," Ferguson said. "Something. I don't know. We need to go into the other room." He gasped having trouble sucking in the air. Each breath seemed to draw the dark into him. The dark hated each of the them. It felt visceral. He instinctively felt its rage and desperation. He led Abby into the parlor. With each step, the oppressiveness lifted and the air cleared.

"There has to be a rational reason. There are no ghosts. Imagination? Air trapped in a house unopened for seven years?" he said to convince himself as well as to reassure Abby. "Maybe we can find some brandy or something." He turned up one of the lamps, and together they rummaged in the kitchen and found a bottle of claret and two glasses. A fire had been set, which he lit to take the chill from the room. He put his jacket around her shoulders since she wore only her nightgown.

Ferguson and Abby sat on the floor in front of the fire. After a few minutes staring at the fire, he could see she remained quite upset. "Tell me about you, your family or about being a doctor."

In the quiet, she said, "After my husband died, I finished my medical degree. I learned more about Jung and managed to work with him in Switzerland. He had been put in charge of one of the camps where men who fled to neutral Switzerland were interned." After a few seconds she continued, "They brought the horror of their war with them. Some of them had experienced

…too much. Jung found that their brains coped in various ways. It is often seen as weakness or cowardness. Jung understood that the brain had been swamped and didn't know how to reset itself. He tried to understand and find techniques that worked, that actually helped the men."

Another pause, "John, am I right in thinking you went through some bad experiences during the war? Of course, it's none of my business, and I appreciate if you'd rather not talk about any of it."

In the calm quiet of the night, he found himself telling her more than he'd ever shared with anyone of his struggle. "As a captain in the Royal Scots Fusiliers, I fought in Belgium and France. I commanded a company of young men. They looked up to me, and we had truly been very lucky for such a long time. These boys decided we stayed alive because of my decisions— my cunning and intelligence. I think I started to believe it. The magical thinking that anyone lived or died in that hell for *any* other reason than sheer dumb luck is a trick your brain plays on you. They were just boys, not even twenty. Miserable conditions. We struggled always with constant water in the bottom of the trenches, seeping through our leather boots. Sleeping underground, constantly worrying the ceiling of the trench would collapse on us. Dullness, boredom followed by sheer terror, charging into machine gun fire. All of it. We kept surviving. At the second battle of the Somme, it looked like the Germans were going to overrun our position, and we were ordered to retreat. Hundreds of us marched away from the battlefield all day. A beautiful day, we were joking and horsing around." John became quiet a moment before he continued.

"I don't remember coming home from the front. Rather, I don't remember being sent from France to a mental hospital." It seemed to Abby he squirmed a bit before continuing. "Actually, I don't even remember how that battle ended. I had to read that we won. I'm lucky to have been sent to that hospital. They did as much for me as they could and sent me back home to Scotland to get better. I was determined to get better."

His voice picked up, "I have a mentor at Scotland Yard, who made me into a pretty fair detective because he is a great detective. He gave me a chance to come back to the Yard last year and gave me one chance to show I could be useful. That I could be a detective again. If I failed, I would be out. I nearly did fail because several times I found myself leave reality to be suddenly transported to some terrifying battlefield with no warning. I had no control.

I desperately needed to figure out what happened that destroyed my brain, and I just knew if I could do that, I would be on my way to recovery. Finally, I dreamt the horror. One young man died so suddenly and unexpectedly that my brain shut down." Telling that upset him more than he was prepared for. He wiped a tear with his knuckle before it fell. He took a breath and looked up at her. "Discovering that proved me right. Since then my recovery has progressed nicely. Nothing left of the flashbacks. Now it's only occasional nightmares, and those are getting more rare." He found her so easy to talk to. It felt wonderful, freeing, maybe even forgiving to actually say all of it.

Soon they walked upstairs, and Ferguson took his torch and lit the room where the two maids slept the night before. He moved beds and dressers. No odd vents or loose metal. He went into the burgeoning water closet, where they met the night before and rapped on the cast iron porcelain tub. He looked into the hole in the floor where a toilet would be. His torch lit up only the piping and the walls of the water closet below. Nothing sounded close. Then he thought about it and looked up into the black hole that had been the stairway to the servants' quarters. He jumped up on the tub and grabbed the edge of the hole, but the hole remained too high to climb into. "First thing," John assured her "when workmen arrive, I'll check out the attic."

He looked at Abby, watching him. "Where's Dickie…uh Inspector Geever?" He went and opened the door to his room. Geever slept quietly.

Abby wished she could ask him to sleep in her room, his warm strong arms holding her so she could get a good night's sleep. She stopped herself saying that aloud by blurting out, "John, I feel there is more going on here than mechanical noises. Something different. More." The look on his face revealed he didn't want to hear that. "Of course, it must be explainable really," she added feebly, not believing it. They both retired to their rooms. Abby appreciated why he sought something rational. She hated that sometimes she seemed as clairvoyant as her mother. John Ferguson would not like that. He would not believe that. She wished it wasn't true. But she had come to trust her visions. Carl Jung believed her. Something is haunting this house.

Chapter Seven

Early morning as the sun rose, Dobbs walked down the drive from the manor house with Alan and Sukie. She ruminated about the goings on in the dower yesterday. That detective didn't see no portrait reflection, she thought to herself. He saw the ghost of that poor, dear Jenna whose last moments were here in this house. She loved Lady Edra's precious Caden as much as she loved her own son Keyan. She never killed nobody. Is she haunting this house? Why would Jenna haunt it? Dobbs didn't believe it and thought, that made no sense. Course there just ain't no such things as ghosts! Must be just the plumbing. Dobbs wrapped her sweater about her against the early morning chill. Alan unlocked the back door to the dower house, and they came into a chilly house before anyone was up and started their morning work. Fires needed to be lit in the parlor and the Doc's waiting room and office. Table to be set and tea to brew.

Sukie hung up her sweater and said, "I'm so glad we snuck out and slept at the manor in our own rooms. I got a good night's sleep. No more ghost noises and smells. Cor, our room stunk the night before."

Dobbs said, "We didn't sneak out. And there aren't any ghosts you daft girl. Remember, I only came with you so you didn't have to walk in the dark up to the house alone."

Last night, Alan thought Dobbs had been stepping pretty lively escorting Sukie up to the manor, but didn't voice his opinion. He reflected, something did seem queer about the dower now. Before, I loved working here. He mumbled, "I loved working with Jenna." He thought about her laugh and the kisses they stole. Before she had the baby and all that, but he didn't care. "I would have married her."

Dobbs said, "None of that. We've work to do." Alan hadn't realized he had spoken that last part.

Once the three who remained in the dower last night came down, breakfast finished quickly and rather quietly. Geever mentioned he had another bad dream. "Did either of you have any disturbance last night? Ferguson and Doc Abby glanced at each other, nodded, but neither wanted to add anything more. "I had another round of the vicious dog dream. It really rather leaves me shaken. I'm not one to have nightmares." He looked to Doc Abby first, then Ferguson. Neither commented. Abby had no wish to share her dream of being strangled this morning. Geever assumed neither had suffered nightmares again.

A few minutes later, Doc Abby went across to her surgery to prepare for the morning patients. Ferguson and Geever left for the police station. As they walked, Ferguson asked Geever, "Of all the people you spoke to yesterday, who do you think might give us information now that we know more. We need to know who had a grudge against Geran Inch. Who might still care seven years after his disappearing act?"

Geever said, "I think Jory might have some good suggestions who might have a grudge, or someone who knew him well. I'll speak to him."

At the police station, Ferguson phoned his boss, Allistair Howell, about the case. "We've established the identity of the dead man as Geran Inch, even though his face was so disfigured, and no one's seen him for about seven years. His mother identified him through a unique medallion she gave him and he was known to wear all the time. We sent the fingerprints yesterday. I'm thinking possibly he lives in London. His train ticket said he departed from London. Maybe he served in the war. More information could help us. Perhaps there's someone there with a bit of time to research."

"DC Patrick Mullins just finished up on a case and can do some leg work on that."

"Perfect. Tell him Geran Inch might have been working somewhere with horses. He had been a groom at one time here in Cornwall. And to call me here when he finds anything."

"Any motive for the murder yet?"

"Not yet. Inch hasn't been seen for seven years, not even a letter to his mother. He was not popular. We need to find someone who still hated him seven years later enough to so violently kill him."

"Keep at it, Ferguson. This is one we want solved. No fairy-tale explanation living on and making the Yard look foolish." Ferguson didn't figure Howell wanted to hear about someone trying to scare them by making the dower appear haunted. Howell wouldn't hear about that until Ferguson figured out the who and why of their experiences.

After hanging up, he found Jory and Geever discussing the case. Since identifying the murdered man, they figured the murderer probably came from Woodcomb or the surrounding area. Jory suggested questioning Merryn, the woman who took Mrs. Inch home yesterday. "She maybe had a fling with him. He had been popular with a number of young women. Don't know for sure about that, but she knows all the gossip about everybody in Woodcomb. We can go question her if you like."

Geever said, "Yes, fine idea." Then to Ferguson, "When Crocker gets back from looking into some mischief at the school, you need to talk to him."

Jory said, "Good idea. When I think back I remember he got pretty upset when Geran started on his daughter, Eva." Jory and Geever left then with the police car. Ferguson agreed with Geever's surprisingly good idea to question people who had been involved with the dead man—without being prompted. Something a real detective might suggest. Shortly after they left, Crocker returned as Ferguson finished writing up his conversation with his boss.

"I been over to the school. Some vandalism. Nothing serious," Crocker said. "A brick thrown through a window. Nobody seems to have even gone into the building. Just an opinion about the math teacher probably. He's real strict and so not liked by many students. Probably one of the older lads. Headmaster's going to quiz some likely suspects."

Ferguson nodded at that before asking, "What were your feelings toward Geran Inch, Crocker?"

"Like most. Couldn't stand him."

"Why would that be?"

"He was such a cocky git. Never got how any of 'em fell for what that blowhard said."

"Who do you know who fell for his charms?"

"Lots of silly girls." It seemed personal the way he said it.

"Any close to you?"

"I got a daughter, Eva, and she bought it for a bit, but then she wised up."

"Eva? Is she married to Arthur Penrose?"

"Aye."

"I met her briefly yesterday."

Crocker looked down at his hands and rose to get himself more tea. He seemed not to want to discuss this further. Later, Ferguson would be questioning Eva and would find out how much she bought of Geran's games. He left the station since he got nothing from Crocker, and thought this might be a good time to talk to the men who were working on remodeling the dower. They'd know something about Geran Inch. It wouldn't take long to question them. Maybe they could clear up the reasons for the strange noises. After that he'd question Lady Edra more about her relationship with Inch and maybe find out from Keyan when the man died. They'd probably be at the manor.

Construction noise again greeted Ferguson as he entered the dower. A patient checked in with the ever-cheerful Sally, then Ferguson asked her, "Do you know who is in charge of all this work." She popped up, walked to the kitchen and returned with a tall thin man with brown hair, aged about 40 wearing bib overalls. A pencil stuck out of one breast pocket, and a folding rule stuck out of a side pocket.

"This would be the man in charge. Wilber, Detective Ferguson would like to interrogate you, I believe." She smiled and nodded, satisfied.

"Thanks, Sally," Ferguson said as she resumed her place at her desk.

Turning to the man, he said, "No interrogation, Mr...?"

"Wilber Trew, sir."

"I do have some questions about the work being done on this house. I understand you're the foreman. Are you a full-time builder?"

"No, sir. Not enough carpentry work around here for full time. Although after this, I'll be working at the Crown repairing the damage done by that fire the other night."

"And when you're not being a carpenter, what is it you do, Mr. Trew?"

"Most time I'm up at the manor farm, or I work on upkeep here on the grounds."

"The manor farm? Would that be the farm directly across from where they found the murdered man? Run by Arthur Penrose, correct?" A nod from the foreman. "I've an odd question for you, Mr. Trew." Ferguson looked around and took a deep breath before asking, "Do you think that anything from all this remodel might create a sort of eerie, deep moaning sound, almost human, coming from somewhere in the house? One that grew to be deafeningly loud and then quit suddenly?"

Without any strange looks or pauses, Trew answered, "Oh aye. The timbers in this old place could be complaining about all this bother. Nobody's been taking proper care of the place these past few years. It's rare, but I've seen it happen. Things settling into the new arrangement. Is that happening here, do you think, sir?"

Ferguson smiled and relaxed. "I think so, Mr. Trew. I definitely think so. While I have you, please follow me into the dining room. I need to interview every man working here about the man murdered Sunday."

They sat at the table. "Mr. Trew, did you know Geran Inch?"

"Aye. Married to Lady Edra, he was. Ran off years ago. Left her and his son. A real toe rag, he was, sir."

"We've identified the man killed Sunday night as Geran Inch."

"No! What would he be coming here for? Geran Inch? Killed Sunday night, and we were right across the road mad harvesting." A troubling thought occurred to him. "You don't suppose he lay there dead even as we walked away to the fire at the Crown, not 20 feet away in that ditch?"

Ferguson said, "That's quite possible. We don't have an exact time of death. He could have been coming here later, after you left. How did you know where the body lay?"

"As we came to work Monday, we all saw Jory and Crocker dealing with the body. Practically right across from the manor farm they was. Most all the men you see working on the dower here today, work at the farm and then sometimes on the manor grounds, when we're needed. Otherwise, we work on our own places."

Then he added, "Penrose stood in the middle of the road in front of his place, caught us coming to work first thing. He turned us before we even got to the farm. He gave us our new job fixing up the dower. Men had to rush back home for tools. Penrose and Lady Edra and me came over early, and she opened up the place. She had paper and ruler with her. We drew up a plan right then and had it ready when the others returned. She had that footman, Marrak, sent to Truro for building material, and we got started on tearing down walls and such. She thought up this scheme after the fire destroyed the Doc's surgery and apartment. Lady Edra wanted her moved in here. It's only been a few years no one's lived here. Mostly we're adding plumbing. Electricity will come after we get the harvest in. After that Doc Abby will have a telephone. But for now she's still getting any calls through Abe Court over at the Crown."

"The Crown looks like it needs a lot of work. He still has electricity and a telephone line?" Ferguson asked.

Trew nodded. "It's mostly the roof and the top floor with all the damage. Abe's covered the roof with a lot of tarps, so he can still run the pub, so he'll be fine till we get to him."

"Now, Mr. Trew, do you have any idea what would have brought Geran Inch back here?"

"No, sir, I do not."

"You worked on the farm on Sunday? Is that usual? Do you always work Sundays?"

"We work Sundays during planting and harvest. Sunday was a long day. There were trucks and wagons bringing in grain all day that needed shifting into the granary. Then about supper time, we had a grain truck, loaded to the absolute maximum, dump its load of oats all over the ground. The fool driver backed into a corner of the granary. That had to be shored up before we could scoop up the mess and properly store it. The storm hit, making it all worse, with the wind blowing our tarps, and then the rain hit. Finally, we're quitting, and I'm about to get a ride home. My wife, Merryn, brought the wagon to take some of us home. We're tired, but we could see the Crown was afire. All hands on for that. I fell into bed soon as I got home. That's for sure." Trew shook his head remembering.

"I bet you did. As you were leaving the farm Sunday night, did you see anyone walking, coming down the road from Menadue Wood?"

"Didn't even occur to me to look up the road, sir. Is that the way he came, do you think?"

"Yes. We're pretty sure about that. Where do you live, Mr. Trew?"

"Just north and west of town. Straight up High Street, on past the Crown." He paused, and when Ferguson didn't ask another question, he said, "Sir, if there's nothing else, I best crack on with all this."

"Thank you for your time. Could you tell me who the plumber is?

"That would be James Jones. We'll both be to blame for whatever mistakes there are with the plumbing." He grinned at that and rose to get back to work. "I'll send him in to you, sir."

Another bib overall clad man came into the dining room moments later. This man, no older than 30, was tall and thin, and sported a dark full mustache. "Did you want to see me, sir?"

"You are James Jones, is that correct? The plumber?"

Ferguson discovered that Jones only knew of Geran Inch, and had only heard bad things about him. He worked on the farm on Sunday, saw no one coming into Woodcomb from Menadue Wood, and had been sent to work on the dower the next morning before even getting to the farm.

Ferguson questioned the other workers with the same story. He learned that no one cared about Inch being dead. He got no closer on the murder case, so Ferguson felt the time for questioning the plumber about strange noises had arrived. He found Jones working in the upstairs water closet. "Uh, Jones…if you have a moment." Jones turned toward him waiting. "We were awakened here in the dower…by a strange bang and very loud clanging that sounds like someone striking metal on metal. Could the alterations in this building you're making with the plumbing pipes, or anything else that you know of, possibly create such sounds?"

Puzzled, Jones responded with a shrug and a shake of his head. "Nothing I know of could do that, but I'll give it some thought."

Jones' answer disappointed Ferguson. He hoped for a construction explanation. If nothing having to do with the plumbing is responsible then someone must have made them. I can think of no other reason to manufacture strange sound in the middle of the night other than to scare those of us staying here. He wanted to figure the source of the noise and figure out the why later. He asked to borrow a ladder and a piece of pipe. He collected the torch from his room to hunt for a possible explanation in the attic.

Jones obliged, curious. He climbed the ladder and through the hole with his own torch after Ferguson. They stepped onto the remaining attic stairs. A tiny window at the top of the stairs let in a bit more light, adding to their torch lights. Looking behind, Ferguson saw how the new back wall of the water closet cut off the last of the stairs to the attic. It also took some space from the bedroom he now slept in.

"You're closing off the attic entirely? Won't this area still be needed for servants' quarters?"

"We needed this space to jigger in the water closet. The thinking is there's room enough for servants near the bedrooms with whoever occupies the house, like the Doc. Nobody has as many servants now as they did in times past. When we're finished, we'll create an attic accessible panel, where the hole we came through is now. We'll also create a set of stairs later at the back of where the servants are sleeping now, to reach the attic, if they decide to open it again."

At the top of the stairs, Ferguson and Jones found several small rooms still furnished with abandoned iron bedframes, mattresses, small dressers, some wash basins and little else. They stepped across footprints in the dust from the plumbers working on the stairs that led to the new plumbing vent pipes, rising from the new water closet ceiling. More footprints led to the other vent pipes, where more plumbing arose. Ferguson used the pipe he brought to hit the new vent pipes, resulting in a reverberating, tinny sound. It did not sound even close to the clanging sound from two nights before.

Jones watched curiously. "Why are you banging on the pipes, sir? I guarantee we know what we're doing, and everything will work just fine."

"No, no. I'm sure, Jones. I'm just trying to replicate the loud banging and figure out what made the noise in the middle of the night that woke up every one of us."

Jones looked puzzled and shrugged.

Looking at all the men had accomplished—piping for plumbing in the attic and first floor as well as walls taken down and new walls erected—Fergusson asked, "How did you get so much done in a couple of days?"

"Everybody's working hard on this for Lady Edra and Doc Abby. And we're needing to get back to harvesting before we lose the weather. Then there's the Crown needing its roof."

Ferguson nodded, then asked the plumber for one more favor. "Could you bang as hard as you can with the pipe, while I climb down into the bath and out into the hallway?" Jones thought the request odd, but obliged. It produced clangs that were similar to the nightly clanging noise, but no matter how hard the plumber hit an iron bedpost or the plumbing pipes, the sound could barely be heard below.

"Will this help solve the murder, sir?"

"Frankly, I doubt it has anything to do with the murder case, but the loud noise was troubling, and I'd hoped it could be simply explained. I hope no one is trying to disrupt our investigation."

Jones looked like he couldn't understand what loud noises could possibly have to do with murder, but was willing to learn. "I'll keep thinking about it."

He thanked Jones for his time. "Glad to help, Inspector." He returned to his plumbing job looking rather proud of himself for helping with a murder investigation.

Ferguson climbed back into the attic but found no air duct or hole of any kind which might amplify the sound to the floor below. He searched for an entry point some intruder might have used to secretly enter and hide up here. A fire escape chain rope covered in cobwebs lay unused across one back window. All the windows still opened, and footprints could be seen in the dust on the floor, under a couple of the windows. Sticking his head out one, he found quite a drop from there to the ground. He would check outside for footprints or ladder indentations. Why would someone be trying to scare them? Did they imagine we might flee in terror, abandoning our investigation? Another thought occurred. Possibly the opposite, perhaps someone wanted them to investigate the old murders. When he climbed out of the attic and entered the hallway, Sukie stood staring at him with a questioning look on her face.

"All's well then, Detective, sir?" Ferguson nodded. "I reckon we can all sleep safe here tonight," Sukie said smiling brightly. She turned and walked down the stairs, reassured all was well. Walking around the exterior of the building, Ferguson found plenty of boot prints, suggesting nothing more than workmen doing their jobs. He found no indentations from a ladder.

He had found out all he could about the strange noises.

Now Ferguson needed to run down Keyan and ask about finding the body. He figured his best shot lay at the manor, probably with Lady Edra. He found them in the same room in the children's part of the house as yesterday. Keyan wrote something from a book that looked to be about history. "I need to ask him some questions." Lady Edra nodded and closed the book they had been working from.

Ferguson sat in a chair facing them. "Keyan, would you mind telling me about finding that man's body."

Keyan seemed embarrassed and looked at Ferguson and then at Lady Edra, who nodded and smiled. "It's okay, Keyan," she encouraged him.

They could tell he pictured the sight as he spoke. "I thought I saw just a dead animal. I walked up. Then…I saw." His eyes were saucers.

"Was it getting dark when you found the body? Was it raining and blowing?"

"No, sir. It was early morning. The grass was still wet from rain the night before."

"Do you often walk up to the bridge at the edge of Tredwen property? It's opposite from the direction of the school and very out of the way to get to the manor house, if you were going to see Lady Edra."

"I don't usually go anywhere near where Tommy Penrose might show up." Keyan's face clouded up, and he looked at Lady Edra. "I got up really early so I could watch the mama otter and her babies from the bridge before Tommy left for school. The otters slide down into the water, then they climb out and do it again. The young'uns also like to wrestle. They're funny." Keyan smiled at that.

"Before I got to the bridge, I saw the man. He looked…broken. He was dead. I ran as fast as I could to tell Baba, and she sent me to Jory, Officer Moon." Ferguson still found it amazing that everyone in this village, even children, called the local policeman by his first name.

"Were you frightened?"

"Of what, sir?"

"Many people seeing a dead body would be scared."

Keyan thought that an odd reaction, so he couldn't answer the question any other way. "I just thought Jory would take care of it."

"Someone told me that Sunday night you had one of your spells at the Badger. Do you remember what you said?"

That embarrassed Keyan, "I just mumble stuff. It just comes out from my brain."

"Well, I think you're a very brave young man," Ferguson said. That made Keyan beam and Lady Edra smile.

"Lady Edra, I do need to formally interview you now. Is there a room here, or would you prefer at the dower?"

She sighed. "The conservatory. I'll meet you there in two minutes, after I give an assignment for Keyan to work on."

As Ferguson waited for her, he stood looking out the French doors at the beautiful grounds and the magnificent oak at its center. Penrose and the men from the farm kept it all in excellent condition. He turned when Lady Edra entered, and they sat facing each other in two comfortable, chairs.

"Tell me about Geran Inch and your marriage." Ferguson took out his notebook.

A deep sigh, but Lady Edra had steeled herself to answer his questions. "He was handsome, clever and exciting. I was barely eighteen, starry-eyed and had a ridiculous amount of power to make my own choices. My mother had died just months before. I had no brother to inherit. As her nearest relative, by my great grandfather's will, I inherited the manor and the title. Geran had no pedigree or formal education, which scandalized Father, and undoubtedly made him more attractive to me. I fell pregnant. That appalled my father. He saw to it that we got married to stave off that scandal, but Father made our lives miserable. Gran came up with the idea of the two of us moving into the dower house for everyone's peace. She moved to the dower with us."

"She chose the dower over the grand manor house? Why did she do that?"

"I don't know. She never really got on well with my father. Geran soon began staying out late and finding women, or girls really, to entertain him. Once Caden was born, I no longer cared as much what he did. Gran and I so enjoyed little baby Caden. Jenna, a maid who worked at the manor, also fell pregnant. She never did tell anyone who the father was." He could tell, Lady Edra found it perplexing that Jenna refused to name the father. By tradition, for turning up pregnant, she should have been fired with no references. Whoever she named as the father would also have been fired.

"Gran liked and trusted her. She felt Jenna would be the perfect nurse. She came to the dower with us and became the nurse to both her baby, Keyan, and my Caden.

"Did you force Geran to leave you?"

"No. And a divorce would have been more scandal. Much as my father wanted him gone, a divorce was not discussed."

"What did happen? Why did he leave such a posh position, and abandon his son."

She sighed, "I came home to find him packing. He said he needed more excitement. I wouldn't go to London. He told me he felt imprisoned by this stuffy place, and I no longer interested him. I knew he cared nothing about Caden. The way he left, I figured he'd try London awhile and come back. I never heard another word from him. It devastated me for a time. I thought maybe he died, but he's been alive all this time. A couple of years ago, I hired an investigator to find him. By then I would have divorced him scandal or not, but he couldn't be found. Now it's been seven years, and we were in the process of having him declared dead. I wanted to be free of him. Free to marry if I choose. Amazingly, I got the telegram Sunday declaring him dead. The same day he actually died."

Mary Inch had baked pasties early as usual for the morning crowd. Now she worked on the lunch pasties. Staying home helped nothing. She needed to be here working. She couldn't stop thinking about Geran returning. Why did he? She folded meat into its dough envelope and set it on the baking sheet. He had to know how shocking it would be. Why not send a letter? Tell someone first. Let the people here adjust. She spooned meat into another pastry envelop, pinched the edges shut, and set it on the baking sheet. He must have had a very important reason. What could it have been? Did he need to tell me something? Another pasty set onto the baking sheet.

Dobbs worked on a list of things she needed to bring down from the manor house. She tried to concentrate. Additional serving spoons, a soup ladle and more sugar went on her list. She found herself alone in the kitchen for the moment. The carpenters' noise seemed distant. She could reflect for a minute. Those sounds yesterday, that horrible moaning. Whatever that detective saw on the staircase. Maybe it *was* a ghost. She set down her pen for a moment. "Jenna?" she said aloud into the quiet, looking around. "Jenna are you here?" Silence in the kitchen allowed her to close her eyes, and listen for a voice, a whisper, an image. Nothing. Shaking her head at her silliness, she went back to deciding what to add to her list. She needed to add more starched napkins. She looked at the list and saw MURDER scribbled across the paper—the ink just drying. She jumped up, turning over her chair, heart racing, terrified. Had she unconsciously written the word? She must have.

Alan came in the back door and stopped abruptly, noticing the upturned chair and Dobbs shocked expression. "What is it, Dobbs?"

"Nothing…nothing." *No. I didn't write that word!* she thought terrified. Her skin crawled and she looked around. Alan stared at her. He would not understand about this and would dismiss it. But who? Ferguson wouldn't believe her. Detective Geever? She had a better idea. She put on her coat, took her purse and left the dower immediately. She would visit Liza Zelly, who had been their cook here at the dower seven years ago. Dobbs remembered a story from back then, about Liza's friend Mary Inch—the gypsy. Some around here have Mary Inch read her tarot cards for them.

As Ferguson left the manor heading toward the dower, he spotted Dobbs leave and head toward Woodcomb on some errand. Entering, he found Doc Abby sitting in the dining room, reading something while having her lunch. He sat across from her. "Anything interesting?" he asked.

She set her book down. "No. Anything interesting in the attic?" Abby had a sly grin on her face.

"Uh, no. Nothing…nothing strange up there. Dust and iron headboards and some old dressers." Was she laughing at him?

"It is important for you to check." She didn't seem to criticize or mock. It seemed more—something light to make conversation or to make a connection. The smile and a twinkle in her eyes made him wonder though.

"Yes. I thought it would help explain…" His voice trailed off.

"Thanks for taking care of that." The grin again. Did he detect sarcasm?

"The foreman said the noises, uh, the moaning noises are simply what old houses do sometimes. So that's good." He tapped his fingers on the table absently.

"Definitely, that's good." A gleam in her eye.

Her gentle teasing confused and unsettled him. It challenged his professional detachment. It challenged his general detachment and unwillingness to connect with people in a deeper way—especially a woman.

Especially while he worked on a case. It surprised him how keenly he wanted her approval. He wanted to impress her, yet had no idea how to do that. It had been a long time since he admitted to himself that he cared about someone, that he was attracted to a woman, and he didn't want to blow it. He decided to leave before he said something stupid. "Well, I best get to it." He stood abruptly.

"But you haven't eaten lunch yet."

"Ah," he said clumsily. "I'm going to the kitchen to see what…" She made him nervous.

Abby rang a small bell, and Alan appeared. "Oh, Detective, ready for lunch. Right away." Ferguson eased back down into his chair.

"You seem quite at ease with the servants. Going into the kitchen, their domain."

"I grew up on a great estate. My father was the head ghillie there. He still is as a matter of fact. My mother works as a seamstress for the marchioness mostly, but the rest of the family too sometimes. As a lad, the staff indulged my roaming around below stairs. Lord Charles took an interest in me and made sure I got an education." He stopped, then added, "Even without that experience, I find the servants know what goes on in every big house."

"From there you became a detective in Scotland Yard?" Abby showed some of her concern from last night. "I'm glad you're here." She said it quietly and pointedly.

"Even though I'm rummaging around looking for everyday explanations for things, instead of looking for the supernatural?"

Staring directly into his eyes, she said, "Absolutely. That's why I'm glad you're here, and I very much hope you solve the mystery of this besotted house, as well as who murdered that poor man."

Ferguson merely nodded. His lunch silently appeared, and Alan disappeared into the kitchen. He wanted her to stay and keep talking. He wanted to know more. "What's your story? Where did you grow up?" he asked her.

"My father is the viscount of Keady. It's a small estate in Northern Ireland, nothing grand."

"Doesn't that make you Lady Gobnait of Keady."

She smiled at that. "Actually, I think the whole of my name becomes Doctor Lady Gobnait O'Rourke Maguire—of Keady. Or maybe lady comes before doctor. I can't remember. My husband's name was Randall O'Rourke.

When he died, I added my maiden name, Maguire. We hadn't been married long." She seemed embarrassed about it. "I don't know if that's the right thing to do, but that's what's on my medical license. It just seemed best." She brightened up after explaining and said, "Only my feisty granny ever called me Gobnait. You can see now why Doc Abby is perfect for me."

"What about you husband?"

"We met in medical school. He was ahead of me. When he graduated, we married," she said quietly as she remembered. "He had a bright future as a surgeon. When the war broke out, he felt compelled to join the Irish Guards. Ireland remained neutral, but thousands of Irishmen joined the war. They dispatched Randall to a hospital in Belgium. He died six months later in an incident that involved a bomb being dropped on the medical tent."

Then she added, "That's what drove me, after graduating with my own medical degree to go to the prisoner of war camp in Switzerland. Besides all the terrible injuries and surgeries, I learned so much about how the brain copes with trauma. There is a critical connection between trauma and neurosis.

Ferguson chose to change the subject. He didn't want to get into questions about the war or about trauma. "Do you think you'll stay here, so far from home?"

"If you mean stay in this house, then yes, if your great detective skills solve our noise problem." Another smile. "If you mean Woodcomb, yes. It's a lovely place. Where else can you find a baroness like Lady Edra who is not a ridiculous ponce? She is intelligent and caring. Also, many of the other small villages near here have welcomed me, grateful to have a physician nearby.

"I think Edra's ideas about Dando and his murderous raids help her cope with the traumatic murders years ago and her husband's abandonment. Helping Keyan these years since is also a very positive thing, essential to her healing. The knowledge that Geran Inch is dead will ultimately be very beneficial to her mental health. She will be able to truly move on." She paused, then, "I best get to it." Abby picked up her book and left the dining room. Ferguson watched as her fine figure and her glorious hair disappeared.

Jory drove Inspector Geever to Merryn's house two miles west of the village. The modest, well-cared-for farm lay along the west arm of the cliff that rose from Woodcomb's cove. The English Channel could be glimpsed far below, out beyond the bay. Geever noted three fat pigs in a sty next to the sturdy barn, and he spotted two milk cows who ate grass contentedly in a field. Next to the well-maintained house, a huge kitchen garden sprawled before them laid out with neat row upon row of vegetables. Merryn knelt pulling out carrots as they arrived. She came to meet them still holding the wicker basket full of produce as they parked. Jory explained the reason for their visit. "Merryn, we'd like to talk to you about Geran Inch."

Geever said, "Beautiful farm. Very peaceful up here, isn't it? I remember you helped yesterday with Mary Inch and Keyan. I need to ask you some questions, if you don't mind. We're questioning everyone who might have known Geran Inch."

She smiled and nodded. "Let's go up to the house and sit down. I'll make some tea."

As they entered the house, Geever asked, "I assume you are married, Merryn?

She added water to the kettle on the stove. "Yes. James is my husband. James Jones."

"Where is he today?"

"You've probably met him. He's one of the men working on the dower. Most of the time we farm, but he's a good plumber and gets work around, as more and more people are getting running water piped into their homes. James always helps Penrose's harvest, as well as planting. It's good money when there's a project on at Tredwen."

"A busy life," Geever remarked. "Is it just the two of you?"

"We have two girls seven and nearly five. In school right now."

"Did you know Geran Inch?" Geever thought her seven-year-old could possibly belong to Geran Inch.

She knew that would be his next question. "Oh yes, I knew him. He was somewhat of a show-off and dare devil, when we were all in school. We all thought him fun and exciting to be around. He took me on wild horseback rides with him. I was so impressed that he chose to take me along," she paused remembering. "I saw him with other girls, including the grand Lady Edra. Once he had charmed her, we all became nothing to him. Devastated me at the time. Later, I was so glad that happened because I could've been beguiled and abandoned by him instead of her." She shuddered thinking about it.

That interested him. "Do you know anyone else he captivated, someone else he abandoned for Lady Edra?"

"I think it could be nearly anybody our age. Boys, too. They thought he was great. Wanted to be just like him." She looked at Jory to agree, and he nodded. "I'll give you a couple of ideas." She stated three women's names, and Geever wrote them down.

"Would you have any idea why he came back here?" Geever asked. "Who might he want to see after all this time? It seems he didn't get in contact with anyone, not his mother nor Lady Edra. Did he think maybe you might be sympathetic to his visit?"

"God, no! He left such a mess behind. Suddenly he disappeared. No one wanted to see him back." The way she said it, Geever believed she certainly didn't wish to reconnect with him.

"We may have questions for you later, but for now, thank you for your time, Merryn, Mrs. Jones." He smiled pleasantly. "One more question. It just occurred to me. You seem quite far from the manor farm where your husband worked late. How did he get home so late on Sunday night?"

She hesitated a moment wondering why he asked before she answered. "Usually he rides our horse, but I needed Old Jude hitched up to our wagon," she nodded toward the barn, " to take a load of produce and canned vegetables to market. So, I picked him up in the wagon. I also gave Smitty a ride. We had to help Abe Court because of the fire at his place."

Jory asked, "And before the fire started, you waited in Penrose's yard with your wagon?"

"I turned Old Jude around in Penrose's yard and waited in the road, yes."

"Did you chat with Mrs. Penrose?"

"No. She would have been inside putting her kids to bed."

"And you saw nothing unusual?"

She shook her head, "Nothing. Several men rode in the back of the wagon with us as we raced to help with the fire at the Crown. "

"Thanks again, Merryn."

As they drove away, Geever asked, "One more person who found Mr. Inch distasteful? Jory, were you one of the boys enthralled with Geran Inch?"

Jory said, "I sure wished I had his talent for impressing girls. But in those years, I spent most of my time out on my uncle's fishing boat. Then, I concentrated on being a brand-new constable."

"Do you think if she suddenly saw him Sunday night, she could have struck out at him?" Geever asked.

"I don't know. There did seem to still be some pain there," Jory admitted as they returned to the station.

Jory told Geever the addresses of two of the women whose names Merryn gave them. Crocker gave him directions and left Geever to find and interview them. Ferguson had waited for Jory's return to reinterview Penrose, and they drove off immediately. As they neared the manor farm, Ferguson said, "Workmen told me Penrose stood in the road Monday morning and turned them to the dower to get to work on the remodel. Did you go to his place and tell him what you were doing?"

Jory said, "We didn't inform him of anything. We concentrated on the body lying in the ditch. He did come out shortly after we got to the body, crossed the road and asked what was going on. After he saw the body, he didn't just wait in his house. That's when he stood in the road and turned all the workmen back to the dower as each one showed up. Lady Edra had decided Sunday night, after hearing about Abe Court's place, that she wanted the dower remodeled even before they finished the harvest. She really wanted Doc Abby to move into it and have her office there." They pulled in near the house and saw Penrose coming to meet them from the granary.

"Do you think he knew about the body before you did?" Ferguson asked as they watched him approach.

"Why wouldn't he tell us if he did?"

"He sure is angry about something. Maybe Penrose knows something."

Penrose motioned to stop them as they got out of the car. Jory said in a loud voice, "Penrose, inside now. No more of your nonsense." He pointed his finger toward the kitchen door. Penrose stopped. His face flared red. He looked from Jory to Ferguson then slowly walked inside. "Sit down," Jory ordered him. "Where is Eva? We need to talk to her too."

"She's out. Running errands," he glared at both men. "You're lucky you caught me. I don't have time for this. I'm trying to get as much harvesting done as I can with most of the work crew at the dower house. Truly, I don't know anything!"

Ferguson said, "Nevertheless, Mr. Penrose. This will be brief, if you simply sit down and answer my questions. Did you know Geran Inch?"

"What? That slick wanker what used to be married to Lady Edra?" Ferguson thought he seemed sincerely surprised. The news that the body had been identified as Geran Inch hadn't gotten to him. Odd. Or maybe he's a great actor.

"You hadn't heard? His mother, Mrs. Inch, identified him yesterday afternoon by a medallion she gave him years ago."

"No great loss then."

"Did you know him well?"

"Well enough to know everything always became himself. He truly cared for no one and used everyone he could."

"Did he use you somehow? Did he treat anyone you know badly?"

Penrose became uncomfortable, squirming in his seat, "No. All you need to know is how he treated Lady Edra. Total scoundrel."

"Did you see his body Sunday night?"

"No." He acted offended that they might think he would see a body and not report it.

"You sure? The body lay in the ditch, directly the other side of the road, in front of your farm."

"We were awful busy that night trying to get a lot of our harvesting done. We had a truck back into a corner of the granary." He turned his head looking at the granary through the kitchen window. "The wind whipped up about that time and drove a downpour to us. It was pretty powerful there for a while as we tried to clean up. Then we spotted the flames shooting out, up at Abe Court's inn. We all ran to help put that out. The rain still poured when the men left Sunday night. I certainly didn't go stand in the road, while the storm blew around me."

"How did you know early Monday morning that Lady Edra needed the men to start work on the dower, instead of finishing the harvest first? Did she walk over here at daybreak or send somebody with her plan very early?"

"She sent Wherry over. When I returned from Abe Court's fire Sunday night Wherry sat here having a cup of tea. Told me Lady Edra had a plan for the dower and would be using all the men working on it."

"Surely she had barely regained consciousness then."

"I know nothing about that."

"She couldn't telephone you?"

"We don't have a telephone." Penrose looked from Jory to Ferguson. The question seemed absurd to him. "Very few places do have one."

"Did Wherry have to walk down the drive to the Tredwen entrance and come back up the road past your place?"

"No. There's a gate right at the edge of Tredwen Manor. I'm sure he came through there."

Ferguson remembered the rail fence that ran for the first few feet from the boundary of Tredwen before the fence became the rock wall. The purpose must have been as a short cut from the far corner of the manor to the farm. He had overlooked the gate when originally examining the crime scene. That gate made it easy for anyone from the manor to have come through the gate about the time Geran Inch came down the road—which made all the people at the manor more interesting—both staff and family. "We'll leave you to get back to work. Thanks for your cooperation."

Walking back to the car, Ferguson considered that Wherry now needed questioning about delivering Lady Edra's new plans to Penrose. Wherry had crossed through a gate to practically where they found the dead man. Ferguson reasoned there was a fair chance Wherry walked right past the body of Geran Inch. He was nervous about something when I spoke to him. Maybe the valet-chauffeur had reason to kill him that we don't yet know about.

From Penrose's place, the policemen drove on past Menadue Wood and spent the remainder of the day interviewing the folks who lived along the road. Most were tenants of the Bandrys for several miles along the road to Plymouth. They learned nothing new.

Chapter Eight

Dobbs and Liza Zelly were about to enter the pasty shop when they stopped to allow the police car to pass, heading for the police station. "Hello, ladies," Mary Inch said smiling as they came in, "I'm about finished with lunch. Can I fix you something?"

Liza seemed very excited. "No thanks, Mary. But I have some exciting news. I can't hold it in any longer. My son, you both remember Joseph? He's coming to visit for a few days all the way from Australia! I haven't seen him for years. I just can't wait!"

Mary said, "That's great news, Liza! Hasn't he been working somewhere with horses?"

"Yes. He loves horses, as you two know, and when my brother asked him to join them on their station—that's what they call a big ranch there in Australia—he just left here immediately. Right now he's in London on a buying spree. Nason, my brother sent him on this important trip. He's been going around to horse farms, race tracks and all the rest of it." She was bursting with pride. "He'll be here tomorrow for a few days before he takes it all back to Australia. I hope you'll both come over to say hi."

"Of course we will. That's such good news!" Mary Inch said.

Liza stopped, remembering that her friend only yesterday found out the dead man was her son, Geran. "Oh, Mary, I'm so sorry to be blabbing on. I heard about…how are you doing?"

"I'm doing okay. It's been hard to take in. He never once wrote to me or told me anything about why he left so suddenly. Now I can't ask him." She gave them a tiny smile to reassure them she would be fine.

Dobbs decided enough small talk. She could barely contain herself and jumped in, "Mary, I have an important thing to ask you. In the couple of days we've been back in the dower, strange things have been happening. We feel…or I feel anyway, the house has become haunted." She glanced at both their faces and then hurried on. "It had been such a lovely place to work before. Before the…deaths. Jenna. And Caden. Now that we're moving back in, it's become, well…terrifying, really." She stopped. "It's haunted." Her chin jutted out daring anyone to doubt her. "I know that's crazy, but really scary things are happening to us. Loud moaning, bad smells that come and go. Nightmares. Just hear me out, Mary." Dobbs sat silent a moment before she continued, "I believe your Jenna is haunting the dower. She feels wronged. She never hurt anybody in her life, and she didn't commit suicide." Dobbs, stopped, expecting a great deal of doubt. Liza Zelly stood beside her nodding her head, hoping Mary would understand.

Mary looked from one to the other rather bemused. "What? Why are you saying these things."

Dobbs rushed on. "Jenna's angry that anyone would dream that she murdered a little boy in her care. She wants, no, she needs, to be vindicated, cleared. And I think you, Mary, can help us, if you would." It hit Dobbs that she would be asking Mary to exorcise the ghost of her own daughter, if she was right about what was happening.

"And how would I do that?" She found it hard to believe they even asked her something so preposterous.

"You read fortunes for some around here, with your crystal ball or whatever."

"I don't have a crystal ball," Mary answered evenly, becoming wary.

"However, you do…read…or tell their fortune."

"I've never done such a thing in my life, Kerra Dobbs."

"People have told me you help them with problems. That you're very good."

Liza Zelly added, "Remember you told me Joseph would do quite well working for his uncle and, well, just look. My brother trusted him enough for this big important job."

"I listen to whatever one of my neighbors is having trouble with or worries about. I do a reading with someone, and it quite often helps them see where they can move forward and how to do that. It was certainly no mysterious leap for the tarot reading to predict that Joseph, your sharp, hard-working lad would prosper, Liza."

Dobbs asked, "What're you reading that tells you things?"

"I read the Tarot cards. It's not fortune telling."

Dobbs looked from Mary to Liza and back. "Then that's what we need. You can read the Tarot cards for Jenna." They held their breath as she considered.

After a moment, Mary Inch quietly said, "Okay. I'll do it. It's crazy, but I'll do a reading for my Jenna." Liza Zelly and Kerra Dobbs smiled triumphantly. Mary Inch looked skeptical but made a decision. "Tonight, I'll try to do what you asked. The dower dining room table at nine o'clock."

Ferguson had been convinced that he must attend the séance, and he reluctantly joined the group around the dining room table. While the others waited for a message from beyond, he thought perhaps he could expose how the phony haunting worked. Primarily he agreed, if he was honest with himself, because it seemed important to Abby. At nine o'clock, they all sat around the dower's dining room table. The gas lights in the dining room and the parlor had been turned down, and for the first time, the double doors into the parlor were closed—in spite of his objections.

Mary Inch insisted, "It creates a more beneficial atmosphere." Some candles had been placed down the center of the table reflecting a golden glow on each face. Seated were the people who had been staying there, plus Alan who knew Jenna and minus Sukie, who refused and went up to the manor house after dinner. Although they hadn't spent nights there, Lady Edra sat with Jory by her side.

From his seat at the foot of the table, Ferguson could watch each of them. Mary Inch sat at the head of the table closest to the kitchen door, with a deck of tarot cards in front of her, and looked around. Lady Edra sat at Mary's left with Jory next to her. Geever, Abby, Alan and Dobbs filled the rest of the chairs.

"Kerra Dobbs thinks this house might be haunted," Mrs. Inch began, "and I have been persuaded tonight to try to help in some way, although I don't know what you think I can do or how I can help. I know nothing about contacting the dead or hauntings. I've never even seen a séance. Growing up Romani, as a girl, my grandmother taught me about palm reading and tarot card readings. I brought the Tarot with me. Before you dismiss these as carnival tricks, you should know these are traditions with deep roots, hundreds of years old in my culture, which we are all taught growing up. I not only learned my ABCs, but my family, especially my grandmother, helped me develop my psychic abilities as part of my education. We also learn from childhood about the power of dreams and how they affect our daily lives. None of it was ever structured as a classroom. We learned to trust it as a part of daily life. There would be many days when I couldn't go out to play because someone in my family had a 'warning dream,' in which they saw something that indicated a person might have an accident. The history of my ancestors' connection to the supernatural taught me the practice of spiritual therapy. This tradition and my education shaped me into a Romani spiritualist, or *drabarni* in our language. Any time I've helped a neighbor around here, it's never been to predict the future or speak to the dead, only to help answer questions about their lives. I've learned how to intuit things. I've tried to teach my children and Keyan these things. Geran never cared, but Jenna believed. Keyan, I think, has special abilities. He is very intuitive. He could become a *drabarno* one day."

She stopped for a second before continuing, "I have to ask, were there any strange things happening when any of you who lived here before?" Lady Edra, Alan and Dobbs all shook their heads. "What then has changed? What could be causing these things?" No one ventured an opinion. "Six years ago, my daughter, Jenna, died here. Do any of you think Jenna became a ghost? Surely not little Caden? An angry spirit?" A pause. "Do you believe that?"

Dobbs, said, "I think it's her. She was a sweet, loving young girl, but something is wrong. She wants us to hear her. If she did murder a little boy and commit suicide, her soul has become tainted by it and turned evil by her sins. Or it's the black soul of the real murderer's thirst for more blood."

"I don't know ghosts," Mrs. Inch said. "I have heard that if a person's been wronged, they can't rest, and their ghost becomes venomous and dangerous. If this haunting is about my beautiful Jenna, she is vengeful because she didn't do anything bad. We can do a reading for the spirit that is here. As I said, I trust dreams. Although, no dream warned me about my beautiful daughter's and little Caden's death, still, I'm happy Keyan won't go to school on a day that I've had a troubling dream. I think he's trusting his own feelings when he doesn't go. He knows he would have a bad day if he went. Perhaps your dreams in this house are trying to communicate something to you. Maybe they're messages. They might be clues. If you tell me what you have been dreaming about in this house, then maybe I can help." She looked at Abby first, sensing some kindred abilities.

Abby nodded, "The first night I slept here, I dreamt a horrible fur-covered monster with sharp claws searched for a baby to kill. I couldn't save it. It was awful. But, last night's dream terrified me more." Her voice trembled. "I remember only dreadfully powerful hands choking me, while he repeatedly smashed my head against a wall. It was so real, I couldn't breathe." Her hands went to her throat. "John found me in my surgery banging my head on the cupboard door, and woke me, petrified. I was gasping for air." Her eyes searched John's face. He stared intensely at her and she could feel the strength he sent her.

Mrs. Inch seemed shocked by Abby's dreams. She couldn't help but notice Ferguson's intense reaction to Abby after she spoke so she next asked him to recount his dreams. "I've simply been having my familiar nightmares about the carnage of war. Nothing else." Mary stared at him a moment deciding whether he spoke the whole truth.

She moved on. "Inspector Geever?"

"I have been barely aware that others were having nightmares. They didn't share how horrifying Doc Abby's were. My dreams have been of a prowling menace of hatred and death searching for something. As if it's looking for me. It seems closer each night." He glanced at Ferguson, then looked at his hands a little embarrassed wondering if he had shared too much. Ferguson was indeed surprised by what Geever disclosed. It didn't seem like a very— unshakable Scotland Yard detective—thing to say. However, Ferguson had been so focused on Abby's experiences that he hadn't paid attention to anything Geever had mentioned about his nights. When he had checked, he found quiet and assumed Geever to be a very sound sleeper.

After absorbing Geever's words for a few seconds, Mrs. Inch said, "Dobbs?"

"We only stayed one night, me and Sukie. Alan doesn't have a room, so he's sleeping in his room at the manor." She looked at Alan who nodded. "I only smelled something vile and dead, but Sukie said she felt a stalking presence lurking near us."

Alan shook his head. "I'm only here because I thought of Jenna as a friend. I haven't experienced anything. I just want to help."

She turned her gaze and asked, "Lady Edra?"

"I haven't had any dreams." She wilted, depleted. "I haven't spent a night in this house since we returned that year from our Christmas holiday in Ireland to find my world ended. The little, peaceful, happy world Gran and I created here in this house had turned to a horror. It made no sense. I still find it hard to even think about. I had no idea these dreadful dreams came each night to you." She looked at them as tears fell onto her cheeks. Jory placed his arm around her shoulders, and she leaned into him. When Mary glanced at him, he simply shook his head, indicating he had never spent the night in the dower house, and implying that he came merely as support for Lady Edra.

The quiet suddenly shattered as a terrified shriek came from Keyan, the other side of the parlor door. He had been crouching, eavesdropping. Ferguson leapt from his chair. By the time he had the door thrown open, Keyan disappeared. They heard him yelp. It sounded like someone pulled him, bumping him up the stairs. A small cry erupted from him with each step. Ferguson reached the dark staircase first. From moonlight streaming in through the Palladian window, he saw Keyan dropped on the landing facing them. Jory followed directly behind Ferguson as they hurried to the top. Jory asked, "What is it, Keyan? We're just talking to your Baba. No need to …"

"The beast grabbed me!" His eyes were huge, and his breath came in gasps as he spoke. He shook as he leaned against Ferguson grasping his coat sleeve. "It yanked me up the stairs. It wants me dead. Just like the tree wants me dead." He began to sob. "The monster wants us all dead!"

His grandmother stood resolutely at the bottom of the dark stairs. "We will try to contact this fiend," she declared in a commanding voice. "We will do a reading for the presence in the house tonight. Now. Everyone back into the dining room. Keyan, you sit next to me."

Ferguson declared, "These doors remain open," referring to the parlor doors, as they reassembled in the dining room. Jory pulled up a chair for Keyan next to his grandmother. Mary Inch took a deep breath then turned her attention to the others and picked up her deck. "This reading is for the spirit haunting this house," she announced. "Please help us to understand you." She unfolded and laid a sheet of paper with a five-point star drawn on it in front of her. "I need each of you sitting here to be aware of any sensations you have, as we do this." She looked around at each of them. "We will do the pentagram as the reading for whoever is here, trying to communicate with us." Next, she chose the top card in the deck and placed it in the center of the star. "I have chosen the Hermit as your significator." She addressed the spirit and spoke, looking above their heads. The card showed an old man dressed in a long robe, holding a staff in one hand and a lantern in the other. "The Hermit asks you to search deep within your soul to help you find your way again. When one is in need of understanding, the Hermit will help find the answers you seek, and help us sitting here to understand what it is you seek."

She shuffled the deck and chose Lady Edra to cut the deck. She held the deck next for Dobbs to cut the second time and Geever the third. She placed the first five cards from the top of the deck at the five points of the pentagram face down. She turned over the first card saying, "This card represents the Spirit that guides this reading." The card showed four horizontal swords, with a fifth vertical sword bisecting the others. "This is a card of conflict. You seem to have gathered clouds of negative energy. I feel you are resentful of something and have been pushing and pushing, but no one is listening. The card is reversed and indicates you may be ready to stop fighting, if we hear you." She closed her eyes a moment waiting.

Ferguson watched their faces trained on Mrs. Inch. Silence moved through the darkness, the only sound Mrs. Inch's voice. He strained to hear or see any hint of trickery or manipulation in the space.

Turning the second card over, she said, "This is the Earth card. The Five of Wands represents your present situation. It indicates you are in the midst of a battle. Something is keeping you in place or even holding you back. What is it? Are there forces at play here that are preventing you from moving forward?" She looked around the room. The whisper of the gas lights, the only answer.

"The third card is the Water card about your unexpected personal energies." She turned over the Five of Pentacles, a card showing two very poor men, a tall, older one in rags and a younger man on crutches trudging through snow. "This card points to misfortunes to overcome. It indicates you feel isolated and alone, rather like the two figures on the card, as if you have been left in the cold. Are you wondering why no one is helping you?" She raised her voice. " We want to help you. Tell us what can we do?" She waited a few moments with her eyes closed. The others looked around at each other.

Abby watched Ferguson's intense focus on everything except the reading of the tarot. It pleased her that he watched as their protective doubter. He did not believe in the power of any of this, yet he seemed to her again the most powerful force in the room.

"The fourth card is the Fire card and shows you the immediate future." She turned over the Hanged Man. It showed a young man in medieval clothing, hanging upside down with one leg tied to the branch of a tree and the other leg bent. He held his hands at his side. "The Hanged Man calls you to release old behavior patterns that no longer serve you. This is the Universe's way of helping you see your situation in a new light. If you resist, you will meet more obstacles along the way. Allow opportunities to flow effortlessly to you. Let us be your opportunity. How can we help you?"

She asked those around the table, " Would each of you close your eyes? Open yourselves to any image you are shown." The others sheepishly looked at each other, and then one by one closed their eyes, except Ferguson. He noted that Geever looked around the room over the heads of the others, searching for something false before submitting.

"What image did you see? What were you feeling?" They each looked to the others. When no one spoke she continued, "The fifth card is the outcome card." She turned over the Death card reversed, which elicited a few low gasps. The Death card showed a skeleton dressed in black armor, riding a white horse. "Death is about endings and beginnings, birth and rebirth, change and transformation. It symbolizes the end of a major phase that is no longer serving you. It opens up the possibility of something far more valuable and essential. You must close the door to your past. Close the door on all that has befallen you. Close the door on your anger. You have awakened those of us here to your injustice. We need to be enlightened about how to help you. Your hatred and rage are merely terrifying everyone. We will try to get to the bottom of your injustice. Jenna, my beloved daughter, if this is you, we need to know how. What happened to you?"

Geever jumped up from his chair shouting, "I smell smoke!" Ferguson leapt up and threw open the door to the kitchen to discover a fire raging, flames leaping near the tall ceiling, from a large pan set on top of the stove. The men threw water on it, and dropped a cloth on it quickly dousing the fire. Smoke flooded the kitchen and drifted to the other rooms.

The others stood in the doorway looking shocked. Keyan said in a barely audible voice, "It wants us all dead."

Ferguson stepped through the water on the floor to the back door and opened it. "This door wasn't locked. Anyone could have come in and started this while we were in the dining room." He thought it suspicious and particularly thoughtful of this vengeful ghost to set a containable fire, causing minimal damage. It rather unnerved him that this had been accomplished so totally quietly.

Lady Edra said, "I think we have our message. This is a dangerous place. No one is sleeping here. We will all be staying at the manor for the duration."

"I'm not," Abby said. "If Mrs. Inch is right about dreams, then maybe our dreams are how whoever is haunting us can communicate. It can show me."

Ferguson said, "I already decided I'm staying. I'd like to catch whoever is doing this."

Geever calmly said, "I agree. I'll remain, also." He said this with no trace of haughtiness. Ferguson reflected how Geever seemed less of a prat all the time.

Lady Edra asked Abby, "Won't you please come with me. These dreams of yours are so terrifying my dear Abby."

"Thank you, Edra, but if we can end this, if I can understand maybe we could solve what happened to little Caden." She hugged Lady Edra who left quietly with the others.

Geever turned the lights up in the parlor and turned off the other unused lights. Ferguson checked that the front and back door were secured once the last one left. The three who remained sat before the fire, subdued.

Ferguson said, "I'll be sleeping in your room, Abby. Last night you were sleep walking. I want to make sure you're safe." That felt awkward. He added, "Perhaps we all should stay in one room." He looked at Geever.

"I'll be sleeping right here in the parlor near the fireplace. If someone gets into the house, I shall sound an alarm."

Geever went to his room and brought down a blanket, a pillow, his notebook and his torch. Before settling down, he entered the darkened kitchen and shone the torch all around the baseboard, in all the corners, even under the counter and under the stove. Maybe Ferguson had a point. Some person must have set the pan alight. Ghosts don't do that. Of course, there are no ghosts. What am I saying? He found some clean rags and mopped up the water from the floor. He lit up the corners and crevices in the other rooms and found nothing but extra dust, around where the workmen were building the water closet in the hallway, and in Doc Abby's dark surgery. Geever thought calling her Doc Abby fit. He found her to be a properly serious woman who should be respected. Arranging his makeshift bed, he sat down and wrote up the interviews he had with women and men who had been involved with and deceived, in some way by Geran years ago. It always surprised him how carelessly many of the men that they hunted down, hurt people, and Geran Inch had racked up a good number.

He decided to get a book from the shelves in the doc's waiting room—formerly the dower library. Looking at the book spine titles, a sullen hostility grew in the darkness behind him. He spun around, shining his torch everywhere at once. He stopped and said, "This is absurd." He thought the whole evening had created these spooky thoughts. He turned back to the books, chose one calmly and returned to the parlor and settled in on the couch.

Ferguson checked the upstairs bathroom and found it nearing completion. Walls were patched, and an access panel had been installed. Taking his torch, he removed the hatch, climbed onto the edge of the tub, where the hatch had been created a little lower than the hole had been. He could now pull himself through to check the entire attic without a ladder. Satisfied no one lurked there, he climbed back down, replaced the panel, and checked the bedrooms, making sure all was secured. Ferguson went to his room leaving the door ajar and spent a half hour writing up his notes about the progress made on the case, omitting the séance-tarot reading and the nightmares.

Crossing the hall, he knocked lightly on Abby's partially open door. "Come in, Ferguson." She lie in bed and had changed into her nightgown. He sat in the chair next to the bed, took off his shoes and loosened his tie. "I planned to stay alone in the house, even if you left," she said.

"You were pretty sure, though, that I would stay with you, weren't you?"

"I hoped you would," she smiled. "Won't you be terribly uncomfortable sitting in that chair?"

"I'll be fine." He stretched his long legs out in front of him. "Lights out?" She nodded, then blew out her lamp. The moon's radiance filled the room with a serene, bluish glow making it easy to fall asleep.

Two hours later, Ferguson awoke to violent knocking from somewhere and muffled terrified screams.

He found only the tangled covers of her bed—no Abby.

He grabbed the torch. The sounds led him to the bath. She pounded from the other side of the wall. "Abby!" Still, she pounded and scratched at the wall. "Abby! I'm coming!" He removed the access panel, which quieted her, and climbed through.

He found her on the bottom stair that had been left of the partial attic stairway. "Oh my god, how did I get here, John? What is this place? It's so dark." She clung to him shaking and sobbing. He helped her through the panel. She oriented herself. "The bathroom?" She looked at the opening that John had pulled her through. "How…?" John shook his head. How indeed he wondered. He could barely climb through the panel, standing on the edge of the tub. She couldn't reach it without a ladder. The panel also couldn't have been set back in place from inside the wall. She looked at her closed hand and slowly opened it. It held a necklace, a medallion. Exactly like the one Geran wore. One like Mary Inch said each of her children had. The one that came from Geran? He reached into his pocket and pulled out the medallion taken from Geran's body. They stared at each other.

There was nothing to say. Ferguson went back to his chair, and Abby to her bed. "Can you go back to sleep?" he asked her.

A small trembling voice, "I'll try." The silence in the room allowed Ferguson to close his eyes.

"Ferguson?" a quiet voice asked in the dark. "It would be so much easier to fall asleep if you lay down beside me."

"Of course." He lay on top of the covers next to her. He found it so much more comfortable lying in the bed that he slept shortly after they lay down. She snuggled next to him. She loved the substance of him, his strength lying beside her, listening to the rise and fall of his breath. He smelled wonderful. The intimacy allowed her to feel safe and protected, and she soon fell asleep.

When Ferguson awoke to grayish light as the dawn broke, Abby lie sleeping peacefully next to him. Sometime in the night, she had thrown the covers over him. She lay against him, her arm over him, breathing quietly next to his ear. It felt so good to be this close to her. Her beautiful mahogany hair lay across her shoulder. She looked so peaceful, her lips slightly parted, sleeping. He untangled himself, and got up before it felt too good to be next to her. He searched the bedrooms, turned on the torch and climbed into the attic. There were only Abby and his own prints in the dust. How had someone carried her there and left no indication—other than a medallion that Jenna had been known to wear?

Downstairs as Geever awoke and sat up he heard Ferguson walk into the kitchen. He followed. Before Ferguson could check the lock, "Wait," Geever said, touching the door first. "I stuck a hair from my head across the opening. He showed Ferguson that it remained undisturbed.

"How did you get that hair to stick without tape?"

"Brylcreem. I discovered long ago that my hair product could be used to make sure no one rummaged around in my personal property, undetected when I wasn't around. I have a brother. Enough said."

"Huh, Brylcreem," Ferguson shook his head and chuckled at that. Brylcreem that kept Geever's hair perfectly, gleamingly combed back had proven its usefulness on the still locked front door as well. A commotion in the kitchen alerted them to the morning return of the servants.

Chapter Nine

Walking to the police station with Geever after a subdued breakfast, Ferguson wondered about telling him of Abby's experience last night, but decided it could wait. John had no idea how to explain it rationally to anyone. They needed to focus on their job. "I'll call Howell with a report about our progress, or lack thereof, unless you would prefer to report to him."

"No, no that's fine. Uh…John, my father's 60th birthday is today, and I wondered if you would accompany me to a luncheon with the family?" He seemed embarrassed.

"What? Of course not! We need to make some progress today!" Geever fell silent. John went directly to the telephone to report to Howell, after acknowledging Crocker with a nod. No Jory yet this morning, Ferguson noted. A few minutes later, after ending his telephone call, he emerged from Jory's office looking between mystified and angry. Glaring at Geever, Ferguson said, "It seems Lord Geever, the Earl of Truro, has been granted permission from the head of Scotland Yard, himself, for you *and I* to attend a grand birthday luncheon today!"

Geever shrugged his shoulders. "Sorry."

Totally ignoring what John just said, Crocker piped up, "I'm off for a bit of fishing with my son-in-law and grandkids." John shook his head. Crocker seemed more alive and chipper than he had ever seen him. "Don't worry. We'll be back by tomorrow night."

"Great!" John said sarcastically. "Wait. Your son-in-law, Penrose? Penrose is going fishing? I thought he seemed desperate to finish the harvest?"

"Can't do much of anything with most everyone working on the dower house."

"You'll be off when exactly?"

"Noon today until tomorrow afternoon."

John wondered where Jory was this morning. It seemed like everything about the case had come to a halt—not that Crocker would be missed much. He'd have to have Jory questioning and requestioning more people, since Geran had left such a lot of people disliking him a great deal. They needed also to find out how the men harvesting at Penrose's got home that night, and did any of them just happen to have a spade handy when suddenly Geran Inch appeared. At least one of the men working on the dower knew of someone they had questioned who hadn't shared the whole truth. Time to start getting to the gossip.

Ferguson sighed. "I'm going to interview Lady Steran now. I need you, Geever, to formally interview Sir Vinson about his movements Sunday night. Point out, we believe he is lying to us. Let's shake him out of his smug detachment. Can you do that before he leaves for Chough Hall?"

"Absolutely. The name of his paramour would give him his alibi, and we could eliminate him." Geever marched out of the police station, shoulders squared, prepared to conquer the cagey Sir Vinson. Plus he escaped John's wrath.

John left notes for Jory. A few minutes later, he stopped off at the dower to pick up his notebook. His bad mood led him to yell at a workman, kneeling hammering at something at the bottom of the stairs. "Move it man. I have a birthday party to get to!" Several men turned at the commotion. Taking the stairs two at a time, he found other workmen standing in front of the water closet door who slowed him down. "Out of my way, please! I must achieve something before the important party, boys!" His short-tempered sarcasm, mixed with his frustration, drew sly grins from the workmen.

A few minutes later as Ferguson nearly lifted the knocker on the manor front door, Jory opened it. Startled and confused by finding Jory letting himself out of the manor, early in the morning, John wordlessly stared his questions at Jory. The unspoken questions involved—are you sleeping with the Lady Edra—is this the first time or has this been going on for some time—are the servants aware? How did I not see your relationship was more than just your concern for a distraught friend? A dead husband makes you a contender for the lady's hand—not to mention the lady's land and title. Jory Moon you have made yourself a person of interest! Maybe even the person with the most to gain by Geran Inch's death!

Jory understood every question John's thoughts intended. He nodded, and said, "I know, but later. I need to get to the station." As Jory left him, a footman appeared, and John requested to speak to Lady Steran. The grandfather clock chimed nine times reminding him his morning was already slipping away with no progress. At first, she refused to see him, especially at this hour, but when he prevailed upon her maid, Mrs. Deane, to convey the importance of a timely interview, she relented. It required him to only wait another half hour. A half hour that fueled his annoyance around the lost afternoon.

"Inspector Ferguson, what is so urgent that we must meet at this hour?" Lady Steran demanded.

Through nearly clenched teeth, he responded, "I have an important appointment this afternoon. An assignment given me by Sir Arthur Newburg, the very chief of all of Scotland Yard!"

His abruptness surprised her. She wasn't used to being spoken to in such a manner. She did, however, want this unpleasantness to go away, and Ferguson struck her as someone who might be capable of solving the murder. "Please, sit Inspector. What is it you wish to know?"

He let out a puff of air calming himself and started to ask her how long Jory and her granddaughter had been…what? He stopped himself. Jory would be questioned later. He asked evenly, "I need you to tell me all you know about Geran Inch leaving suddenly. A man is dead, savagely murdered. I need to know what made this selfish, thoughtless man, living such a posh life, suddenly disappear. As far as I can see, he used people, laughed at them, betrayed them, yet he suffered no consequences. Then suddenly, he's gone without any explanation. None that seemed plausible either to his wife, or his mother apparently. Did no one look into his disappearance? Did no one investigate?"

"Why don't you ask Sir Vinson about that?"

"Because I don't trust anything that comes out of his mouth." They exchanged glares.

Lady Steran sighed and looked out the window as she began to speak. "Vinson hated the cad from when he first found Edra attracted to him. He tried to dissuade her in every way possible, but nothing worked. My daughter, Edra's mother, had died, and a sixteen-year-old girl became a baroness with a remarkable amount of power and self-determination. Such power has been granted to sixteen-year-old young men who have done ridiculous things with that power for hundreds of years. She was no different. I felt it best for me to support the besotted child, since I couldn't make her see sense. I can't prove it, but I think Vinson gave Geran a great deal of money to disappear forever." She paused briefly, "I also believe he paid the creature more money over the years. But I have no proof of my suspicions."

Ferguson thanked her and left to confront Sir Vinson. Lander met him and said, "Sir Vinson is in the oak room this morning preparing for his visit to Chough Hall. Follow me to the south wing." They continued past several closed doors to the end of the hallway. Lander left him in a very masculine room of dark oak. Paintings of horses and photographs of horses, lined the walls. Statues of horses and trophies won by generations of Bandrys were displayed on the bookcase and other pieces of furniture. Sir Vinson gathered up some last-minute things. He held papers in his hand, about to drop them into a case.

"Ferguson, what is it? I'm rather in a hurry to leave. Geever interrogated me only minutes ago," he scowled. Geever must have done a good job. He had upset the man. "Please, sit Inspector. Can I get you anything…?"

John interrupted, "Did you pay off Geran Inch to leave your daughter for good?"

Sir Vinson peered at him, speechless for a few seconds, then "Why, of course not."

"And didn't you pay him several times over the years to remain gone?"

"Absolutely not!"

"I can obtain copies of your bank statements," Ferguson said, without any knowledge about whether he could dig into the affairs of a baronetcy over their objections. "Perhaps you grew tired of paying blackmail to this scoundrel, lured him back and ended it once and for all."

"Nonsense. No such thing happened!" John wondered if his outrage was genuine. "My accounts, Bandry accounts, would show no such thing. I must ask you to leave now."

"Then let me examine them."

"I have no intention of allowing you into our affairs!"

"We'll see." There was certainly something he did not want to come to light. As John stormed out of the manor, he considered Sir Vinson to be in contention with Jory for having the best motive for killing the man who had become his son-in-law, while consorting with other young women and, importantly, flaunting it. Probably most critical to Sir Vinson Bandry's thinking, his daughter's marriage had become such public humiliation that he could no longer abide the situation. Ferguson needed to find some proof of his theories.

"Detective, can I have a quick word?" Kitto, the young stableboy, met him as he left the manor. "I wanted to catch you before we left. It's probably nothing." They walked back to the stables and watched as the older groomsman, Mitch Tink, put a saddle on Sir Vinson's glorious white gelding. Kitto stood beside a wagon that looked to Ferguson to be everything needed for the horse and the competition tomorrow.

"Are you taking Asif to the earl's for Sir Vinson? He mentioned he was about to depart."

"Sir Vinson's chosen to ride him to Chough Hall. Tomorrow he'll be competing in the dressage competitions. We're going up today so both Sir Vinson and Asif will be rested and ready to go tomorrow. We're bringing the tack and everything else up in the wagon."

"Does anyone around here go to watch the competition?"

"From Woodcomb, you mean? No, not really. The matches are for toffs. Me and Granddad will be there though. We'll be in charge of Asif's care, and bring him and all this back home. Wherry will be driving the car up later. He's not just the chauffeur, you know. He'll then do all the valet stuff for Sir Vinson. He needs dinner clothes and all the rest of it. First though, he'll drive Lady Edra this morning on some errands."

Ferguson returned Kitto to the subject he wanted to talk about. "You had something you wanted to speak to me about?" Kitto nodded, and looked around making sure no one could overhear them.

"Sunday night, the night of the murder, after everything calmed down about Lady Edra's fall and all the rest of it, Wherry showed up here at the stable. The thing is, I was about to go back to my room, over in the back of the big barn. I wouldn't have still been over here except for the commotion. I don't know, maybe he thought I had already gone, but anyway when he saw me, he asked about Asif here. Sir Vinson had just got home. He had been riding Asif, and I brought the horse back to the stable, and I was brushing him. Wherry just stood there, then said all serious, 'What's on his hooves?' and I looked at them. He said, 'is that blood?' and I said 'probably just mud,' and he left just like that. I thought that a bit queer. I wiped at

Asif's hooves. It looked kinda reddish and wet, but blood made no sense to me. The horse had not been hurt. I just let it go and went to bed. But I been thinking, since you asked if anything unusual happened. They said the body had been stepped on by a horse. Probably nothing." He grinned uneasily, rather hoping Ferguson would find this information of no importance.

"What time did Sir Vinson get home?"

"After ten, I'd say."

"Thanks, Kitto, for this information. Probably nothing as you say." Ferguson remembered the bit of horse hair he had picked up from the murder scene, pulled it out of his pocket, and handed it to Kitto. "These were found where the body lay. It's small, but does this match any of the horses in the stable?"

"It's dark like Asif's mane, but I couldn't say from only those hairs. It makes you think, though, don't it, sir?" This had obviously disturbed Kitto. Ferguson needed to consider if there might be another reason that Kitto told him? He didn't think Kitto seemed to be tattling to see if he could get Wherry in trouble, but he didn't know about the dynamic between the two men. Kitto was ten years younger than Wherry, and a stableboy. That didn't seem to equate to Kitto being jealous of Wherry's position in the house.

They turned toward the voices they heard outside. Sir Vinson, Lady Edra and Keyan were coming toward them chatting. Lady Edra and Keyan smiled. Sir Vinson refused to look at him. The man was peeved by Geever's and John's rude questioning.

"Sir Vinson, you're personally riding Asif to the earl's estate? How far is it?"

Grudgingly he answered. "About twelve miles. It'll take three to four hours, but the horse needs to be there and rested for tomorrow, and besides, I love riding him."

"Well, good luck tomorrow," John said. Sir Vinson looked at the detective with a side eye and sniffed, as his only reply. He mounted Asif and said, "All right Tinks, I assume you are both ready. Let's go." Sir Vinson nodded and tipped his hat to his daughter as they passed her. Both she and Keyan waved as the entourage left the estate.

Kitto and Mitch waved from the truck to a young man they spotted standing at the front door of the dower. The man stood hat in hand and waved his hat in greeting to the Tinks, who continued following Asif and Sir Vinson. The man probably wanted to talk to him, Ferguson thought. He turned to Lady Edra first and asked, "Are you going to watch your father tomorrow." Lady Edra had also noticed the man and stared at him. "Do you know who that is?" John asked.

"I'm not sure. He may have worked here in the stables. But to answer your question, no. I'm not much interested in the competition. We'll be here, won't we Keyan? Let's go saddle Naazim and do some practicing on her. Then I really must get ready for my day." Keyan smiled broadly, and the two walked into the stables, leaving Ferguson to cross the lawns and meet the man.

Quietly he asked, "Are you Detective Ferguson?" John nodded. "My name's Joseph Zelly. I used to work in the stables here at Tredwen with the horses. Me mum said you probably wanted to talk to me. I think I know who killed Jenna and little Caden six years ago."

After being momentarily stunned, John regained his power of speech. "I would very much like to hear your story Mr. Joseph Zelly. Why don't we go inside and talk." The workmen's clamor greeted them, as Ferguson ushered the man past the drawing room, into the dining room and took his notebook from his pocket.

Joseph looked around curiously taking in the commotion. Ferguson was about to explain, when Joseph glanced at him and pointed his hat vaguely around and said, "Mum told me the dower was getting a remodel so as to keep the doc here."

Alan appeared. "Some tea and perhaps some toast?" He recognized Joseph and exclaimed, "Joseph! You back?" Alan smiled broadly. Ferguson gave him a stern look. "Sorry." He disappeared back into the kitchen.

Joseph took a deep breath and began, "Again, my name is Joseph Zelly, and I used to work here in the stables with Geran and Mitchell Tink before Kitto. I moved up and became a groomsman for the Bandrys after Geran Inch scarpered the year before. He left a lot of bad feelings when he just disappeared. I kinda thought maybe he'd been murdered, and whoever did it buried him quite well. I got his job though and thought good riddance."

"You both worked in the stables. Were you chums?"

"Not really. He was too wild for me."

"Okay. Continue."

He paused, "That Christmas morning a year later in 1915, I was leaving to start my new life, and I had a train to catch. That was the year the whole Bandry family went away to Ireland for the holidays. All the manor workers usually get a day or two off at Christmas, but that year, we got a whole week. Time to spend with family and friends. The entire staff was right jolly that year. The animals had to be seen to, course, and the house occasionally checked, but no one paid much attention other than that. Only Jenna stayed with her babe and Lady Edra's Caden. She never resented it that she had to stay at the dower. She could run across the road to her mum's with the two boys if she wanted some company.

"The day I left, I'd been staying in the village with me mum. I came back to the stables early, just before light, to feed and water the animals and pack up everything I owned because I had the early train to catch. I was off for my adventure with my uncle Nason in Australia. He has a big station there. They call the ranches there stations, and my uncle raises horses for the army and all sorts. That's why he wanted me to work for him, me knowing horses and all. He sent all the horses he could for the war effort. Thousands of horses from all over were used by the armies. Breeding them, training them and such, and that was what we did. Everyone, including me, thought I'd be back within a year, but I love it out there. Never looked back.

"You see, Detective, that year we all enjoyed our long Christmas holiday. The day after Christmas, Boxing Day, everyone had to get back to work. The family would be coming home that night."

He squirmed a bit on his seat remembering. "This is my first trip back to England. Uncle Nason sent me as his representative to scout out and buy new stock and look at some new equipment. It surprised me to run into Geran Inch, working for one of the racehorse trainers at the Ascot race-track. We got together for a couple of pints and got to talking. He said he hadn't been home for six or seven years. Seeing him reminded me about the murders. I asked him if he knew about the tragedy there. Mum wrote to me about it, but I didn't get her letter for months with the war and all, and mail being spotty at best. I had an exciting new life with so much to learn, and the work is exhausting. I still just drop into bed at the end of the day. I never put it all together, until I sat there drinking lager with him. It made me remember what mum wrote to me, and I told him what her letter said. Jenna and little Caden—Geran's son—had been murdered. It gob-smacked him. I told him some people thought Jenna killed the boy and committed suicide because she regretted what she'd done. Most didn't believe it, but nobody could explain what happened.

"When I told him, Geran became absolutely enraged that anybody could believe his sister, Jenna, could do anything so gruesome, and I agreed with him! Why did anyone believe that? Believe Jenna would murder that little Caden? I had practically forgotten it, but talking to Geran, I remembered I saw Sir Vinson that Christmas morning, as I left to catch my train." He stopped with his chin out daring Ferguson to not believe him. "None of them, the family you know, was supposed to be back, but there he stood. Christmas morning. A day before the Bandrys all returned. No servants, cold house, nothing, but there he stood. I thought it queer. But it were none of my business. I was leaving and excited to get on with it.

"After feeding the animals, I had to pick up my luggage from the stables, and drag my trunk with all my gear to the train station. I stopped for some breakfast at the Inch pasty shop. Then on to the station. I almost ran into Jenna practically running, dragging her little son Keyan with her. I asked her why the hurry, and she said Sir Vinson just showed up at the dower and told her a terrible accident just happened at her mum's shop. He told her maybe she should check it out. See if her mum needed help. Sir Vinson told Jenna to go, he'd stay with his grandson. Spend a bit on his own with the lad. A fire, I think he told her. We could both look down at the quay, and see the shop looked fine. I thought that odd. I told her I just finished breakfast there, and there had been no problems. That stopped her dead in her tracks. Eyes big as saucers. Something was terribly wrong. Jenna fairly threw Keyan at me. She turned and ran back to the dower house. She screamed, as she ran for me to drop Keyan with her mum. She yelled she would pick him up later. All this commotion made me almost miss my train, so I just dropped the lad off inside the door, and he ran to her. She had customers. She was busy. We just nodded to each other. I never even thought or wondered. So wrapped up with my new adventure. Never looked back or thought about it.

"Geran said he would come back here, and tell them all what really happened. He said I should too, so they'd believe him."

Ferguson asked, "This happened very early, about dawn Christmas day, and you're sure you saw Sir Vinson?"

"The sun shone right enough. I'm sure who I saw standing by the front door of the manor house."

"Did he see you?"

"I think he probably noticed me half dragging me trunk and all."

"You say at just after dawn on Christmas morning. Mary Inch didn't even take that day off and had some hot pasties for you?"

"I told everyone I saw for weeks about my trip. I spoke to her the day before, and she said she'd have some ready to eat and carry on the train. Always a nice lady. Besides, she had customers when I dropped off Keyan. Some fishermen going out early. Even on Christmas morning."

"You didn't mention your surprise at seeing Sir Vinson standing at the front door of the manor house?"

"No. Him standing there was naught to me. I had picked up my pasties. When I dropped off the lad, she just nodded, seeing little Keyan, and he ran to her. She wished me the best, and I thanked her. Ask her."

"I will. Thank you, Joseph, for speaking to me. This is an amazing story."

"I thought maybe you'd not believe me, but I swear it's the truth."

"A few things. First, Joseph, perhaps you were escaping the draft by running off to Australia in the middle of the war?" John knew thousands of Australians had fought and died. Running away to Australia wouldn't have kept him out of the draft. He wanted to see what Zelly had to say.

"Heart murmur. Made me exempt. I didn't run from nothing."

"Fine. Second thing. How'd you get out of England on a ship in 1915. That seems nearly impossible. Liners were being sunk by U-boats all the time."

"I don't know about that. I departed from Dublin on an Irish ship—Ireland was neutral. Maybe that's the reason, I don't know."

"Finally, it did strike me that you're about the same age as Jenna Inch. By all accounts a lovely young woman who had a baby out of wedlock. She seems to never have revealed who the father was. Perhaps you left rather suddenly, since maybe she had decided to reveal you as the father. Your Australian adventure would have been dashed to pieces if you suddenly had a wife and a child to support."

Joseph looked at him with disappointment as he shook his head. "I would have married her in a heartbeat. I don't know who she wanted, but it were never me."

John nodded. "Thank you, Joseph. I'll not discount what you've told me. I will investigate." He watched Joseph put his hat back on and leave. He took the notebook from his pocket and noted Joseph Zelly's name and a few sentences about the story he told. What a stunning revelation, he thought. How convenient he has come home just now. Could anyone possibly forget reading a letter about a murder of someone he knew? Someone he says he cared about. Why make up this story? Ferguson had to consider the possibility that Sir Vinson had wronged Joseph, and this was his revenge. John could understand if his story involved Geran Inch murdering people. He seemed to be despicable. But, Sir Vinson? John tried to conceive of the distasteful, arrogant, shallow man plotting such an elaborate, devious plan. The motive also seems mystifying. Kill a powerless servant girl? Maybe he had fathered the child. These things happened all the time. Maybe she threatened to reveal his terrible behavior. But kill his own grandchild? His male heir?

Ferguson had some questions for Alan and asked him to come into the dining room. "Alan, were you and Joseph Zelly friends?

Alan smiled, "Yeah, we were mates. He came around the dower then a lot. His mum, Mrs. Zelly, was the cook while we lived here. Him and me went to the Crown for a pint every now and again."

"Did you two like to hang out with the popular Geran Inch?"

"No. We didn't really party. Geran was always getting squiffy and poncing about. We figured he'd get some girl up the stick." He turned bright red at that. Probably remembering, Ferguson thought, that it was Lady Edra who turned up pregnant.

"Besides," Alan continued, "we had little time off and not much money. Geran was pretty much a wanker. And then, he became our boss."

"Thanks. You can return to whatever you were doing." Alan quietly left him.

Ferguson stepped out of the dower where the happy voices of Lady Edra and Keyan across the lawn interrupted his thoughts. He walked over to the paddock where Keyan sat astride a brown filly, with black mane and tail. Lady Edra stood this side of the fence encouraging him. This was another attractive Arabian. Not as magnificent as Asif but very nice. The nine-year-old boy looked awfully small to him, beaming as he sat on the powerful horse circling the paddock. "Lady Edra, I need to speak to you right now." He said it quietly but she caught the ominous tone. They stood next to the fence and talked, while watching the boy, who concentrated on starting the horse with his legs and making a clicking sound with his tongue, then stopping the horse with both the reins and his voice. He practiced it repeatedly.

"I'm sorry to be so abrupt, but I need you to think very hard about the Christmas Jenna and your son died. It's very important. That Christmas, the whole family did what exactly?"

Lady Edra hesitated a moment, wondering why he asked, then said, "We went to the far north of Ireland for ten days that Christmas and stayed in Cliffony House, with a friend of the family."

"You went on vacation in the middle of the war, and to the north of Ireland in the middle of winter? It had to be freezing cold." Ferguson found that a truly surprising decision.

"Father wanted a respite from the whole war thing. Our home sits practically overlooking the Channel." She gestured with an outstretched arm toward the cliff at the edge of Tredwen, which fell to the Channel. "German ships and the danger, so close every day. We had spent years, most of my teen years, going to Cliffony. It is surrounded by woods and gardens. It's truly a lovely, quiet place. I went on long rides every day."

"Did your father leave at any time to return to Woodcomb, to Tredwen Manor?"

"No." It seemed to Lady Edra such an absurd thing to ask. "Why would we go over Christmas to escape, and then him return early?"

"He remained with the family every minute?" Ferguson asked her.

She thought about it a bit. "Wait. He did leave us to meet someone in Dublin about business. He didn't return that night. He didn't make it back until Christmas night, actually, fairly late. I remember because we waited to open our gifts until he had returned. No one thought anything about it. I barely remember it. We then all came home together Boxing Day."

"I just met someone who swears he saw him here on that Christmas day. At the manor house."

She looked stunned and confused. "That can't be true. No one stayed at the house. The staff, servants, everyone had Christmas holiday off. They only had to be back early on Boxing Day, to get everything properly in order for our arrival that night. And my father came with us on the train to Waterford, and the ferry across to Cardiff, and the train home from there. We got home late. I'm sure of that. I can't even imagine the man, *my* father, showing up to a cold house without his valet beside him. Much less making the trip the day before."

"Was Wherry his valet then? Did he go to Dublin with him?"

"Yes, Wherry was his valet. Occasionally, father travels alone if it's strictly business. Whatever the details of the meeting, it was strictly business. He wouldn't have needed dinner clothes or help changing. I don't remember whether Wherry went with him or not. Are you insinuating he masterminded such an elaborate plan, and came to kill my beautiful little boy, Caden? Can you possibly be asking me if my father killed his grandson—his only grandson? The heir to Tredwen? Are you saying he killed Caden's nanny, Jenna, too? That's too preposterous. Who told you this?" She looked toward the dower where Zelly had stood before speaking to John.

"I'm merely asking if it were at all possible for Sir Vinson to have been here on that Christmas day? I'll speak to your father about it. I've no time now. I need to get on." He glanced at the dower. "We'll speak more tonight."

Lady Edra watched Ferguson's back as he walked across to the dower, wondering about their astonishing conversation. "Unbelievable!" She turned back to watch Keyan and Naazir prance around together. She started thinking about Cliffony House, where they stayed. It had been miserable cold, and it rained most of the time they were there. The Gallaghers had been friends of the family her whole life. In winter Sir Roger had hunting weekends, which her father sometimes attended. But there hadn't been hunts during the war. She remembered the trips they took there years ago in the summer. Her mother was alive then, laughing and taking the sun. They swam in the Atlantic and hiked and we rode. Why had her father decided they should all go that Christmas? There were German ships patrolling the North Atlantic, round neutral Ireland, so close to their enemy Britain. U-boats were the terrifying bane of the British Navy. One destroyed a ship, killing over a thousand people off the Irish coast earlier that year, including many Americans. The navy had to patrol the Irish Sea, the narrow waterway separating Ireland and Britain, so people could safely travel between them. How could that trip have possibly lessened Father's worry over our safety? She remembered riding to the end of the peninsula where the house stood, and spotting a U-boat cruising directly off shore. She had never questioned it. Then there was the unheard of ten days off for the entire staff. Had she missed a blackness, an evil hidden behind it all? Hidden in her father? Not possible. She shook her head and looked at the huge smile on Keyan's face. She smiled. "Keyan, it's time to go. Let's put your horse away. I have to get ready to go."

Returning to the dower to prepare for his afternoon with an earl, Ferguson entered the kitchen and asked for a basin of water to be brought to his room to wash up. Dobbs and Sukie both smiled slyly at him with delight and said nothing.

Alan beamed, proudly holding two buckets of hot water. "The new water closet next to your room is nearly finished, sir. You can use it. Inspector Geever has finished taking his bath. There's no hot water there yet, but we're taking buckets of it up."

John stood mute at this unexpected information, as Alan passed him. He glanced at Dobbs and Sukie, who suddenly wiped the grins off their faces. Following Alan, he noticed covertly snickering workmen, and an openly curious, smiling Sally who nearly followed him upstairs. He figured they found it humorous because he had been storming about all morning, cranky about losing half a day for this frivolity. Now he would get a hot bath. He passed Wherry coming downstairs caring two empty buckets.

"Good morning, sir. If you'll get ready, we have shampoo and soap already in the water closet." Looking both ways down the hall, Wherry quietly asked, "Sir, could I have a word?"

"No time right now. But, I've got questions for you as well. This evening when we return." Entering his room, Ferguson found his extra shirt had been pressed and hung up already. The new bathroom still needed paint, but a very recently added toilet made the room complete. Even a gilded mirror had been temporarily affixed. He smiled as he undressed and slipped into the hot water. When he emerged after his bath, he met Geever, looking dapper in a three-piece suit, oiled hair, Brylcreem reapplied apparently, and Ferguson had to admit, Geever smelled marvelous.

A gleaming new Rolls Royce sat languidly purring at the front door, awaiting Geever and Ferguson. Like the fine footman he was, Alan announced the automobile and held the door for them. He joined all the workmen as well as two patients waiting to see Doc Abby who all had noses to the window watching and smiling as the chauffeur, in livery, held the car door open for the two detectives, then slowly pulled away.

John wondered if Abby watched this spectacle—probably also smirking at how upset he got over this diversion.

"I'm terribly sorry about all this, Ferguson. I tried to cancel, but it only roused my father to include you," Geever said.

"Well, here we are now. Tell me, what Sir Vinson told you about Geran."

"He hated Geran and encouraged his unhappiness at being stuck in such a dull place as Woodcomb. He tried to get him to leave. Sir Vinson didn't say anything about how he proposed to get him to leave. He adamantly refused to tell me who he captivated with his charm last Sunday night."

"Fine. We'll keep after him. Eventually I may arrest him. Then he'll probably be ready to give himself an alibi—if he has one." He considered telling Geever about Joseph Zelly's story, but decided it could wait for now. "Tell me what you found out yesterday interviewing people."

"Geran Inch seems to have been a cad, but one with an amazing amount of charm. Lots of people, both female as well as male were attracted to the young man and felt betrayed and used when he lost interest in them. Nothing specific. I did learn that Merryn Jones took their wagon to pick her husband up. He's the plumber. It made me think. I reckon their wagon might have possibly had a spade in the back. She had a spade with her yesterday in her garden. She could have spotted Geran entering Tredwen land. She still feels her betrayal strongly. Perhaps while she waited for her husband at Penrose's, before everyone ran to help put out the Crown fire, she avenged herself. Or her husband avenged her treatment at Geran Inch's hands years before. It made me think, others may have gotten rides home late that night. Lots of people could have seen Geran Inch show up late at night, and dispatched the cad. We might be looking at more than just the men working on the harvest. Yet no one admits to even seeing the body."

"Indeed. Perfect opportunity, in the confusion of the wind and rain, the overturned oats, and the darkness, to strike. None of the workmen admitted to anything more than barely knowing the man. Geever, good job uncovering more suspects. Now you need to eliminate some by reinterviewing them all. Wait. You said Merryn is married to the plumber, Jones? The clanging sounds from the first night that sounded like metal against metal. Something about it. Could Jones be the one deceiving us? Still, he would have needed a place to hide."

Chapter Ten

A winding lane led from the road to the grand estate of the Earl of Truro, which could be glimpsed through the symphony of autumn colors on the trees and shrubs. Ferguson spied the earl's house in intermittent patches through the trees and found it to be properly impressive, even before seeing the entire house. He thought it to be more than double the size of Tredwen manor. "Chough Hall, the ancestral home of my family for four hundred years," Geever announced. Elizabethan brick work, elaborate chimney pieces and stone-mullioned windows with small diamond-shaped glass, ran across the front. The car drove past the house and out buildings to an arena, which could be glimpsed behind and off to the left of the main house. They passed a horse and rider just finishing up performing in the arena, and noticed several people watching sitting in a group of stands. The car stopped in the midst of a crowd of activity, people chatting and attending to horses on this bright warm afternoon.

"This is dressage weekend. I hadn't realized until Sir Vinson mentioned it," Geever said. Under a huge marquee tent, Geever led Ferguson to meet his parents. Many people either in riding gear or beautiful, expensive clothes, chatted in small groups, most enjoying a glass of wine.

An attractive older woman in an expensive wool suit, who spotted them, tugged on her husband's sleeve, then held her arms open wide, and came toward Ferguson and Geever. She looked delighted to see her son and gave him a kiss on the cheek and a hug. "Darling, it's so good to see you," she said to Geever. She wore diamond earrings and necklace and had gold bracelets on both arms, which jingled as she shook Ferguson's hand.

"You must be John Ferguson," she said. He nodded and smiled. As she spoke, the older man next to her, slightly balding and wearing a fine tweed suit, turned from the small group he had been holding in thrall with his conversation,. He smiled upon spotting his youngest son. The people, who had been listening to the man, turned to see what the earl smiled at.

"Ah, Richard, my boy, you've made it." He gave his son a hearty slap on the back. "Your very presence today is my favorite birthday present! And, you brought your friend. How very nice. Look everyone, Richard has brought a friend."

Farther down the tent marquee, they heard a laugh, and then a snide, "For once, he brought a friend," from a man who looked a lot like Geever. A couple of others near him obligingly snorted. Geever ignored the remark. "Ferguson, that would be my older brother, William." The brother saluted with his glass, but didn't excuse himself from his friends.

"I'd like you to meet my father, Sir George Geever and my mother Lady Jane. This is my fellow detective, John Ferguson." Ferguson smiled while shaking Geever's father's hand.

"Welcome John. I'm glad you could make it. Come join us. I'm so glad you both could spare the time for an old man's sixtieth birthday." He pulled them into the group he had been chatting with. "Richard, this quarter's dressage competitions are being held here at Chough and on my birthday!" He turned to Ferguson smiling. "Official competitions today, and tomorrow morning will be the seniors' time to show their stuff. I'll be in that group, of course. We will not be in as good a shape as this crowd, but our horses aren't seniors." The remark drew polite tittering at the earl's witty remark. Noticing Ferguson look around at the elaborate preparations, he said, "We'll soon be sitting down for a very informal luncheon after the next round of judging in the arena. More people will be arriving a bit later for the late afternoon's competition."

"Will they all be staying over? Where will you put them all?" Ferguson asked.

"No, no. Gracious no. These people and their fabulously trained horses will all have been judged today. The official rankings will be announced later tonight and awards given out. Most will be leaving then. A number of the senior riders and horses are arriving this evening. We will have our chance tomorrow."

Others in the earl's group were then introduced to Ferguson. They all seemed to know Geever. One of the women said, "Richard, it's a shame you no longer compete. He was exceptional, Detective, before he moved to London. You might be surprised to know that he nearly won the Duke's Cup just a few years ago." That indeed surprised Ferguson. He hadn't bothered to imagine Dickie Geever before he became the bane of his existence.

The earl explained to the group, "Richard filled an important spot at Scotland Yard with so many men gone to war." The others nodded and smiled admiringly. Ferguson tried to not look stunned, after learning Dickie had saved Scotland Yard during the Great War. The conversation now centered on dressage horses.

Ferguson patted Geever on the shoulder and motioned that he would look around and leave him to chat with his parents. A footman offered him a glass of white wine, which he refused. "No thanks, but I could use something cold to drink." The footman returned momentarily with what Ferguson found to be a wonderful fruit drink. He sighed, relaxing, glad no one felt like chatting him up. He thought the others probably couldn't imagine what to say to him. What could they possibly have to chat about with such an ordinary person as himself, and a policeman at that. He agreed. He had no small talk either for these nobs. Geever stood surrounded by the lord's friends, yet his brother didn't reach out to speak to him or to Ferguson.

He walked to the arena and stood at the near end, close to where two men and one woman wrote on clipboards and conversed with each other. Apparently the judges, he thought, but he couldn't see what they wrote. A tall brown horse, with a woman in her thirties, ran the course of various jumps situated around the arena. Her horse knocked a rail off one of the jumps, causing a murmur from the spectators. Horse and rider next completed several maneuvers to apparently show how well horse and rider mastered them. The horse and rider team then stopped in front of the judges, and the woman dipped her head in a bow, while the horse stuck one hoof out and bowed impressively. The crowd clapped and cheered when the judges held up the scores. Apparently, she had done a good job. Turning from the arena, Ferguson wandered over to the stables looking for Sir Vinson and the Tinks, since they hadn't come across them while driving here. Inside one stable, he found a lot of noise and commotion. A long aisle led down the middle with stalls on each side. Some held horses. Grooms talked quietly to some of the horses while they brushed them. It seemed to him, the commotion upset many of the animals. A man Ferguson believed to be a coach spoke excitedly to what appeared to be a nervous dressage rider who kept nodding to the man. Geever's older brother, Sir William, and his friends, stood near the entrance. They seemed to be talking in hushed tones, but Ferguson overheard only the word "Asif." Sir William spotted him. "Detective. Are you enjoying yourself?"

Ferguson said, "I overheard Asif. Sir Vinson's horse. Sir Vinson is riding him to Chough today. Has he shown up?" Sir William and his friends shook their heads no, uninterested. Ferguson added, "We didn't pass him on our ride up here."

Sir William answered, "You wouldn't have passed him. They would stay off the main road and come through the woods and lanes. I think it'll be awhile before he shows up. He certainly has a handsome horse." They all nodded.

Ferguson asked, "Is Sir Vinson any good at dressage?"

A rather tall, blond man with a scant mustache spoke. "He's not bad. His horse, however, is truly magnificent."

"Absolutely. Asif is a beautiful animal. Is your interest simply admiration or is there something more?" Ferguson asked.

Sir Willam seemed impatient with John's questions, "If you must know, I would love to buy Asif. But, Sir Vinson refuses to sell him at any price. Don't you agree he could be a champion dressage horse with a younger rider such as myself?"

"I couldn't say. I don't really have any opinion. I don't understand how dressage is judged." They nodded, then lost interest in him. "If you'll excuse me, I think I'll return to the party." A nod from Sir William. They turned to watch Ferguson as he walked out of the barn. Ferguson pegged Sir William as a very sly character and wondered about their conversation. What would Sir William be willing to do to acquire what he wanted? From first impressions, Ferguson felt it may be whatever he needed to do.

Walking away from the barns, he noticed a stir closer to the main house and walked toward it. A truck, with Jackson Plumbing written on it, sat in the drive, surrounded by several men. Two of the young men, who seemed to be footmen, wore Chough livery, an older gentleman wore the classic butler morning coat, and two men in coveralls put tools back into the truck. Ferguson recognized one of the plumbers.

"Jones! What are you doing up here? Don't they need you at the dower any longer?"

Jones smiled. "I get plumbing jobs wherever I can get them, and the dower water closets are near enough finished that I figured I could take this extra job."

The other plumber, older and larger, at least in girth, asked, "And who might you be, and what business is it of yours what's going on here?"

"This is the detective who's investigating the murder in Woodcomb." The others looked impressed. "Detective John Ferguson, this is Davy Jackson who owns this here truck. And this is Smith the butler, and Blair and Foiles a couple of footmen." They nodded interested.

The butler said, "We had a problem with water not coming out of one of the sink faucets, the one in the kitchen, if the police need to know that for some reason. And that absolutely would not do for the earl or for Chough Hall, with several guests staying the night."

"You solved it, I assume."

"Course, everything's fine now," Jones said.

"Perhaps then you have a moment to answer an odd question." The two plumbers and the other men looked at each other and waited. "Jones, I brought this up before, but I'm still wondering what a man could bang on, with a metal pipe, in a house, that sounds like he's banging the pipe on something metal, that could make a very loud clanging sound. A disturbingly loud sound—loud enough to be disturbing in other rooms?"

The men stared as if Ferguson had lost the plot. What a crazy thing to ask. Jones said brightly, "I've thought about your problem, sir. Slam that pipe onto a copper bathtub. That'd do it. The sound would reverberate around the tub like a bell and could be very loud. He looked at Jackson who smiled and nodded his agreement. " You got a copper tub?"

"You just put in the new bathtub, and it's porcelain."

"Yeah, but they had a copper tub—kid size, like—and it'll sing! They had one for the babes years ago. I hadn't seen it since we been working there, but I remember they had one. Find it and try it. That'd do it alright." The older plumber nodded slowly, agreeing, and both were very proud of themselves for solving a problem on a case for the police. The other three men smiled and nodded. They turned expectantly to Ferguson, awaiting the next important police problem for which their help might be required.

"Thank you. That might just do it. I'll try and find the copper tub." The group seemed disappointed when he merely turned and walked away. Ferguson considered what Jones had said. There is no copper bathtub in the dower. There's no washtub that I've seen, much less a fancy copper bathtub. There's only the shiny new porcelain tub just brought in. Dobbs will know about tubs. I'll ask her later. He spotted Geever across the way approach his brother and friends, now standing near the arena. Walking toward them, Ferguson watched Sir William barely acknowledge his brother, but the other men appeared genuinely to like Dickie. They were laughing together, and one patted him on the back. It again surprised Ferguson that, barring his hostile brother, Dickie Geever is not only liked but respected here. He excused himself from his friends when Ferguson met up with him.

"I think my father is about to announce his birthday luncheon. Shall we join them?" The meal was served informally at several tables under the marquee. Perfect bouquets of mums decorated each table. A line of gloved footmen stood at the back of the tent to serve. This was referred to as "informal" in fine homes, yet china and silverware were laid out on white tablecloths with place cards. Everyone found their place and sat. Ferguson smiled at the conundrum of the place cards. Where should they place him? Who must be assigned to sit next to this common policeman? He had been placed far from Geever or his brother or either of their parents. On his left sat an older lady, and on his right a mustached man of about forty-five. The footmen brought plates, loaded with salads and fruit and chicken, while people chatted. The older woman pleasantly asked, "Have you been to Cornwall before, Detective?"

"No, but the free-standing granite tors rising from the gentle slopes impressed me as our train passed through Bodmin Moor. They are so unique." She seemed pleased Cornwall had impressed him.

She answered, "I've always thought everything about the moors seem so alien and mysterious. You know, I think Sir Arthur Conan Doyle chose Bodmin for his atmospheric tale "The Hound of the Baskervilles" because he felt the same way about them."

Ferguson thought about it a moment and agreed, "I think you're right about that."

She seemed pleased with his answer, nodded to him and turned to chat with the person to her left.

The man to his right declared himself to be a banker, which interested Ferguson immensely. "I wonder," he asked the man, "if, say, a police inquiry led to questions about the finances of a person of, say, the aristocracy… perchance. Would a judge issue a warrant, hypothetically, in such a case for that policeman. If he wished to acquire bank statements over the objections of said aristocrat?" Ferguson tried to look as if it were a rhetorical question—just chatting.

The banker roared with laughter, causing everyone to look at them. After taking a drink of his wine, he answered, "Not if it's an earl, my boy."

"How about a request about a baronetcy?"

"Not impossible, but you'd need a sympathetic judge. If we're talking about the Bandrys, they're not as well connected as some, nor are they terribly popular. They have broken with the centuries-old tradition of strictly male heirs inheriting, you understand. I don't know. Sir Vinson is in favor enough that he can bring his fabulous Arabian and run him through his paces tomorrow against this lot. It might be possible though. What is it you're looking for?"

"Seven years of bank statements."

The banker looked astonished and shook his head. "You'll probably have better luck trying their estate agent or maybe their accountant or lawyer. He might be persuaded to dig that far into their past. Otherwise, if the Bandrys have something to hide, and who doesn't," a knowing smirk, "I think they would advise their lawyer to fight the proceedings. Do you know who takes care of their business affairs each month?"

"Hicca Stark is the Bandry estate agent."

"Ah, Stark. He does work for a number of estates near here. I believe he's very loyal to the Bandrys, though. His family has been connected to the Bandrys for literally hundreds of years." That did not bode well for the success of Ferguson's hope to discover Sir Vinson's secrets. He'd have to see if Lady Edra would allow it. After all, she was the baroness not her father. More food arrived, which ended the discussion.

Later, as the luncheon drew to a close, Ferguson noticed Sir William and his group chatting with Geever, and walked over to them. One of the men joked, "Richard! It's just great to see you, old man. Too bad you're not competing, and your bumbling brother here is. You and…what was your horse's name, Richard? Anyway, you and that horse were great. What's happened to your horse?"

Sir William's answered rather caustically, "Artemis. That is Richard's horse's name. I shall be competing on Artemis today." An awkward silence followed for a moment. "Now, if I could get Sir Vinson's Arabian away from him, we would be the champion rider and horse. But I can't seem to convince him to sell him to me. I may have to resort to desperate means." That struck Ferguson as sounding surprisingly serious. The others laughed nervously and glanced at Ferguson.

The friend changed the subject. "Yes, you were quite a competitor until you lost your mind and decided to play detective." Everyone chuckled at that except Geever. "Couldn't they spare you for a few competitions?" The group looked at Ferguson, as if he caused Geever's lack of free time.

Geever replied seriously, "I don't think jobs work that way."

Sir William pointed to Ferguson. "This is the type of person who should handle distasteful things like murder. They understand such things and such people. They come from such people." Ferguson simply stared at him, refusing to respond until Sir William turned away with a hearty laugh, flinging words over his shoulder as he walked. "Sorry. Just a joke, old bean." His mates sheepishly followed.

Ferguson and Geever stood silently watching them. How had it not occurred to him that Geever might be anything other than the bore taking up space in his office. Geever simply turned. "I think It's time to say our goodbyes and get back to our distasteful jobs, don't you?"

On the quiet drive back to Woodcomb, Geever said, "I came to Scotland Yard because I wanted something more than just idle amusement for my life. I realize I skipped the queue, was fast tracked, and my promotions were because of my father. My choices, however, have created something I didn't predict. It's something quite strange. I don't really fit with my brother's crew any more. They seem rather, I don't know…shallow. Yet, I never really fit with you fellows at the Yard." He smiled, but Ferguson didn't think it a happy smile. Geever continued, "What would you call such a strange character as me."

"A man. A thinking man. And a policeman. It's time we got back to our job, don't you think…uh, Richard?" It sounded strange as it left his lips, and yet he thought it felt right. No more Dickie.

Doc Abby's waiting room stood empty just now, and she sat with her legs stretched out before her, in her small office space next to the consulting room. Her day had been full. She usually didn't see nearly as many patients at her office in the Crown, before the fire. People had shown up, even from nearby villages. She is the nearest doctor, but still she had seen several more patients than usual in the last couple of days. She wondered if perhaps people were curious about what the dower house looked like inside, and the commotion of the workmen made it all the more enticing to visit the doctor. Sally had been helping her a couple days a month with the books and ordering supplies. She was glad Sally had agreed to come every day. She was such a cheerful and efficient help. Sally showed up then, with a hot cup of tea for her, and left quietly, closing the door to the office with a smile. Doc Abby took a relaxing sip and said to herself, "Yep. That girl is wonderful!" Her hands still shook a bit. It had been difficult to get over last night's horror. She probably wouldn't be sleeping any more in the dower, as the trouble seemed to manifest with her. Yet, if she managed to be brave and stayed alone, she believed the spirit might communicate something about why it haunted the dower. She gazed vacantly at the windows directly in front of her. Something caught her eye, something about the series of three tall mullioned windows, each covered by a lacy curtain. The center one looked slightly different. She discovered it was not a window but a discreet door. "A French window!" She walked over and tugged at it. Finally, it gave way with a sharp loud bark. Pulling it open, she felt no one must have used it in a very long time. It had a lock which probably hadn't been locked in a long time. It hadn't been secured last night. She stepped over the threshold onto a lovely, flagstone terrace, slumbering under decades of disuse, and half hidden here on the side of the dower. A wooden trellis covered in ivy provided a shady spot. Brushing away leaves, she sat on a small brick bench. Her view opened onto the imposing, ancient Tredwen manor, standing steadfast guard over all this land from its hill, as it had for hundreds of years, which for some reason calmed and reassured her. Between her and the manor house, the poplars and willows paraded their autumn, golden splendor, and the magnificent oak on the far side of the manor flaunted its fiery red crown. The languid quiet afternoon relaxed her, and she sipped her tea while watching high, wispy clouds float overhead. Lady Edra's chestnut mare, Sadeem, watched her from the nearby fence. The gentle horse's brown coat reflected reddish in the sunlight. The white strip down Sadeem's face seemed extra bright in the afternoon sunlight.

It surprised Abby to see Wherry drive up to the manor house front door and let Lady Edra and Jory out. They kissed briefly and walked arm and arm into the house. That surprised her. She slyly thought about the kiss. There's a story there. I hope they plan to tell me what's going on, at dinner. Where have you two been? She watched as Wherry moved the car further along the drive, parked and entered through the servants' entrance on the side. Abby wondered why Edra and Jory had needed to use it for the afternoon. She supposed Wherry would now finally drive to Chough Hall and become Sir Vinson's valet again. Only a few minutes later, Wherry emerged with a bundle of what appeared to be clothes, tucked under one arm. She thought his movements seemed furtive, for some reason, as if he didn't want to be seen as he exited through the gate at the far edge of the property. "What's that about?" she asked herself.

Sally stepped through the French door onto the terrace, marveling at the new discovery, looking around. "What a delightful find!" She gazed briefly at the view. "Sorry to interrupt you, Doc, but it's Tommy Penrose."

"Again?" She moaned quietly.

Sally nodded. "Looks like his face is bruised, and he has a gash on the side of his head. He's holding his arm. Must have hurt it too."

Abby sighed. "I'll be in in a second." Time to return to work. A moment from yesterday came to her as she rose from the bench and stretched. She could feel Ferguson's strong arms pulling her from the blackness of the attic, rescuing her from whatever had happened last night. Ferguson had enfolded her against his chest as she sobbed. Later, she watched him sleep, his face looking serene with his hair falling across his forehead. She smiled, remembering the look on his face as she teased him about his diligent search for rationality in this besotted house. She stepped back across the threshold of the French window, wondering what it would be like to fall in love with John Ferguson. She pulled the snug door closed behind her and locked it. She would tell him about the unlocked door when he returned.

Entering her consulting room, Doc Abby said, "Oh Mr. Penrose! I expected your wife. She always brings your son in. So, tell me what happened to Tommy this time." The sight of the boy shocked her, even though she had seen what his father did to him several times before.

Tommy sat hunched over, looking forlorn. His nose had been bleeding but had stopped, leaving a ring of drying blood. He had a nasty gash on his forehead that looked to possibly need a stitch, and he held his arm.

"What happened, Tommy? How did you get hurt?"

"He fell…uh, out of a tree. He's such a problem. Won't be careful."

"Tommy, is that how you got hurt?" The boy said nothing as usual.

"I'm telling you that's what happened. Now fix him up." Penrose sighed to calm himself. His voice became pleasant, and he said, "The kids and me are spending the weekend with their grandparents. We're doing a bit of fishing. Both of them love to visit their grandparents and we'll do a bit of camping."

"I'm surprised you're taking time off during harvest," she said as she swabbed at the cut with disinfectant and checked it. The bleeding would stop without stitches.

"Can't get nothing done and all with nearly every man working here. I hear there'll be enough men finished near enough by Monday, so's we can get back to work. My Eva's nerves are at her again, so I agreed to take the kids off her hands and go camping and fishing for the weekend. Give her some rest." He seemed rather agitated. The camping plan didn't seem to be relaxing to Penrose. An angry man who often loses his temper, while Tommy often becomes his target.

Today it disgusted her. With everything else, it seems too much, and she raised her voice. "He certainly needs to get patched up a lot, maybe too much. This doesn't look like he fell from a tree. What did you do? Do you hurt your son, Mr. Penrose?" Tommy looked up, shocked by what she had said.

"How dare you!" Penrose shouted as he rose from his chair and stepped toward her. "Who do you think you are? I told you what happened, stupid woman."

Quickly, she opened the door and backed out into the waiting room. Penrose threw the chair he had been sitting in against the wall. He knocked the bottle of disinfectant off the table. Sally rose from her desk, shocked. Abby caught Sally's eye, and quietly said, "Go! Get someone."

Sally raced out the front door and looked around. She saw Crocker standing outside the dower, oddly not in uniform. She screamed, "Help! Piran, Help! Arthur's gone crazy!" Crocker stood stunned. She saw Jory leaving the manor house and ran toward him, still screaming.

Chapter 11

The earl of Truro's chauffeur returned Ferguson and Geever to the doorstep of the dower and the Rolls Royce glided back to Chough Hall. Sally met them as they entered, obviously very upset. "Thank God you're back! Arthur Penrose has gone mad! He's nearly accosted Doc Abby! Jory arrested him. He's in the jail now."

"Is she alright?" Ferguson demanded.

Hearing the commotion, Abby rushed out. "John, I'm so glad you're back."

"Are you alright?"

"I'm just a little shaken. I'll be fine. Sally, go home now. I'm fine. The detectives will handle everything. I'll have Alan walk you home."

Sally paused a beat before answering. "That's not necessary. I'll walk." Sally wondered about the doc. At first, she seemed exhausted by Mr. Penrose's terrifying fit. Now she seemed practically giddy, speaking very fast. Penrose sat behind bars, but Sally was not reassured the doc was fine. Sally smiled weakly at the Doc, then glanced at the detectives before grabbing her coat and leaving.

Ferguson could see by Abby's glassy eyes she was still in shock.

"What's happened?" Geever asked.

"Arthur Penrose brought his son Tommy in hurt…again. I see poor Tommy a lot, but he's never been brought in by his father, always his mother." She spoke fast, excitedly. "I think Penrose is violent towards, not just his son, but probably his wife Eva also. Although I've never had to examine her, and I've never had to see to any injuries from their little girl Claire, just Tommy. Eva always tells of Tommy's *accidents*," she stressed the word, "as if he was a very clumsy boy. Tommy always sheepishly agrees, so there's nothing I can really do. But today, Arthur brought him in. I asked why he brought Tommy in today. He mumbled something about he and the children going fishing for the weekend with the grandparents. Eva is staying home alone. She needs a rest according to Penrose. Maybe she is too bruised up to bring Tommy in today. I don't know.

"I shouldn't have accused him of anything, but he made me angry looking at poor Tommy, sitting with his forehead bleeding, holding a cloth to it and then holding his arm. Once I said something, Penrose jumped out of the chair. He threw the chair! He knocked a bottle off and broke it. He started shouting that it was none of my business and came toward me. I opened the door, ran out telling Sally to run get help." She rushed on. "He was totally out of control. He grabbed Tommy by his hurt arm to storm out, but Sally had found Jory. He hauled Penrose off. The boy's grandparents, Piran and whatever Mrs. Crocker's name is, were waiting for them outside, and they took Tommy. They left for their fishing trip."

"Perhaps you could rest. Maybe lie down a while. If you're alright to alone, we need to go to the police station and talk to Jory."

"I'm fine. I'm fine. I just need to calm down. Go." She smiled weakly at both men, turned and marched up the stairs to her room. Ferguson watched her wondering what was going on in her mind and hoped she calmed down. He wanted to reassure her, but right now he needed to get to the police station and talk to Jory.

Inside the police station with Geever, Ferguson first noticed a young constable he had never met sitting in Constable Crocker's chair. Jory came out of his office. "I'm writing this up and will charge Penrose with assault."

"I never touched that cow! Let me out of here right now! I need to get to the camp site!" The three men stared at his outburst, then turned and went into the office, followed by the new constable, and Ferguson closed the door.

"This is Constable Sam Colley. Crocker's off for his camping trip. He's here till Crocker returns." Ferguson and Geever nodded to the man. Penrose could still be heard shouting.

Ferguson told Jory, "Definitely, hold him and charge him. This is my chance to talk to Eva without his looming presence. Maybe I'll get some straight answers."

Jory asked, "Do you want me to go with you?"

"No. I want to question her alone. If Penrose calms down, see if you can get a straight answer out of him. Don't release him. Keep him overnight at least. Geever, go back and check on Abby. See if she needs anything. Geever nodded. They left the station. Ferguson headed to the manor farm and Geever to the dower.

Eva Penrose let him in and she seemed calm. She directed him to a chair in the sitting room and sat on far end of the couch. He could see no bruises anywhere on her.

Ferguson explained, "Tommy went with your parents. Doc Abby got him patched up. He's just fine now. Not to worry." She sat with a small smile on her face and nodded. "I understand you've been feeling were very nervous, and that things were bothering you. Arthur told us he and the children were going camping to give you some peace and quiet. Their trip is to give you some time to rest and relax for a couple of days. Your children have left with their grandparents to go camping." She looked at him placidly, waiting. She seemed to Ferguson to be only vaguely concerned about his visit. "We have your husband in jail for attempting to assault the doctor."

That shocked her. Her eyes were saucers, and she kept shaking her head. "He never assaulted nobody! What are you talking about?" Eva looked around anxiously. "He'll be so cross with me. You can't keep him there. You have to let him come home. This'll never work."

"Eva, calm down. Please sit back down. I need you to answer some questions." She sat but kept shaking her head. "Did your husband hit Tommy?"

"No, course not."

"Then who hit him? He looks beat up. Did you do that?"

"No, never. I wouldn't." She became outraged at the suggestion. "He's so clumsy. Arthur says so. The boy is just clumsy."

"I don't think Tommy did this to himself. Does your husband need to discipline the boy a lot?"

She started nodding. "Yeah, he needs so much discipline. Arthur disciplines him. Because he's a good father."

"Eva, what would you say if I told you I think your husband believes Tommy is not his son? What if I said, I think maybe Geran Inch is Tommy's real father. I think Arthur believes that, too. Maybe he doesn't want Geran's son here."

Eva appeared dumbfounded and momentarily at a loss for words. "What? What are you suggesting? No. That's not true. No. Why would you say such a thing?"

"Tommy has dark hair and coloring. You and Arthur both have light hair and complexions. Arthur's hair is practically white. I noticed Claire's hair is also very blond. I think it's not believable that Arthur Penrose is Tommy's father. Geran had coloring nearly identical to your son's."

She stood up and spat out, "Geran was a terrible person. He hurt people." She sank back into the chair.

"I agree. I think he hurt you. I think he abandoned you, left you pregnant, and you needed someone to marry you."

She started sobbing. "Arthur saved me! What would I have done? Arthur and my dad agreed. I was just a silly girl. I need Arthur to tell me what I should do."

"Did Arthur find that disgusting excuse for a man, Geran Inch, actually returning here where he had ruined everything? Did he kill Geran for you, Eva? Geran who abandoned you, when you only believed the things he told you. Arthur has always taken care of you, hasn't he? He took care of Geran for good, didn't he, Eva, so he couldn't hurt anyone again? So, he couldn't hurt you or your son."

Shocked into jumping out of her chair, she cried, "Of course not! He never did that! He's not like that! Get out of my house now! Go!"

"Eva, I need to know. Did Arthur kill Geran Inch?" She shook her head violently pointing toward the door. Ferguson could see she would tell him nothing further.

"I'm so tired. I'm just so tired," she mumbled. Ferguson watched Eva walk up the stairs as he closed the door behind him and walked back to the dower, hoping she got some rest in the quiet without her family.

Walking back from the Penrose place, Ferguson noticed Wherry, in the Bentley, slowly exiting the manor. He put up his arm and stopped him. Wherry rolled down his window. Ferguson said, "Just going to Chough Hall now, Wherry?"

"Uh, right. That's right, sir."

"Why so late? Didn't Sir Vinson expect you earlier?"

"No, sir. He knew I had to drive Lady Edra and Jory Moon to Truro today. Busy day. But he'll be waiting." He fidgeted a little. "I really need to get going."

That surprised Ferguson. He didn't realize Jory had gone to Truro today with Lady Edra. To Wherry he said, "I thought you wanted to talk to me?"

"Oh yes, that. It's just that Sir Vinson came home the night of the murder with a bit of blood on his riding pants and some on his boots. When I asked him about it the next day, he asked 'what blood?' He assured me I had mistaken mud for blood. It was mud. Just mud. That's all. Mystery solved. I really need to get going, sir, if there's nothing else."

"No, I suppose not. Wherry, you seem a little nervous. Is anything wrong."

Wherry peered at him wide eyed, as if caught out in something, before regaining his composure. "Not at all, sir, I'm just in rather a hurry. You understand."

Ferguson understood something made Wherry nervous. "Of course. Carry on. Sorry to slow you down." Wherry rolled up the window and slowly left the manor.

Ferguson planned to check on Abby first, but Alan met him at the door with, "Detective Geever is in the dining room with Marrak, sir, if you'd like to join them. Said he needed to speak to the detectives." Ferguson would need to find out how Abby was doing later after finding out what Marrak wanted to tell them. He sat down next to Geever, across from the footman at the dining room table.

"This is Joseph Marrak, the footman at the manor. Go ahead, Marrak. Tell Detective Ferguson, what you just told me," Geever said.

"Well, sir, I told this detective I seen something queer. I don't know, but it might be important—or probably not." He looked at them waiting.

Ferguson said, "Why don't you just say what you came to say and let us decide?"

Marrak liked that. "The thing is, next day after the murder, on Monday you know, as I passed Howel's room…"

"Howel? Is that Sir Vinson's valet, Howel Wherry?" Ferguson interrupted.

"Oh, yes, sir. Sorry, sir. The door stood open, you understand to Howel's room. A crack. Anyway, I stepped inside to said hello, and he not only looked surprised by me, but sorta guilty, you know. He was stashing what looked like maybe Sir Vinson's riding pants behind his dresser. I don't know, but why stash 'em? Maybe to clean 'em later? I don't know. Anyway, I overheard Sir Vinson remark to Howel, he wanted those pants packed for the day at Chough. But they're not in his room anymore. I kinda checked. The riding pants Howel packed for Sir Vinson were not the hidden ones. Those were still stashed. But they're gone now. You understand? Maybe he's protecting Sir Vinson from something. Anyway, thought you should know." He straightened up after that and breathed a sigh of relief. Ferguson thought maybe a second pair of pants would explain why Wherry looked so worried as he left. The bloody ones were somewhere else—for some reason. Maybe he would blackmail Sir Vinson, and the pants were proof of something. Or more probably, Wherry finally got the stains out and he is even now taking them to Sir Vinson for his dressage ride tomorrow. Although Kitto said Wherry wanted him to know he thought Asif had blood on his hoofs. What was Wherry up to? Why point that out to Kitto unless he wanted Kitto to start to think maybe Sir Vinson was the horse rider who had his horse trample the body. More questions. "Thank you, Marrak. If that's all, we'll look into it as soon as Sir Vinson returns from Chough. You've been very helpful." Both detectives stood, then Marrak stood.

"Thank you. I'll get back up to the house now. Back up to my job. Hope it helps. Thank you."

"I'll just accompany you, if you don't mind, and I'll have a look at Wherry's room," Geever said smiling. "Shall we go?"

He considered whether the valet and the groomsman could be working together with their stories suggesting Sir Vinson as the horse rider who trampled the body. Usually the valet working with the master's person and the man working with the horses and mostly in the barns had little in common to become allies. He had to consider that until he had proof of their stories being factual, but for right now he needed to see about Abby.

Ferguson said, "I'm going to check on Abby. Get her out of here. Marrak, please inform Lady Edra that Doc Abby needs a room prepared this evening."

"Lady Edra had the staff prepare rooms for each of you already, sir."

"Great. Thank you."

Alan stuck his head through the dining room door. "When should we go up and bring down supper, sir?"

I don't know, Alan. I wouldn't worry about it. We may all be going to the big house tonight." Alan looked surprised by that, but merely returned to the kitchen. Ferguson went upstairs and knocked on Abby's door.

Wide eyed and excited, she threw open her door. "John, I think the ghost is really trying to connect with us. With me. Especially with me." She still spoke rapidly. "I need to sit in the parlor by the fire. And wait and listen, you know? I think tonight I'll know if it is Jenna. I can know what has happened here in this house. Everyone else must go of course."

"You can't stay here anymore." He spoke calmly and quietly. "Each night you seem to be targeted and more violently each time. Abby, after last night, how can you even think about staying?"

"It'll just be me and Jenna. I'll stay awake. She's ready to tell me who killed her. I can stay here if I choose!"

Abby stood near the wall, and as he moved closer to her, she backed up against it. He put his hands either side of her on the wall and put his cheek against hers. She quit babbling. He said, "I think that would be ill advised." He tried to calm her. "What will happen if you wake up being strangled again or inside a wall in the blackness of this house? I will be sleeping soundly in my room at the manor. No one will hear you."

She felt his whiskers rub her cheek and felt his warmth as he held her closely there. She felt calmer as the frazzled feeling drained. Finally understanding she couldn't stay alone here, some different feeling occurred to her. She took a deep breath, "I have been hoping you might kiss me at some point," she whispered into his ear.

John closed his eyes briefly and dropped his head, eyes closed.

He answered her nearly in a whisper. "You know I want to very much, but I'm here as a policeman. There can be no contact between me and you or anyone associated with the case." He still held her.

"You seem to be having contact right now. John, I obviously have no association with anyone. How could I have known the dead man?"

"You could be very scheming," he teased her seeing she was, indeed, calming down. "Maybe you are a seductress."

"A what? Maybe you, Ferguson, are a seduct--or."

"That would be a seducer, I believe." Abby smiled at that. He said, "Maybe you knew him as your lover years ago, and he abandoned you like all the others."

She squirmed away becoming rather indignant. "Perhaps I met this horse groomer, Geran, while I lived in Switzerland during the war, and we had a torrid love affair. Maybe I knew him in Dublin when we were both medical students." He still stood very close to her. She saw him grin.

"You never know. In court you could say I seduced you to get something."

"Something?" she asked.

"Information. I seduced you so you'd give me a clue. You might say I seduced you for information."

"Right. Information." Now she smiled also. John took a step back, became serious and simply stared at her, with the only question on his face he needed answered right now. Would she go with the others to the manor house?

Abby understood what he wordlessly asked but said nothing. He stepped near and pulled her close. They kissed. A long passionate kiss that surprised them both. Then they just stared at each other. She felt all the keyed-up energy drain from her. The face of the rage-filled Arthur Penrose flashed before her, then the terror she felt from the menace of the utter darkness of last night encircling her, caused her to shudder. "All right, I'll move to the manor with you."

John opened her wardrobe door and simply stared at her, until she grabbed a bag from it and threw in some clothes. She swept the things from the dressing table into the bag. "Fine. Let's go," he said. He grabbed his things from his room, and turned down the sconces on the stairway. They walked downstairs.

"Before we go, I'm sending the servants out of here." John left her standing near the front door, and walked to the back of the hallway, and pushed open the door to the kitchen. The three servants sat silently and looked up expectantly at him. "Let's all stay at the manor tonight as Lady Edra suggested. Right now. No arguing. No one is to be in this house tonight." They didn't need persuading. The three of them stood, picked up their things and left by the back door. Alan handed him the key, and Ferguson locked it. He turned down lights as he went through the dining room and parlor. Doc Abby turned off lamps from her reception area. He went to the front hallway as Geever came in and stared, questioning why they stood under the only light, in the front hallway. "Geever, we're all staying at the manor. Get your things. We're leaving." Geever took the stairs two at a time and returned in a flash—with only one cordovan leather bag, Ferguson noted. The sleeve of a shirt had been caught out when the bag was slammed shut. Ferguson locked the front door as they left to walk up to the manor. Stars were emerging but no moon had yet risen. No one turned around as they walked, neither the servants ahead of them nor the three of them. The dower stood apart, inky black against the night, silent.

———————

Ferguson, Doc Abby and Geever were ushered into a large, brightly lit drawing room, still clutching the bags they brought. A lively fire radiated warmth. The contrast from the silent darkness and the forbidding dower seemed surreal, and the three of them stood stunned and mute. "Oh, there you are!" Lady Edra said. She and Jory sported huge smiles and both held champagne glasses. Lady Edra's grandmother sat quietly, less excited, holding her glass.

Lady Edra said, "We wondered when you'd get up here. We're so glad you've decided to stay here and not at the dower." She noticed they stood mute clutching their bags. "Please put your bags down. We'll have your things placed in your rooms. Lander, see to this please." Marrak gathered the bags from them and left. Lander held a tray with champagne for each of them.

Lady Edra said, in a sing-song voice, "We have a lot to tell you." She took Abby by the arm and sat her on the sofa next to her. "Down, Sheba." The dog got off the couch to make room for Abby and came to stand in front of Ferguson. Lady Edra ordered them to sit. "Drink up. We're a glass ahead of you." The two detectives found chairs and sat dazed, sipping their champagne absently, awaiting the announcement. John distractedly stroked the dog's ears, and glanced at Abby over the rim of his glass. She watched him over the rim of her champagne looking as puzzled as he was.

"Or perhaps we are two glasses ahead of you," Jory added. Their smiles only grew brighter as they looked at each other.

Lady Edra said, "Go ahead, Jory darling. Tell them."

"Okay." He looked at each of them. "The Lady Edra," he held up his glass, "and I am now officially engaged." He paused then added, "Well, actually we've been engaged for such a long while. Now that Geran Inch is officially dead, we can openly announce it to the world. Well, what do you think?"

Ferguson was thinking Jory had become probably the number one suspect for the murder of the man who had stopped him for years from marrying a baroness and living a life of prestige in the manor. He glanced at Geever who also understood the implication. Ferguson wondered why he had so discarded the idea that Jory could be a murderer? He hadn't discarded it. It had never seriously occurred to him. Everyone around Jory trusted him, so Ferguson did too. No, that wasn't the reason at all. It was because Jory Moon had policed the south coast of England during the war and protected Cornwall from all evil. He respected that immensely. Now they had to think, possibly, that same man might have killed for love or money or prestige.

Abby said with genuine happiness, "That's such wonderful news! I'm so happy for you both. Not that it's much of a surprise to me. I know how much you care for each other. Are you surprised, Lady Steran, by this news or did you suspect, like me, all along?"

"I've known these two had strong feelings for a long time. I'm quite happy for both of you." She smiled warmly at both Jory and her grand-daughter. Both Ferguson and Geever mumbled congratulations, and each took another sip from his drink. Geever watched, waiting to see what Ferguson would do. Ferguson said brightly, "So tell us all about it." Ferguson glanced at Geever who understood. Tonight they would be happy for Jory and Lady Edra. Tomorrow, they would question—interrogate—Officer Jory Moon for murder.

"We went to Truro today to arrange things for our wedding," Lady Edra shook her head. The truth of her statement seemed to surprise her. With obvious joy she continued, "We went to the printers to order invitations. The date will be," she looked at Abby, "in three weeks from today. We're sending invitations to everyone we know, including everyone in the village. We went to the jeweler, and I was sized for my wedding ring. Oh Abby, it's so lovely. Wait until you see it. We also had to see my dressmaker and choose material for my dress. It won't be a long formal design. It is appropriate to a second wedding."

Jory added, "We've also spoken to the vicar, Harrison, and asked him to officiate. The wedding is to be in Woodcomb's church."

Ferguson had to admit Jory's delight didn't seem tinged with any kind of concealed guilt, nor did Jory seem to realize how this situation looked, in an open murder investigation, in which he had the most to gain. Ferguson thought about Jory's behavior since they arrived in Woodcomb. He appeared totally open and honest, as he always did. Perhaps that's why Ferguson had missed the obvious strong feelings between him and Lady Edra.

Keyan sat cross legged in the dark quiet of Menadue Wood, patting Oscar and Blue who sat quietly next to him. "Look at all those stars, dogs. There must be a billion—a kazillion thousand!" He glanced at each dog. They never seemed impressed by the stars. The trees sighed softly with the gentle whisper of the wind. He loved it. He felt calmed always by the woods. The blackness around him wrapped him in its gentle embrace. Sometimes, when things got to be too much, he liked to walk around here or just sit and listen to the sounds. He liked the woods during the day, but he loved the night. It made his brain happy. He never woke up in Menadue after losing himself in one of his spells. Sometimes the dogs would catch a sound or scent and race off, but then they quietly returned to his side. Baba was always so busy. She had to get ready for her early mornings. Tonight, Lady Edra had also sent him off on his own. She was very excited about something. She would tell him why tomorrow. She promised.

Oscar sniffed the air, then stood. Blue followed suit. Keyan said, "Settle down. What do you see?" He strained to see or hear what alerted the dogs. They stayed by his side instead of running off to investigate. That usually meant other people walked in the woods. Quiet voices floated from somewhere. He spotted them, as their torches flickered into view and vanished between trees, coming nearer to his spot. They were too far away to recognize. They weren't kids. He couldn't see clearly enough to decide if they were men or women. He knew, for sure though, that there were two of them. He held Oscar's and Blue's collars. Something was off. Beside a small Christmas tree not much taller than him, they spent several minutes digging a fair-sized hole. They dropped something in, covered it up, stamped down the dirt, and kicked debris over it. Next, they used the back of the shovel to hammer in something metal that clanged as one of them hit it. They looked down at what they had done, and walked back where they came from. Keyan released the dogs, and they ran to the spot and sniffed all around. He followed them and found where the dirt had been disturbed. He saw a metal stake that only stuck up three or four inches from the ground. He took off Blue's collar and placed it around a branch on the little pine tree, so he could find the right Christmas tree tomorrow. The tree bent slightly from the addition. He would come back tomorrow and dig up the treasure. The dogs ran ahead and back to him, as he walked on the road and over the little bridge at the edge of Tredwen. The dogs disappeared through the gate at the back corner of the manor. Keyan stopped before crossing through. He had never seen the gate open at night before. He looked down the road to where he could see the path to his house and back to the gate. He decided to follow the dogs. He could climb over the stone fence directly across from his house, and go home that way. The dogs ran to the barn, where they knew they usually found Kitto. Keyan could see a light remained on. He would stop and see what Kitto was up to. Wait. Kitto and old Mitch aren't here. They're at Chough Hall. Perhaps they left a light on for the dogs. He let the dogs in and closed the door. He felt a chill thinking of the dower at his back across the lawn from the stables. Could he brave a glance? A quick look over his shoulder. It seemed a safe distance. The house stood completely dark and cold looking. He wondered why the policemen weren't there. Why wasn't Doc Abby there? It wasn't that late. Something felt very wrong. Before he could pull his eyes away, he thought he could see an image in one of the upstairs windows. It almost looked like the outline of the terrifying thing. He needed to tear himself away from looking at it. He tried, but he couldn't force his body to not look, and to run away. He screamed, "HELP ME!" but no sound came out. Everything went black, and he seemed to be falling. Falling toward the dower. Sucked into its blackness.

Chapter Twelve

At the western edge of Scotland, beyond the groomed grounds of the sprawling, ancient Culzen Castle, along the far brink of the estate, a seventy-five-foot cliff dropped sharply to the Firth of Clyde. Lord Charles, Marquess of Ailsa, liked the spot to whack golf balls. His preferred spot ran along the boundary cliff edge. Much of this periphery gently descended to the sea and became overgrown with shrubs and bushes, but not the spot his lordship preferred. Not one bush grew here. Neither did it gently descend to the water below. Here there was a straight plunge to the boulders below. The lord loved the magnificent view out over the Firth of Clyde. His preferred partner for this sport was the fourteen-year-old John Ferguson, who now sent a ball arcing out over the edge.

"Good one, John!" the lord roared. Thwack! Lord Charles drove another ball far out into the water. Brilliantly blue sky shone over the sparkling water below. A fairly strong wind blew up and over the cliff edge this morning into their faces. John was always proud and happy whenever his lordship spoke to him, or he got to accompany Lord Charles for any reason. "We're trying for the Isle of Arran over there, Boyo! Can you do it?" He was a vigorous man of action in his fifties. Tall and in good shape, he fancied some sport this morning. The ghillie's son whacking golf balls and laughing with one of the richest, most powerful men in Scotland always thrilled John—which was nothing compared to the amazement of his parents whenever it happened.

Thwack. John nervously watched him edge closer to the dangerous rim of the cliff with every swing. Lord Charles' right foot slipped a little off the edge. John almost yelled for him to be careful and stand back. But a boy telling something to a lord? He kept quiet. The next hit unbalanced Lord Charles a bit, and he began to slip off the edge. "John!" the earl screamed, throwing his club and trying to grab the very air to stop the fall. John dropped his own club and reached out, nearly missing catching his arm, but the momentum pulled them both sliding over the edge. Their plummet to the bottom had been stopped by a tiny ledge fifteen feet down, and they both turned around slowly, carefully, bellies hugging the cliff face. The schist broke off unable to bear both of their weights. The lord fell a few more feet down to another ledge, pulling John with him. John slid further before his feet hit another ledge. John's head rested even with the lord's feet. He watched as his lordship swept his hands along the cliff face trying to find a handhold, but the cliff face only crumbled. Small gravel-sized pieces fell on John's head. He remained perfectly still, panting, arms wide hugging the cliff face.

"HELP!" Lord Charles's voice boomed. "FERGUSON! WHERE ARE YOU?" He yelled for John's father, the chief estate ghillie in charge of the woodlands, the hunting and fishing and the general care and wellbeing of the vast estate. There were other ghillies under him, but the lord always counted on John's father. The wind blew the sound to nothing. His father or any of the others could be anywhere. What were the chances anyone happened to be working near this far edge of the castle? John knew his father had men working far from here today. Only his father could be near enough to possibly hear their cries for help. The lord's twisting on the narrow unstable ledge terrified John.

"Your Lordship, stop moving! You'll pull down the bit of cliff you stand on!"

The lord's breath came in gasps. He screamed, "FERGUSON!" again, his voice cracking at the end. "Where is your dad working this morning, John?" Quaking terrified words. Never had he heard anything except command and authority from Lord Charles' mouth. What made it worse to hear; he knew he attempted to sound calm for John's sake.

"I've no idea, sir." His own voice sounded strange to him. A croak barely above a whisper.

Lord Charles shouted again and again, and John joined him. "FERGUSON!" Small bits of gravel again peppered their hair as they clung to the cliffside. John had a thought. "Maybe someone from the house saw us or can hear us."

"Yes. Probably. We shall hope," Lord Charles said. John didn't believe that for a second. Windows probably shut tight. Most of their work was being done below stairs. His father worked outside somewhere and their only hope. John squeezed his eyes shut. As the wind whipped up the slope over them, John

imagined a spirit from the sea in the wind. He mentally sent the spirit to blow through the wild parts of the estate. The spirit searched for John's father, carrying their cries for help. He held tight to the picture of the spirit, driving through the thick trees up the crags and down the hills. He imagined their pleas, carried on the wind, sweeping around surprised deer and soaring over startled foxes, as the spirit searched for his father. He squeezed his eyes tighter, imagining his father stalking one of the estate's great stags, marking its whereabouts and its health, crouched down as John had seen him do so often. He pictured his father turn, cupping his hand to hear the faint sound, and jump up racing to their aid

The earl started shrieking, "HELP!" but it sounded weaker. John shouted with him but his own voice had grown weak. They would need to be very lucky. His father would need to be very close. John tried to hold onto the image of the spirit wind. Tears streamed down his cheeks before he realized he was crying. The lord sobbed an achingly desperate moan, the most terrifying sound John could imagine. The strongest, most powerful man in John's world could not possibly be crying? Be giving up? A man whose booming voice created fear and immediate action from everyone. Lord Charles could handle all things. The man sobbed. John knew they couldn't hold to the cliff much longer. They were about to die.

"YOUR LORDSHIP, JOHN, DON'T MOVE. I'VE GOT YOU!" His father screamed down at them. John's heart leapt---his whole body leapt. He wanted to turn his head and look up at his dad but resisted the urge, resting his cheek again against the rough rock. "I've got to get rope. Stay very still. You'll be fine." They heard his footsteps receding. In a voice still trembling and weak yet commanding as ever, Lord Charles said, "Yes, now we'll be fine, Boyo. Your old man's got us." Brave quivering words.

John awoke, feeling a rising in his chest, at peace with the world, as he always felt after that dream. The dream had really happened. Lord Charles' gratitude had changed their lives afterward especially John's. He gave them the best house on the estate. He sent John to better schools. He made sure the chief constable of Ayrshire took the young man, who was drawn to police work, under his wing, and much more, through the years.

He called the dream his 'Happy Dream'. He usually had it after something positive or particularly pleasant happened. Why this morning? After all the horrible dreams they each had in the dower including his nightmares about the war, why did he dream it this morning in the manor house? It had nothing to do with his progress or rather lack of progress solving the murder he had been sent to unravel. Abby's face appeared to him as to maybe why he dreamt it. Strong feelings for her were definitely emerging. He considered last night's embrace. He could still feel her warm body against his as he kissed her. Perhaps that was it, but another idea drifted by. Hicca Stark. Meeting this man who so reminded John of his father, is possibly what brought on his recurring, happy dream. They were both strong men of high moral values. He shook his head at that idea. Definitely Abby. Abby was the reason. He took a deep breath and smiled.

One of the heavy silk drapes in his room had not been completely closed, and he could see the sky growing light. Dawn light peeked through. In the dim first light, he looked at the unfamiliar, lavish room with a high ceiling, elaborate crown molding and wallpaper flaunting huge white roses on a maroon background. He lay enveloped in blankets, trying to wake up and quit pondering the meaning of his dream. That sounded like something Carl Jung would do.

———————————

Mary Inch awoke to a room easing into dawn before the sun tipped up over the horizon. She found her whole body still ached a little from so much work at the pasty shop yesterday, but she had slept particularly well. She threw off the covers, swung her legs over, and stood, doing a small back bend to loosen everything up. Dressing for the day, she said to herself, "Get that meat packed up, then wake the boy."

Before going downstairs, she stopped for some reason as she passed Keyan's closed door. Mary thought, I don't remember saying goodnight to him. I had been so exhausted after everything at the shop. Delivery screw ups. That new boy working for Caleb is pathetic. The slow water leak at the shop deciding to turn into a flood. How will I pay for that? She opened his door. His bed hadn't been slept in. That surprised her. Maybe he fell asleep downstairs. It had happened before. All his adventures sometimes left him too tired to climb the stairs to his room. He never got up before her, and usually not until she left for work. He must be downstairs already. She called his name as she went down the stairs. "Keyan!" No answer. She hurried through the front room at the foot of the stairs. He wasn't on the couch. The last time I sat on the couch, Merryn made me some tea, and Lady Edra and Detective Ferguson stood right there with Keyan. Now where is he? A thought bumped gently into her search. Aloud she said to the empty room, "Maybe he didn't come home last night. Did I say good night to him? I think so." She had entered the kitchen and found no boy. He wasn't in the house. Did that mean he never came home last night? Her heart beat faster. She looked at the back door, which they seldom used. The back garden stood overgrown. "He wouldn't be there, would he?" The door always stuck, but she tugged the heavy thing open. "Please, please, God." Morning sunlight streamed in. Obviously no one had been out there disturbing the weeds. She stopped abruptly. "He did not come home last night! He would have said goodnight to me even if I was asleep. He's stayed out before. He likes to be in the quiet night, but he always comes home then. He's often with Lady Edra's dogs and he visits Kitto. That's it! Kitto will know where he spent the night. The little devil. Wait till I get my hands on you, Keyan!"

She raced out the front door, throwing her coat on against the early morning chill, shouting his name, just in case he was near enough to hear. "KEYAN!" The crows flapped their wings, hopped about on the branches making fretting noises. As she started running toward Tredwen, she screamed, "KEYAN!" The crows frantically rose from their branches in unison, and fanned out over her head, loudly shrieking their alarm. She rushed to the Tredwen stables to see if Keyan had fallen asleep and Kitto had decided to let him stay. "God, please," she begged as she ran. Rapping on the door only resulted in the sound of dogs whining. "Kitto! Are you in there? Open up!" Still no answer. "Kitto!" She found only stillness and the smell of horses, hay and leather cleaner. The dogs whined and scratched but no Keyan. He would have been roused by the dogs' noise if he had been inside. She left them inside. Backing away from the stable she decided to go tell Jory.

She threw open the door to the police station, and seeing that other constable, the one she didn't know, sitting slumped, half asleep in a chair surprised her. "Constable! Help me. My grandson's missing. He didn't come home last night. We have to find him. Where's Jory?"

"He's up to the manor house." He looked at Penrose in the cell, who sat up when she entered. "I can't leave while I have a prisoner, Mrs. Inch. Go on, and tell Jory." She left confused why Penrose sat in a cell, why Jory wasn't there, and why in the world he would be at the manor at this time in the morning.

Maybe they had another emergency. Maybe he already found Keyan. She rushed up the hill to the manor and started pounding on the door.

John heard a sharp rapping from somewhere near. It wasn't loud enough to be on his door. It stopped. He couldn't make out the words, but a man spoke rapidly, as if relaying an important message. He unwound from the blankets, quickly put on his pants and shirt, and opened his door. Jory spoke to Joseph Marrak, the footman, through a crack in a door nearly across from John's. He listened to what Marrak told him, when Lady Edra appeared next to Jory. Marrak repeated what he had told Jory

"Mary Inch is downstairs. She's very upset. Says you must come, Jory." He turned to John, " You too, Inspector. Keyan is missing."

Lady Edra said, "Marrak, take her to the breakfast room. Get her a cup of tea. We'll be down shortly."

John went to the door next to his and rapped. Geever opened the door. "Mary Inch is downstairs. She says Keyan is missing. I'll meet you down there."

"Righto." Geever closed his door, and John went to finish getting dressed and hurried down to the front hall, but found no one there. He wandered off in search of the breakfast room. Lander came toward him and took him in hand.

"Mrs. Inch is this way." He led the way to the breakfast room. Ferguson could hear Mary before he saw her.

"I don't want no tea, lad! Where's Jory Moon? Where's Ferguson and Geever?"

"Mrs. Inch. Mary, I need you to calm down and tell me what you're saying," John quieted her.

"Ferguson. Keyan is missing. Something is wrong. He didn't come home last night." Her eyes bulged with fear. She shook as she tried to explain. "I can't calm down! I went to the police station to find Jory, and that constable told me you're all over here for some reason. I need you to help me find him." She looked over his shoulder, as Geever entered, followed by Jory and Lady Edra. "You all must come now." She pleaded with them. "We have to search for Keyan. Something's terribly wrong. I can feel it."

John looked at the footman, standing holding a cup of tea. "Marrak, give her the tea.

Mary, sit down, take a drink or two, and slowly tell us what's going on."

She nodded and dutifully sat. The others also sat down and waited, while she took a sip of the hot tea, then started again. "I went to Keyan's room this morning to tell him I was leaving for the shop. His bed hadn't been slept in."

Ferguson asked, "Maybe he got up early and is larking about."

"No. He never makes his bed until after he has his breakfast. I found it exactly as he left it yesterday. I'm telling you, he never came home!"

"How did you not notice he hadn't come home when you went to bed?"

"I don't know." She looked down shaking her head. "I've been tired and upset and thinking about so many things. His door is always open except when he goes to bed. It was closed. I just said goodnight through the door, as I carried myself off to bed. Oh, what have I done? How could I not check?" She looked from one to another, pleading.

Geever asked, "When does he usually come home? Where does he play? Doesn't he come home after dark?"

"Yes. He comes home. Usually at dark. Maybe a little later. He likes the dark. He just walks around. Sometimes down by the quay. Often, he hangs out with Kitto around the stables. I tried to rouse Kitto or Mitch, but I got no answer this morning."

Lady Edra said, "The Tinks are at Chough House with Sir Vinson. They weren't around last night."

That upset Mary Inch even more. "We have to go find him. NOW!" She rose from her chair, but John put his hand on her shoulder, and she sat back down.

"Why don't we go look, and you stay here. We'll find him," he said reassuringly. But it didn't reassure her.

"No. I'm going with you."

"Okay." He could tell she would not be persuaded to wait. "Let's get our coats. It'll be chilly this morning. We'll be right back."

The two men met Abby coming out of her room, and spotted Lady Steran's maid two doors further along the hallway, about to enter one of the bedrooms. "What's going on?" Abby asked.

"Keyan seems to be missing. We're going to go find him. It'd be great if you could convince Mrs. Inch to stay here and drink her tea."

"I doubt that will happen. Let me get my coat. I'm coming with you."

The group met at the front door and walked out into the early morning, greeted by a stunning reddish orange sunrise. Lady Edra said, "There's a lot of barns and stables over here. I'm going to check there." Jory followed her.

Ferguson said, "Geever, why don't you head toward the quay to see if you see Keyan anywhere around there. Abby, you and Mrs. Inch go back to her place and search very carefully. Maybe he felt like hiding and you just missed finding him. Maybe he fell asleep in a quiet corner somewhere."

Mary started to protest, "I looked and called him…" but Abbey cut in.

"Let's look again. We'll meet them back here in a short while." Mrs. Inch nodded and they set off. Ferguson thought of the gate at the back corner of Tredwen. Maybe Keyan had gotten up extra early to watch the otters. Or gone on to Menadue Woods.

Before he moved, Mrs. Inch declared, "He's gone into the dower!" as she and Abby passed in front of it.

"That's impossible. It's locked up tight," Ferguson told her.

Jory had opened the stable door, and the two dogs came bounding out, sniffing Sheba who stood beside Lady Edra. The dogs ran across and began snuffling around the threshold of the dower door, and wagged their tails hoping to be let inside. Jory and Lady Edra followed. Mrs. Inch ran to the door and tried the handle. The dower sat silent just as they left it—locked up. "He's in there. I can feel it. These dogs are usually with him. They know he's in there." She banged on the door calling, "Keyan!"

The boy had a morbid fascination with the dower, Ferguson knew. He and Jory walked around the entire house looking for some sign in the uncut grass for Keyan's footprints or any sign someone had been around. They found lots of flattened grass, but workmen had been all around the house. They also checked to make sure windows were locked. Ferguson didn't know how a nine-year-old could reach one of the windows, but they checked anyway. All ground floor windows were locked up tight. He went to the servants' back door. Locked. The servants hadn't come down from the manor this early. Only Alan had a key. "Keyan couldn't be in there, Mrs. Inch. It's still locked up tight like we left it last night." Ferguson hoped Abby could calm her. He wanted to move on. Then he remembered he had the key. Alan gave it to him to lock up last night.

"Those dogs are always with Keyan. They know he's in there. Get this door open!" Mary Inch ordered.

Geever noticed the commotion just as he reached the Tredwen columns, and turned back to see what the commotion at the dower was about.

Ferguson unlocked and opened the door and Mrs. Inch rushed in ahead calling, "Keyan! Keyan!"

They fanned out. Mary Inch went upstairs and stare amazed at the new water closet, as she hurriedly checked it. No one could hid in here. She went across to the servants' room. She looked in the cupboards, the wardrobe and under the beds. Geever had come upstairs and checked in Abby's room. He checked the large wardrobe. Little boys like to hide in these, he said to himself. He checked under the bed and in a deep chest under the windows. No Keyan. Next, he entered the room Ferguson slept in, and looked under the bed and in the wardrobe. He spotted the murder bag first. Next he wondered why Ferguson had brought so few clothes. Geever then checked the room he had been sleeping in. Nothing. They found no small boy anywhere upstairs. He and Mary walked down the stairs together.

Abby checked her office. While in there, she checked that the newly discovered French door remained tightly secured. There was very little hiding space in her office. The examining table had clean sheets tucked on the shelf underneath, and a clear view that no one hid there. The big cabinet that held all her medicine had no extra space in it or under it.

Ferguson looked in cupboards in the kitchen and found nothing. He pulled aside the curtain in front of the sink revealing the plumbing that had just been installed, but nothing else. He opened the back door and looked farther from the door into the tall grass. None seemed flattened. Looking here, in a locked building, seemed ridiculous. He was about to abandon the dower and head to that back gate, when Lady Edra shouted at them all.

"He's here," she called. Keyan lay fast asleep on the sofa in front of the fireplace. I just glanced in here first and missed seeing him laid out flat against the back of the sofa." They gathered round.

His grandmother came near and sat on the edge of the sofa and quietly called, "Keyan. Keyan, wake up." He stirred.

Lady Edra stood behind her and said, "Keyan, can you hear us? Don't you want to wake up?"

He opened his eyes blinking, first looking toward his grandmother. He didn't seem to focus on her or his surroundings. Turning, he looked toward Lady Edra with such love and happiness and said, "Mother," in a quiet, astonished voice, as if his heart would burst with joy. He seemed to be focused not on Lady Edra, but on someone only he saw. He appeared to be in his own world, not quite awake. "My mother is here." He said with such elation, smiling broadly. His eyes cleared. He sat up suddenly, looked at them all gathered near, and asked, "Why are you all looking at me?" He looked around at the parlor upset. "Why am I in here? How did I get here?" He looked terrified and hopped off the couch. "What's going on? We need to get out of here. Baba, let's go." He grabbed her hand and started pulling her outside. The others followed.

They stood around him. His grandmother asked, "Keyan, why did you say my mother is here? Were you talking about Lady Edra?"

"No. Why would I call her my mother, she is…"

"Why didn't you come home last night? I have been so worried. Why did you go in the dower? You know it scares you."

Tears filled his eyes. "I wouldn't! I didn't, Baba!" He started to cry and ran into his grandmother's arms. He shook his head excitedly. "I didn't go in there. I wouldn't go in there." He rushed outside and looked back at the open front door of the dower. It seemed a gaping, open, black mouth beckoning him. He backed away as Oscar and Blue rushed him. They jumped at him and licked him, tails wagging furiously. That brought a smile. He looked at the others.

Lady Edra smiled, "Let's all go have some breakfast. Then we'll sort this all out. Everything is going to be fine, Keyan. Just fine."

———

Everyone tried to be cheerful, gathered in the breakfast room, watching Keyan gobble down toast and marmalade, completely unfazed and happy. Looking at Mrs. Inch, Ferguson thought it quite remarkable that she knew absolutely he would be found in the locked dower. Could she be harboring a second key? Would Keyan's Baba possibly drug her grandson? Why? Attention? Because she led a drab life lacking excitement? Perhaps she played on the prejudices about her being a gypsy, a seer beyond mortal seeing. One who sees all. Perhaps she was drumming up business for her Tarot cards. Maybe Mary Inch had nothing to do with the plan at all, but someone has a second key and left the lad in there drugged.

Lady Steran entered the breakfast room wearing her robe and slippers, leaning on her cane. "Edra, what is all this commotion?"

"Oh dear! Gran. I'm so sorry we have disturbed you." Lady Edra looked shocked to see how upset she appeared. It was unheard of for her very proper Gran to be in the breakfast room and not awaiting breakfast in her room. More shocking still, her gran appeared in her robe. That had probably never happened in her life. Lady Edra's heart went out to her. "Sit here, please, Gran. We had a bit of a scare. Keyan, here, had gone missing this morning. Obviously, he's fine. All is well."

"Where did you find him?"

"He lay fast asleep in the dower house." She smiled to show he had nothing to worry about.

"I thought they locked it and were sleeping over here because they were having trouble sleeping there. How did Keyan get into a locked house, and why wasn't he home asleep in his own bed?"

Not much gets passed her, Ferguson thought.

Lady Edra said, "That's what we're trying to find out."

"No one should go there," Lady Steran spoke barely above a whisper.

"It's fine, Gran, really. Would you like to go back to your room, now?"

"I think I'll wait here." She spotted Marrak. "Please get me some tea."

Lady Edra turned to Mary Inch and asked if it would be alright for Doc Abby, the professional, to ask her grandson, Keyan, what happened, and Mary said, "Of course."

Doc Abby felt it would be best to question him here in the breakfast room, distracted by eating, unless he became self-conscious of everyone watching him. While he concentrated on his toast, she put a finger to her lips, and looked around asking everyone to be quiet. Then she sat down across from him.

"Tell me, Keyan, what you were doing last night."

He wiped his face and hands, sat back in his chair, and looked out through one of the morning-room, mullioned windows. "An interesting thing happened. Oscar and me and Blue sat watching the stars. We like to do that sometimes. It's quiet in Menadue. Then we saw somebody coming through the trees. I told those dogs to stay with me, and they did. The people, two of them, I remember. Not close enough to know who they were." He took a bite of toast.

Doc Abby glanced at Ferguson, then asked, "Did you recognize them as men or women?"

"They weren't close enough to tell if they were men or women. They didn't talk that I could hear. One of them, the bigger one had a shovel and dug a hole. The ground out there is terrible hard, so it took them a bit. The shorter one handed over a wrapped-up package, and they dropped it in the hole. I saw the place was by a little Christmas tree. One of them stuck something metal into the ground and clanged it in with the back of the shovel. Once they were gone, me and the dogs went to the spot, and I saw it was a metal stake, so they could find it again. That's gonna be too hard for me to find, so I put Oscar's collar on the tree, so we could dig up whatever it was today. We can't get in trouble for that because Menadue Wood belongs to Mr. Stark, and they were not him. I know that for sure." He looked at Doc Abby to see if she believed him.

"What did you do then?"

"I looked for Kitto or even old Mitch. I was going to leave the dogs with them to go home to bed. No one was there. I looked in the barns. I couldn't find them, so I shut Blue and Oscar into the stable by the training paddock. I started walking home." He grew pensive. "I did not go near the dower." He squirmed as he spoke and his face reflected real dread. "I would never go in there! Alone? At night?" he shuddered. "I tried not to even barely look at the horrible dower as I passed it. I did glance at it. It was black and so scary. I think I started to run. I don't remember." He looked frightened remembering. "Doc Abby, what happened to me?"

"I'm not sure, Keyan. Did you talk to anyone?" A shake of the head. "Did you drink anything or take a bite of something different?"

He looked at Doc Abby like she lost her mind. "No."

Ferguson motioned to Doc Abby and Geever to join him on the other side of the breakfast room. "Just a minute, I'm going to talk to the two detectives. I'll be right back," Abby said. Geever joined her and Ferguson. Lady Edra sat in the chair next to Keyan, and his Baba sat on the other side

Ferguson knew from the look on his face that Keyan's utter terror had been real, as he fled the house this morning. The boy wasn't in on the plan— whatever the plan was. He told Geever and Doc Abby, "I believe him. It's possible the people in the woods saw him and somehow drugged him. That would explain him ending up in the dower house with no memory of it. To do all that to a lad, they must have buried something very important. We need to find it."

Doc Abby returned to her seat across from Keyan. "We don't know quite what happened last night," she smiled, "but you weren't hurt. You're fine." She smiled. He didn't look convinced, so she added, "Let's go see what they buried in Menadue last night." He brightened immediately.

"You know it's probably rubbish, don't you?" she cautioned.

"Course. We should go now!" Keyan scooted off his chair, ready to discover what his treasure held.

"Sorry to interrupt," Lander said, "Constable Collie wishes to speak to the policemen, if he could."

"Everyone wait here a minute," Jory said. "We need to speak to the constable." Lander led the three policemen to the front entry, where Constable Colley stood waiting for them.

"I just need Jory, I think." He looked surprised by the other two. "I went and got some breakfast and brought it back for Penrose, who very politely ate it. He's quieted down, asking to go home. I didn't know you'd all be over here." He looked around puzzled. Why Jory had said he could be found at the manor if an emergency came up. What were the detectives doing here so early, and why weren't they at the dower ?

Jory spoke. "That'll be fine, Sam. I'll come with you."

"I'll come too. I have some questions for Mr. Penrose before you release him," Ferguson said. "Geever, I think it's important you find out what's been buried—probably trash, or would you prefer to question Penrose?"

Geever understood Ferguson allowed him to claim the lead. That no longer mattered to Geever. He wanted to solve the murder. "You go interview Penrose. We'll find the buried treasure."

Ferguson and Jory walked with Colley into Woodcomb to the police station. Geever tried to dissuade the women from accompanying him and Keyan. "It might be better if Marrak and I accompany the lad alone. We'll return shortly. Marrak, I need you to come with us and bring some shovels."

Lady Steran stood to return to her room. "Edra dear, inform me of what is uncovered, please."

"Of course, Gran." Lady Steran's maid led her away. Lady Edra and Doc Abby, however, refused to be put off. They would go too. Geever proclaimed it time to go, with a hearty, "Let's go solve the mystery of the Christmas tree treasure!" He knew, if they could identify the two people by what they had buried, maybe they could find out if they were responsible for locking Keyan in the dower. "Let's go through the back gate, the quickest way to Menadue Wood," Keyan excitedly led the group.

They barely got out of the breakfast room before Lander interrupted, "Excuse me, my lady, but your father is on the phone. He seems very upset about something."

"You all go on with Detective Geever. I'll catch you up in a minute."

"I think I better accompany you, Lady Edra. See what Sir Vinson needs before we go," Geever said and turned to the others. "Wait here. This will only take a minute or two. Expedition on hold until Lady Edra answers the telephone." He kept his tone lighthearted so Keyan would not suspect the possible gravity of the search. He followed Lander and Lady Edra to a small reception room, where the telephone had pride of place on a wooden stand. A notebook next to it recorded each call anyone made, to whom, and the person's phone number, date and time. The opposite page recorded incoming calls, date and time. Geever stood discreetly by the door as she picked up the receiver. "Good morning, Father. How are you?"

Before she could add anything, he nearly shouted, "Where in hell is Wherry? Where are my clothes? My things? Where's my car, for God's sake?"

"You mean he never arrived? I don't understand." She looked at Geever blankly. "Probably a flat tire, some car trouble. We've been through the barns this morning. The car is definitely not in one of them. It's not sitting in the driveway. I'll get to the bottom of it. Don't worry." She wanted to calm him down and change the subject. "What time do you ride?"

"I'm scheduled for nine o'clock, which is a good thing. Asif is getting nervous in spite of everything the Tinks are doing to keep him calm and ready. If that isn't enough, he seems to have a bruise of some sort on his leg. I think he's fine. Haven't the foggiest how that could have happened." Anxious and upset, her father seemed calmer for a minute, then, "And I will be competing in my riding clothes from yesterday. He better be near death, or I'll kill him! How can I be my best in yesterday's clothes?"

"You'll be great, Father. I know you will. Beat the old earl! You've the best horse by far. We'll get this muddle figured out in no time." When she hung up, she didn't need to pull the bell, since Lander waited discreetly in the hallway. "Lander, I need Wherry here immediately. Find him. Get Marrak here also. Forget the shovels. We need to get my father his proper clothes and his car."

Lander fetched Marrak. "We need to find where Wherry has disappeared to. Search the house. Maids can help. We need him found now."

Marrak said, "He's not here, my lady. I saw him as he left last night. He had his satchel with him, his clothes and things. He said he was leaving for Chough House."

"When did you see him?" Geever asked.

"Last night maybe eight. He ate dinner with the rest of the staff. I asked him why he hadn't left much earlier, and he said Sir Vinson had called and told him later would be better."

Lander marched over to the log book next to the phone. "There's no such phone call logged in," he declared, indignant at the suggestion. "And I'm very sure I would have answered the telephone, if there had been such a call, and I would have either taken a message for the valet, or fetched him to answer it, had it rung!"

Marrak declared, "Wherry's playing silly buggers with us. All of us." No one disagreed.

Lander seethed, "It won't be silly when he finds out I've fired him, as of this very moment—if Sir Vinson agrees." He nodded toward Lady Edra.

"His door was open," Marrak said. " I checked his room before I came down this morning. He didn't return and sleep there last night. I don't know what he's about or where he could be." Marrak looked perplexed. "If Wherry had car trouble, he would have gotten word to Lady Edra or Sir Vinson before now. Wherry is up to something. The way he's been acting. "

Geever said, "I assume he will be in touch soon and clear this up. Right now we need to find whatever they buried last night. Marrak, shovels. Let's get to Menadue Wood immediately." Geever hoped they found a bag of trash, but began to doubt it. He hoped they didn't find a body.

"Why should we go to Menadue now? We need to find the car and get my father his clothes for the competition. Perhaps Jory could send a man with father's clothes in the police car?" Lady Edra asked.

Geever found that a ridiculous request, to ask the police simply to accommodate Sir Vinson with clean clothes, but to humor the lady, he turned to the butler. "Lander, the number for the police station, please." He dialed the number, and Jory answered. "Jory, this rather beggars belief, but the valet-chauffeur, Wherry, seems to have scarpered with Sir Vinson's automobile, and Sir Vinson's beside himself worrying. Could the police car possibly be sent to Chough Hall, with his proper riding attire, by any chance?"

"What? Not a chance. Not right now. Crocker is still out on leave, I need Sam here to man the station, and Ferguson and I are about to escort Penrose home in the car."

"That's too bad. I feared that may be the case. We'll have to find another way then." He turned with a solemn face and said, "I'm sorry. The car simply can't be spared this morning. Police business. Your father will have to be brave. He must appear in yesterday's riding attire for his competition this morning. Too many odd things are happening. Right now, I think we go to Menadue. "

"I think I ought to remain here in case we hear from my father," Lady Edra stated.

"Probably a good idea," Geever agreed. "The fewer people on the search, the better." He returned to the breakfast room to gather the others, and told them Lady Edra chose to stay at the manor and why.

"Unless you think you might need me to talk to Keyan, depending on what you find, I think I'll let you go without me also. My time might be better spent in my surgery. Tell me what you find. I'm thinking the treasure will not turn out to be police business." Doc Abby smiled

Geever said, "You are probably correct, and I'm sure he'll be fine. He won't witness anything untoward that we find." Turning to Keyan, he said, "Lead us up to Menadue, Keyan." He started, followed by his Baba, Geever and Marrak, who had shown up with two shovels. They went down the back stairs and out through the servants' kitchen door, surprising the staff there, and headed for the back gate. They entered the ancient wood and zigzagged among oak and ash trees, and trudged through brush and around bushes

Chapter Thirteen

Abby stood just inside the dower front door. The servants had arrived. She could hear Alan speaking to the others from the kitchen. She thought how everything seems so normal, so pleasant in the morning here. She walked into the parlor and stood with her hand on the sofa, where they had found the sleeping Keyan earlier. She didn't believe anyone drugged the lad. She thought about all that had happened in only a few days. The nightmares—we've all had. The terrifying sounds and horrible smells. Keyan and I have come under attack more than the others. I believe this house reached out last night and caught him walking too near in the dark. It wants to scare us away. It wants to keep him. He's told us it wants to kill us. I understand Ferguson needs life to be explainable and rational. He deals with evil all the time. He refuses to believe there can be some evil he can't bring to justice. How can I make him see we need to save Keyan? We may have to burn the place to the ground to save the lad—or maybe, I need to burn it down.

Jory and Ferguson stood in front of Penrose's cell. Jory spoke, "You are charged with assault, Penrose. That won't just go away. There won't be a judge in Truro until tomorrow morning for your arraignment. I might let you go home this morning, if you swear to me you can behave yourself, control your temper and stay away from Doc Abby." Jory waited for some diatribe about Abby to erupt. Penrose sat on the cot, head down without stirring while Jory spoke. He raised his head, met Jory's eyes and nodded.

Jory glanced at Ferguson then took the key and opened the cell door. "Are your kids still with their grandparents?"

"Yes. Piran told me they'd head home later this morning, and he'd be back from fishing probably about noon."

"Yeah, I'm expecting him back this afternoon." Jory said. "I'd let you go on out to their camp sight and meet up with them, if you wanted."

"No," Penrose said quietly. "I better see how Eva's doing. She gets nervous, and she won't have done well on her own after all this."

Ferguson asked "She won't do well on her own? I thought the fishing trip had been arranged so she could be alone for a while?"

"She would have enjoyed this time to be by herself had I not been thrown in jail. That will have stressed her. I'm sure of it. Anyway, I need to check on her."

"Sign this paper," Jory led him to Crocker's desk where Sam had typed up his release. Penrose signed it without glancing at it.

Ferguson said, "Jory and I will escort you home, Penrose." He didn't protest, remained silent and looked straight ahead. The three men walked from the police station heading for Penrose's farm. Jory preferred the car remain at the station in case the constable needed it. Ferguson wondered if they would find a woman on the edge of a breakdown, or one totally calm, when they got there.

They spotted Geever with Marrak and Keyan and his Baba enter the road from the back gate of the manor and cross the small bridge marking the end of Treden manor proper, as they passed the dilapidated Inch house. When they reached Penrose's driveway, Ferguson motioned for Jory to join the group heading for the woods. "You can go ahead. I'll follow as soon as I know Eva's fine, and Penrose is fine." He glanced at Penrose who stood mutely beside him. He showed no indication he even heard what Ferguson said. Jory thought for a second, then nodded and left to join the others, while Ferguson and Penrose walked up to the house. Ferguson once again considered the disparity between the Penrose well-kept, prosperous farm, with the cheerful house, looking peaceful in the morning sun, in such stark contrast to the troubled people who lived there.

As Penrose entered the house, Eva turned and stared at him. No hysterics, no smile. She didn't get up to greet him. Penrose showed no emotion and barely glanced at his wife. He looked at Ferguson, then walked over to her. It didn't look like a happy reunion. She seemed at last to notice the policeman standing next to her husband, and smiled wanly. "Detective," she said.

"Your husband is being released, unless you have concerns for your safety, or for the safety of your children when they return."

"For God's sake, Ferguson, I'm not going to hurt anybody." Penrose stood next to his wife, but neither reached out to the other.

"Eva, you look worried. Are you concerned for your welfare?" Ferguson asked her.

"No. No. I'm fine. We'll be fine. His temper flared up yesterday because he's just been so worried about getting the crops in. That's all." She looked at Ferguson as if he had hurt her feelings. "He didn't need to be locked up." Ferguson looked around the house. Nothing seemed amiss except small things. No coffee or tea brewed. If she had eaten, she had completely cleaned up. It seemed to him there should have been something. Did she just sit all night, awaiting Penrose to come and tell her what to do? Something didn't seem right, but she truly didn't seem afraid of Penrose. He could see no reason not to leave them together.

"Then I'll leave you to it. Penrose, you are charged with assault and will need to appear in court tomorrow. Don't add to your troubles today."

"Get out of my house now—please," he said in a quiet, calm voice with a nod.

Ferguson left them thinking something is very wrong there, but he had no idea what. He turned up toward Menadue to find what progress Geever and the others had made. It seemed very unlikely they would find anything important, but what could explain finding Keyan inside the locked dower—a place that terrified the lad? He found Mrs. Inch standing just off the road, on the edge where the wood began, peering into it. She heard him approach and said, "There's too much brush, so I decided I'm staying here." She pointed where they entered, and he left her. He could make out voices and followed them until he found Jory holding a spade, Geever and Keyan watching as Marrak dug.

Just as Ferguson neared, Marrak said, "Whoa, I hit something. I think we found it." Next to the hole lay the metal stake that Keyan heard someone pound in.

"I told you I could find it!" Keyan jumped up and down. "Ferguson, see there's Oscar's collar! That's how we found the treasure!" He pulled the collar from a branch of a three-foot little pine and proudly showed it to Ferguson, who nodded and smiled.

Marrak pulled out a bundle wrapped in a cloth—not a body. Wiping off the dirt, he unwrapped it. A wallet and a pair of pants fell out. Keyan watched with keen interest. Geever picked up the thin, inexpensive, well-worn wallet and opened it. It contained Geran Inch's identification and address, a post office box in London. No money, but a marred, dry blood stain ran across the inside. He found a fingerprint in blood on the back side. Geever held it up saying, "Geran Inch's wallet." He handed it to Ferguson who looked at it and passed to Jory. He unfolded a pair of riding pants and found small amounts of what looked like blood. The pants also had a few spatters on the outside of the pant legs near where the top of a riding boot would have been.

"That's the riding pants I found hidden in Wherry's room!" Marrak declared. "I told you he had hidden Sir Vinson's pants for some reason. It must have been Wherry who hid them here."

Ferguson thought probably at least one of the people who hid these knew who killed Inch. If those pants are Sir Vinson's, perhaps Kitto Tink's story is right, that the blood got on them the night of Inch's murder. If Wherry believes Sir Vinson is a murderer, why hide the pants. Blackmail? Then why bury them? Aloud he said, "They placed the metal stake to be able to retrieve the wallet and pants later. Did you notice you followed an animal trail through here?" No one had. "It would lead them back to the barely visible stake, if and when they needed to retrieve their package." He didn't want the bright, inquisitive Keyan to hear more. "Great job, Keyan. Let's get you back to tell the others." Keyan ran most of the way back to his Baba, waiting at the edge of the woods, smiling broadly. He gave her a hug, thrilled to find such important things.

At the back gate to Tredwen, the men split with Keyan and his Baba. The policemen and Marrak went through the gate with the bundle of clothes and wallet, while Keyan and Mary Inch continued on home. They returned to the manor breakfast room and grabbed some cold toast and slurped down lukewarm tea.

They found Lady Edra and her grandmother in the blue parlor. Lady Edra paced, anxious to hear about the find. Lady Steran, now fully dressed, sat looking worried. They told them what they had dug up, and Ferguson explained, "Whoever hid Geran Inch's wallet and the pants were up to no good. That gives them a reason to drug Keyan, and leave him to wake up in the dower with no memory of how he got there. No one else around seems to have had any glimmer of a reason to touch the lad."

Geever said, "We know Wherry had the pants. We need to find him. He's the most likely to be one of the two people who buried the pants. Perhaps he's the one with a second key to the dower. Perhaps he's the one trying to scare everyone away from the dower."

Jory added, "Wherry's into something. Blackmail? He had Geran's wallet. Maybe murder?"

Lady Edra stood up, shocked by the news, and demanded they show her the pants. She inspected the blood spots. "These pants are my father's brand of riding pants, and I doubt anyone else around here would have pants of this quality and cost. Are you certain that my father's long-time, faithful valet, Wherry, hid them?" She found it hard to believe of the man who had been trusted by them for so long. "Why would he hide them? What does this mean?" She looked at the blood-stained wallet. "Whose is this thing? Is this Geran's blood? What are you saying?" She grew more agitated as she spoke. She looked at Jory, who simply shook his head. "We don't know anything except there were two of them."

Lady Edra had more questions. "Why would Wherry hide Sir Vinson's pants? Did he think my father knew something about Geran's murder? Did he intend to threaten him? For what purpose? Did he hope to blackmail the man?"

Ferguson now added, "I think we need Sir Vinson here, so we can ask him. Now!" Ferguson stood to leave, followed by the other policemen.

Geever said, "I'll telephone Chough Hall and make it quite clear that someone must get him here immediately." They left him to ensure Sir Vinson returned without delay.

Ferguson wanted to check on Abby this morning. He stopped at the dower, while Jory went on to the police station. He entered a quiet house with no workmen and no Sally to greet him. Apparently, finished as it would be for a while. He heard Abby humming to his right. Looking into the surgery, he glimpsed her in the examining room, standing in front of the open wardrobe door, making a list as she went through her bottles, powders and vials of medicines.

"Hello," he said quietly, so as to not startle her as he walked toward her. She looked up and showered a radiant smile on him, catching his heart unexpectedly nearly stopping him in his tracks. "Ferguson, how did the treasure hunt go?" She kissed him on the cheek.

He stood clumsily holding the bag they had recently dug up. "Uh, fine." Did the kiss mean she was glad to see him after last night, or was she merely happy this morning? He thought about how their closeness made him feel and the look on her face as they kissed. His feelings for her were novel. He wanted to be with her more, as he grew to know her better. He enjoyed talking to her—even when she teased him. He wanted to know what she was doing, and where she was all the time. He wanted to share this thoughts with her. That hadn't been true for him in a long time. He chose to believe her kiss now meant something to her as well.

"Well. Did you find anything? Could Keyan really find the spot again?"

"We found these pants with blood on them and Geran Inch's wallet. I need to get these put into evidence and meet Jory at the station. I wanted to make sure you were fine—and keep you up on what we found." She probably knew he had no reason to keep any bystander abreast of police progress. He was unsure why he shared these things. "I'll explain more later. We did release Penrose to his home."

"Oh." Her smile disappeared, and she took a step back, appalled at the mention of his name. "Tell me how that goes. John, I think you're getting close. I just feel it." Another high wattage smile, then she turned to resume her inventory.

Ferguson entered the police station and dropped the pants, the wallet and the sack they had been wrapped in on the constable's desk. "Sam, enter this all into evidence and then lock it up." Ferguson was about to give him details about the items, when the phone rang.

Sam answered it. He looked shocked at whatever he heard. "Can you tell who is it? We'll be there quick as we can, Georgia. Don't touch anything!" He hung up the receiver and excitedly announced, "Sir Vinson's car has been found. It's at the train station, and there's a body inside."

Ferguson stopped. "Is it Wherry?"

Sam shrugged. "She said she couldn't tell who it was."

"We need to take everything you have to deal with a crime scene," Ferguson announced. Jory nodded already heading to a closet. Then to Sam Ferguson said, "Call up to the manor house, get Geever on the line. Tell him what's going on and pick him up, after you drop us at the train station." When someone answered, the constable barked, "I need to speak to Inspector Geever, immediately!"

As Ferguson and Jory walked towards the police car carrying crime scene paraphernalia, Ferguson added, "Tell him to stop at the dower and pick up the murder bag. It's in the wardrobe in my closet. And bring it to the train station." He stopped short and turned back around. "Tell Geever to find an extra car key if there is one—just in case the car is locked. And tell him not to inform anyone else what's happening. We don't want a crowd showing up." Sam still had the stunned, surprised look on his face, but relayed to Geever what had been said.

When Sam came out the back door moments later to where Ferguson and Jory were finished loading and getting into the car, he told them, "Geever said someone from Chough Hall will get Sir Vinson back here within the hour." Sam jumped into the driver's seat and drove Ferguson and Jory to the train station, where five days ago the same car had picked up the Scotland Yard men. He stopped the car behind where the Bandrys' Bentley sat, parked at a strange angle. Ferguson and Jory got out and grabbed the equipment from the trunk, leaving Sam to rush to find Geever.

"That's Sir Vinson's car all right," Jory announced. The car sat at the edge of the gravel parking area, behind the train station, parked at an odd angle, with the left front wheel up on the curb.

A man and woman rushed out to meet them. "Jory," the man said, "We just spotted the car. I knew it belonged to the Bandrys."

"What took you so long to look out and see it?" Jory seemed irritated. "How long has it sat here?"

"Now, Jory," the man said, "It weren't here last night when we went to bed. There ain't no trains early Sunday morning. You know that. That's our only chance to sleep in." He put his arm around his wife. They appeared apologetic. Neither ventured any closer to the car.

The car doors were locked. Ferguson attempted to get in to the right-side car door without destroying possible fingerprints. A man's body lay curled in an awkward position, in the driver's seat. His left leg splayed out, looped over the gear shift. His head pushed down nearly under the dash. "Jory, over here."

Both the man and the woman stood wide-eyed. "Thank you both." Jory addressed the station master and his wife. "I need you to go back inside. We've got it now." They both simply stared at him. "Go back inside, please." Jory started toward the couple, and they quickly started to move back. "Of course, Jory." He took his wife's hand, and they went back inside the station. Jory turned and walked over to the car, peering inside looking at the body.

"Is that Wherry?" Ferguson asked him.

"I can't swear to it with him being all smashed in like that, and I can't see his face." They wanted to try and wait for a key before entering the vehicle. Breaking a window might destroy some evidence. Jory had fingerprint powder and started on the driver's window and door handle. Ferguson walked around to look for signs that the car crashed there. He found no dents or scratches and no marks in the gravel suggesting the car stopped suddenly and skidded. The tires weren't flat. He touched the hood. The cold engine suggested it had not been driven there recently. Jory attempted to get some fingerprints off the trunk handle, as he spoke to Ferguson. "Lots of prints overlapping. Not sure this helps."

Ferguson asked, "Do you have any theory—or any idea what was going on with Wherry? Any whiff that he could have been involved with something illegal or involved with some villainous men?"

Jory had moved to the passenger door handle and concentrated on his fingerprinting. "Nothing I've heard about."

Ferguson wondered if Jory's involvement with the lady of the manor, Lady Edra, had been affecting his policing. Maybe his prospective new life had caused him to be less diligent, less on top of who the criminals were.

Jory looked up to see Ferguson staring at him. "What?"

"I knew you thought a lot of Lady Edra, but I totally missed that you two were trying to declare Geran Inch dead, so you could be married. Do you not see that your relationship makes you the number one suspect in his murder?"

"What! You think I murdered him? You think I could murder a man? I've spent all these years bringing people to justice, no matter where the evidence leads me, Ferguson. Do you think I killed this one instead?"

Ferguson was about to answer when Constable Sam pulled in behind the Bentley. Geever jumped out and headed to the crime scene, holding the murder bag in one hand and the key to the car in the other, while Sam parked and piled out. Ferguson took the key, unlocked the car door and opened it. The body's arm flopped out, and the corpse turned enough to reveal the right side of Wherry's bloody face. His dead eyes peered out, and his mouth hung open at an odd angle. Ferguson pulled on the man's jacket lapels, turning him enough to see that the man had knife wounds across his chest. Blood soaked his clothes. He knelt and picked up the sleeve of the jacket to look at Wherry's hands. Defensive wounds sliced through his palm. He stood, and they all scanned the scene for a minute.

Geever said, "He looks to have been pulled or pushed into this position, probably after he died."

"So, what do we think happened here?" Jory asked. "Wherry took the car. He was supposed to be driving to Chough Hall. Did someone stop him as he left? Did he pick up someone?"

Sam added, "Wherry'd never pull over and let anybody in the car that he didn't know. He loved keeping that Bentley humming and sparkling. I think he liked being the chauffeur more than being the valet. If he stopped for someone, he knew that person. That's for sure."

Ferguson said, "Remember he said he made a phone call to Chough Hall, and according to Lander, that never happened." He paused for a moment. "He should have left for the earl's much earlier. I think he planned to steal this car and never return to Tredwen." Ferguson looked at the others who considered what he said. "He had hours before anyone would miss the car, which would have allowed him to be hundreds of miles away by now."

Geever said, "This Bentley would be noticed wherever he went. People would remember seeing it pass by. He would have needed to dump it, or it would lead directly and immediately to him. He wouldn't be free very long."

"Maybe Sir Vinson's bloodied riding pants had been a bargaining chip to ensure the theft was never reported," Ferguson said. "But then, why bury them?" A possible answer occurred to him. "He buried them in case Sir Vinson went back on the deal and had him arrested. They wouldn't find the pants on him, but Wherry could produce them as evidence if he needed to. He took the car, and Sir Vinson had to let him take it."

Jory seemed stunned by that. "Based on a little blood on a pair of pants, you think Sir Vinson murdered Geran Inch?"

"I'm just trying to make some of this fit into a pattern. Could Sir Vinson absolutely be found at Chough Hall the entire time? We didn't see him there while we were there. Maybe he found a way to return here to silence Wherry. Maybe he truly had nothing to do with this. We need to find out who Wherry had with him? There is another person. Someone who helped bury the evidence and maybe killed Wherry. A falling out, perhaps," Ferguson said, opening the car's back door. Blood had smeared onto the seat.

Geever took the key and opened the trunk. It held a suitcase and a bottle of champagne. When he opened the suitcase, he found only Wherry's clothes and a road map of England and Wales. "Where's the luggage of the second person? Is that who killed him? Whoever it is, they didn't get far before they crashed the car. His murderer is still very near." They all paused considering.

Sam said, "Maybe the second person in the car also helped him bury the stuff in Menadue."

Jory ordered, "Sam, go in the train station and phone the mortuary. Tell Pengilley to get a hearse down here as quick as he can. People are getting up, and we'll have a crowd any minute now."

"Jory," Ferguson said, "Get some photographs of how the car is parked, the position of the body—that sort of thing. Have Sam check the nearby ground and surrounding area for anything dropped or left. We need the car out of here before curious people start showing up to contaminate everything.

Jory snapped, "I do know how to handle this, Inspector Ferguson! I'll lay a sheet over the driver 's seat and, if the car runs, I'll park it in the barn at Tredwen. It'll be inside a barn, at least, until I can find a better place for it."

While the two glared at each other, Geever inserted, "Do one of you want to be the one to tell Lady Edra about this, or should I do it?" That cleared the tension.

"I'll tell her," Jory said, "as soon as I can. I'll drive the Bentley back to Tredwen as soon as we see there's no evidence to be found around the car."

"I'm going to pick up Abby and see about getting an autopsy," Ferguson said. He drove the police car toward the dower and spotted Pengilley's hearse as it turned up the High Street, already heading for the train station. Inside the dower, Ferguson found Abby sitting in her office at her desk, working on some papers. "Hello, again," he said as he sat down next to her. It seemed the best way to inform her of the murder was to just tell her, with no preamble or niceness to soften the information. "We found Wherry and the car," he paused looking into her eyes. She smiled. "We found the Bentley with Wherry's body in the car."

The smile vanished. She looked stunned. "Was it a car accid…"

"No," he interrupted. "He has been murdered." He let that set in for a moment, then, "I would like you to come look at the body, as soon as Pengilley gets the body to the morgue."

"Of course. Why are you so sure he didn't have a car accident?"

"He has stab wounds in his chest, and whoever did it stuffed him half under the driver's seat. We'll know more about what his actions after you look at him." She immediately rose to gather her equipment. He didn't know why her calm demeanor surprised him. She happened to be a physician who had been to war.

While she gathered up her equipment, he stepped into the kitchen and said to the three servants, "I think you should know, we found Wherry's body this morning in the Bandrys' car. He's been murdered." Sukie gasped. Dobbs put a hand to her mouth, and Alan asked quietly, almost in a whisper, "How? Why?"

"I'll tell you more when we find out more. I want you three to know what all the excitement is about that will soon start. I know you will help in any way you can. I especially need you not to tell anyone. Not yet. Not until we know more. Can you do that?" The three murmured their assent, proud to be trusted to do their part. "Thank you," Ferguson said and went back where Abby stood by the front door waiting.

"Shall we?" he asked, as he ushered her out and into the car and once again back to the mortuary. They walked through the reception room back to the embalming room. Pengilley and an assistant, a man who looked like an exact, younger replica of Pengilley, were finishing cutting the clothes off Wherry's body.

"Welcome, again, Ferguson and Doc. This is my son, Michael." They all nodded to each other.

"Thank you for your quick response to pick up the body at such an early hour."

Pengilley said, "Not a problem. We were up working already this morning." Then to Doc Abby, "We need to clean him up before you can see much," Both Pengilley men sponged the man's torso, face and arms while Ferguson watched.

"That's alright, enough for now," she said, scanning the body as they wiped away blood. "Rigor mortis has progressed some, meaning he died last night, but it doesn't help much. We already know that." She picked up his head and felt through his hair. "I don't feel any bumps or wounds. Without his head being shaved or opening the skull, I don't believe he had a concussion or a closed wound. His face doesn't show any injuries from a crash." She moved to his right arm and turned it over, inspecting both the front and back.

Ferguson noted cuts he had spotted earlier along the length of his palm. "Defensive wounds." Abby added, "See the slash in this palm? It looks like he held his hand up to defend himself from someone slashing with a knife. I don't see any redness from his wrists being secured at any point. Bruising won't show up for a while though." She went to his left side and did the same thing to that hand and wrist. "The left hand, you can see has a deep puncture wound near the center of the palm. I think he was stabbed here while fending off his attacker, and when they struck again, he tried to grab the knife with his right hand and received these wounds on his right hand."

That impressed Ferguson. Combat surgeon.

"Let's turn him over now, Mr. Pengilley." They turned him enough to see he had no more stab wounds and no blood.

"There's no slashes back here, and no bruising has shown up yet," Abby concluded. "Please turn him onto his back again." The two men gently laid him again on his back. Abby checked his body from the bottoms of his feet and back, to closely inspect his chest. "I see no wounds other than these three stab wounds on his upper chest. This one," she pointed to one directly above his left nipple and closer to the center of his chest, "I need to cut him open to see it." She opened her medical bag and pulled out a scalpel. She turned to Pengilley, "Could I get some boiling water to clean this before I proceed?"

Pengilley quietly asked, "Does it need to be sterilized?"

She thought a moment, then "Oh. Of course not." A shy smile. "I'm more familiar with live bodies." She cut enough to see the knife wound had indeed cut into Wherry's heart. "There appears to be a superficial nick and one other deeper wound. He might have survived these if not for the one to the heart.

It's what killed him." She looked into the dead man's face sorrowfully, "I'm so sorry, Mr. Wherry. What in the world were you doing?" Looking at his face, she suddenly remembered seeing him walk out of the manor with a bundle under his arm and leave. He certainly looked like he hadn't wanted to be seen. She looked up staring into Ferguson's eyes. "I saw him yesterday afternoon. Later. I'll tell you about that later."

That interested him but he pulled his gaze back to the body and asked her, "Can you tell when he died?"

"From the condition of the body, I'd say last night some time, but I can't tell you more." Pengilley nodded, agreeing with her time of death. Ferguson had never contemplated whether morticians might learn a lot about time of death from experience.

He nodded to Pengilley, "Thank you again for being so quick about this."

"Of course," he said proudly. "Doc Abby, will you be doing more right now?"

She looked at Ferguson. "I could stay and cut him open if that would help. Find the depth of the stab wounds. The width and length of the blade. Any internal injuries or surprises about his brain."

"This'll do for now. You've given me the information I need. Thank you for your help." She nodded with a small grin. "I'll run you back to the dower now." He turned to the mortician and the silent young man beside him. "Thank you again, Mr. Pengilley. Thank you both."

They accomplished the two-minute drive to the dower in silence. He stopped in front of the dower. They both sat silently thinking. Ferguson concentrated on what to do next about this new murder.

"Ferguson, when I looked in Wherry's face just now, I remembered that I saw Wherry carry a package out of Tredwen Manor yesterday afternoon, and disappear through that gate in the back corner."

"What do you mean? When?" Ferguson turned his full attention on her.

"I sat enjoying a quiet moment on my newly discovered little terrace. It surprised me to find out one of the windows in my office is actually a French window! After so many years of disuse, it had become stuck shut, but I got it open. There's a little bench on my stone terrace. It's a lovely, quiet view. I watched Wherry come from the servants' entrance, while I relaxed, and he headed out the gate."

"Was the French door locked when you found it?"

She knew he'd want to know about the door and the lock. "No. But, I locked it when I came back in. I knew you'd be interested, but then I forgot about it. With all that happened. Penrose… and moving up to the manor and you and I…and you and I."

He couldn't think about the passionate moment they had last night. "You're sure this happened yesterday afternoon?"

"Yes. With the scare over Keyan and then the hunt for buried treasure, I never put it together. Did Wherry bury something in Menadue? Did he drug the lad?"

"We don't know anything yet for sure. I need to get on with this." He stepped out of the car. Abby had let herself out before he could get around to open her door. "Best check to make sure the car got put in one of the barns, but which one is it in?" he wondered aloud.

For a few seconds, she watched him stride across to the barns, head down in concentration. She thought about the weight of his responsibilities before she went inside.

When Ferguson found the right barn, he threw open both the wide barn doors to let in more light. At the far end he saw a disused grain wagon, and against a far wall, a fancy four-seat buggy sat abandoned. He walked slowly around the Bentley parked directly in front of him. It hadn't been driven far. He found very little dust on its gleaming exterior. They would have to start questioning people along the High Street to see if Wherry left that way. Perhaps, instead, he had started up the road toward Plymouth, past Menadue. From Plymouth perhaps they planned continuing on to London or taking a ferry from Plymouth to Spain or France. The map they found in the trunk of the Bentley looked like maybe they planned a different route. Maybe the route was to be north into Wales and across into Ireland. He opened the door and sat in the passenger seat, looking at the blood on the gear shift. The contrast between the rust-colored blood of this savage death, and the sublime elegance of the interior of this flawless car, seemed to him another sacrilege added to the murder. He learned nothing, shut the door of the car, closed up the doors to the barn, and returned to the dower determined to make some progress on the murders.

Once inside, Ferguson took the stairs two at a time. He would bring down everything they had collected as evidence, from Inch's murder. What they had, he had stashed in the bottom of his wardrobe. He found Geever standing in his room, and he had already spread the evidence on top of Ferguson's bed examining it. The pile looked pathetically small and minor. Ferguson said, "We're taking all we have on Geran Inch's murder to the police station. It needs to be officially entered into evidence with the wallet and pants." At the bottom of the stairs Ferguson said, "Wait. We need to slow down and think. Into the dining room," he ordered Geever. They both sat, and Ferguson yelled, "Dobbs!" She appeared from the kitchen surprised. "No distractions. We need to think."

Dobbs murmured, "About time and all." He looked at her, surprised. "Please bring us some tea—and hopefully something to eat."

"Yes, sir. I think we can manage some eggs." She smiled as she walked away.

Doc Abby stepped into the dining room and sat down to watch. Geever laid out what they had on the table between them, to inventory, and said, "A medallion, a handkerchief and a train-ticket stub from the first murder. Geran Inch, terrible person. Suspects—virtually anyone who ever knew him. Think about the pants Wherry had hidden in his room that we dug up this morning with Inch's wallet."

Ferguson continued, "This morning, we find Wherry's body. I can't think of Wherry's first name." Ferguson opened his notebook as Alan popped his head through the door to the kitchen, "It's Howel, sirs."

"Yes, of course. Thank you. Howel Wherry, valet and chauffeur." He didn't know how to describe him. "Alan, what did you think of Wherry?"

Alan immediately stepped through the swinging door. "I didn't know him very well. He mostly kept himself to himself. Never heard nothing bad."

Ferguson raised his voice, "Dobbs. You too, Sukie, come here a minute, please." They came through. "What do either of you know about Wherry?"

Dobbs said, "Nothing really. He rarely spoke to anyone at mealtime. He spent a lot of time out in the barn tinkering with the automobile. Nothing seemed odd about him. He didn't seem to ever be in trouble with the master or mistresses." Sukie shook her head and said nothing.

"We found this bundle buried in Menadue Woods last night. We think possibly Wherry and someone else buried it." The three were listening intently. "A pair of Sir Vinson's riding pants with blood on them." That shocked them. "Not that Sir Vinson did anything wrong, and yet according to Marrak, Wherry had hidden the pants in his own room, instead of cleaning them or disposing of them. Can you think of any reason he might do that?"

Their surprised faces and the shaking of the heads needed no words to say they knew nothing. "What about the wallet? It belonged to Geran Inch?" Nothing. "Did Wherry have a woman he was particularly close to?" They looked at each other, and no one could think of anyone. "Not one of the maids, perhaps? Sukie?"

"I never saw him even flirt with anyone."

"Well, thank you," he sighed. "I appreciate each of you for your help, and I would ask you, again, please, not to mention this to anyone else. I need to be the one to share this with them." They agreed.

Dobbs said, "Anything to help you solve this, sir. Now back to the kitchen you two." She shooed them into the kitchen. "We need to make some food to serve these two gentlemen. And of course, Doc Abby here." They disappeared.

Ferguson turned to Geever. "The riding pants. The stable lad…Kitto, told me that Wherry came to him to make sure he noted blood on Asif's hooves, when he returned late last Sunday night, the night of the storm and the murder of Geran Inch. Kitto said he thought it was just mud on the horse, and dismissed it, until we started asking questions."

Geever asked, "It seems Wherry wanted to get Sir Vinson in trouble, but to what purpose? Maybe he wanted a promotion or just more money. That seems elaborate only to get a promotion. The more likely reason seems to be blackmail. If Sir Vinson is who killed Geran Inch, he might do whatever to stop someone blackmailing him. Maybe the deal was Wherry got the Bentley and left Tredwen forever. That gives Sir Vinson a perfect reason to kill Wherry last night. That could connect the two murders. What do you think?"

Ferguson said, "I don't know. Something must connect them. Two murders one week apart. Both connected to Tredwen. Both deaths were violent deaths, stabbings. Neither murder seems professional in any way. No neatly slit throat. No disappearing body. However, professional killers might have made these look sloppy and amateurish to throw us off."

"Now, what makes the two murders completely unrelated?" Geever asked.

"One man lived here. One man hadn't for seven years."

"One man had been universally hated. One man seems to have been unknown to everyone."

It struck Ferguson that Geran Inch abandoned his wife and son about the time the war started. All along the coast between Britain, France and Germany, it became incredibly lucrative for smuggling rings and all types of crime to flourish. "Cornwall has an enormous amount of coastline. Not only did DI Pascoe, until he died, then Jory and his men protect England from invasion, they had to try to control smuggling and all sorts of crime." Ferguson was throwing out ideas. "Smuggling might still be very lucrative today—especially coming through rural Cornwall. Today's smuggling would be about importing, without paying the taxes. Liquor and cigarettes."

Geever added, "Geran could have been sent from his masters in London to handle some problem around here. Sir Vinson, the rather bumbling, innocuous country squire might need money to shore up this costly estate, and could be involved. Wherry, the mysterious Wherry, might be one of Sir Vinson's men." Ferguson realized how seriously Geever studied the possibilities of the information they had.

Geever continued, "A falling out among thieves could have led to all of this. Wherry, killing the man from London, and perhaps Sir Vinson murdering has underling, Wherry, killed because of his blackmail scheme?" He looked at Ferguson expectantly.

Ferguson said, "I doubt Inch was part of big time London criminals. He was practically penniless." He knew the servants would still be listening and raised his voice to be heard in the kitchen. "That man visiting from Australia, what's his name?"

Dobbs entered with their tea, "That would be Liza's boy, Joseph Zelly." She sat down the pot and cups, and left.

"Yes. Joseph Zelly told me he came across Geran working in a stable that trained racehorses. I doubt Inch was a key man in some criminal organization. Also, it would be difficult for Sir Vincent to leave Chough, return here to kill his valet, and return to ride this morning, all without a car and without anyone noticing him."

Ferguson had a thought. Quietly he said, "Jory, the honest, helpful policeman would be perfectly placed to get paid to ignore the operation. And marry the baroness of Tredwen Manor." Geever looked surprised by this possibility. Ferguson looked around. Never had he stayed in the home of anyone connected to a crime. Keep the policemen close. Ferguson had been charmed by the friendliness of the whole village. He lowered his voice. "Maybe we are being sucked in by the helpful attitude. Maybe we are staying in this lovely house, so we can be watched." The three of them glanced at the swinging door into the kitchen. "We need to get this evidence on record now."

"Definitely." They packed up the evidence, and were about to say goodbye to Abby when Alan and Sukie entered, with omelets for them. Ferguson looked at Geever, who said, "Perhaps a couple of minutes for lunch?"

"Sure." The three sat at the table to eat hurriedly, when Jory came in with Lady Edra and joined them.

Alan refilled the tea pot and asked, "Would you like something to eat? Perhaps some tea?" Jory looked at Lady Edra, who nodded to Alan.

Jory said, "I've filled her in."

Ferguson stood to leave and looked at Jory. "From now on, we'll keep you apprised of pertinent developments concerning the murders." Everyone looked at Ferguson as if he lost his mind, including Geever, but he rose from his seat to join him.

Jory objected. "Pertinent developments? What are you on about? Wherry's murder is my jurisdiction."

Ferguson said, "Not if I say it belongs to Scotland Yard."

They stared at each other. Finally, red faced, Jory stood back. "Fine. I'll be in my office at the station." He turned and started to walk away. Lady Edra stared at Jory, confused. "Come on," he took her arm. "You can wait for your father up at the hall." Abby walked with them to the door.

Ferguson softened his pronouncement a little by adding, "I need to separate these two cases from anyone who could possibly be involved—even someone who might simply be a witness. Right now, I believe these two murders are not connected, unless we find evidence that Geran was part of some illegal activity, which brought him to Tredwen, and that it also involved Wherry—and possibly others," he added pointedly. They all stood by the front door staring at each other.

Chapter Fourteen

Before anyone could leave the dower, Hicca Stark burst through the front door with such force it slammed against the wall. He marched into the front hall, fists on his hips, chest out and glaring daggers at Doc Abby, the first person he saw. She asked tentatively, "Mr. Stark, can I help you? Do you wish to see me about something?"

"Don't need you woman!" He bellowed loud enough to be heard throughout the house. "Where's Sir Vinson? I will see him immediately!"

The three policemen stepped forward. "Can I help you, Mr. Stark?" Geever quietly asked.

"Where's the bastard. Is he here with you?"

"Sir Vinson's not here," Ferguson said.

"They told me up to the manor he might be here. Vinson Bandry. That bastard is not a true Bandry, you know. He merely took the right and ancient name for the prestige and money." His eyes moved over their heads toward the staircase, and left into the parlor, and right into the surgery, not concentrating on anyone, searching, moving. "He is a lowly cad. Always was." The others stood mute, amazed and unsure what Stark was raving about. "The Bandrys have always been as proud and honorable people as the Starks. Jacob Bandry, that girl Lady Edra's grandfather, was one of those honorable men. He's the one changed the entailments to allow his daughter and granddaughter to inherit the title and land because he believed Tredwen Manor, title and land should go to someone who grew up on this land, loved it—because they had Tredwen blood!"

Lady Edra stepped forward. "Mr. Stark, what is it? My father isn't yet back from Chough Hall. I'm sure he'll be glad to sort out the problem, whatever it is."

"I bloody well hope so, my lady." He spoke more gently to her. "They told me at the big house that Sir Vinson was not available, and I know he's around here somewhere."

Through the open door, they were surprised as a bright, dark green roadster pulled up, deep growling engine purring, and gleaming in the sunshine. Sir Vinson jumped out of the car before it quite stopped. He looked very upset. Once the car stopped, Geever's brother, Sir William, stepped out on the driver's side.

Stark strode out of the house followed by Ferguson and Geever.

"What's going on here, Mr. Stark?" Ferguson asked.

Ignoring him, Stark roared, "You bastard! Face me like a man." It surprised Sir Vinson and frightened him a little to be greeted in such a manner. He muttered questions and apologies.

"Mr. Stark," Lady Edra appealed to him calmly. "Let's sit down and talk about whatever it is you're here to discuss. Father, if you please?" She held out her arm toward the door suggesting they all go inside.

Sir Vinson straightened up and asked, "What on earth are you on about, Hicca?" He took a couple of steps back.

Hicca took a couple of steps toward him. "You been sneaking around with my wife when I'm not home, you bastard! That's not what a man, not a good man, would be doing."

"I assure you…" Sir Vinson looked shocked at the accusation.

"You have no right to be acting like you are lord of Tredwen Manor. You have been up to no good for years. But not with my Annie, you bastard. And I bet you killed that young man. You think you can do whatever you want without ever having to answer for whatever harm you do. It's time you paid." Stark pulled a pistol from his jacket and shot Sir Vinson in the stomach, before anyone could react.

"Father!"

Ferguson and Geever rushed the man. Ferguson grabbed the gun as Geever laid him on the ground. Stark lay face down in the gravel. "Did I kill him?"

Sir Vinson, bleeding profusely, stumbled into the front hall and fell. Lady Edra dropped beside him, and they heard a low moan. Abby knelt and tore open his shirt, then stood. "I'll get my bag." Ferguson grabbed her arm and looked at her pointedly. She understood he wanted to know if the shot was fatal. She shook her head and whispered, "It doesn't look fatal," then she ran to her surgery.

Ferguson knelt beside Sir Vinson and pulled his bloodied shirt open further. "A gut shot. Couldn't be worse." He shook his head sympathetically. "I'm sorry, Sir Vinson. Nothing can be done. You'll bleed out in minutes. I've seen it before. Everyone, stand back. This is your last chance to clear your conscience. In your last minutes, tell me the truth. Did you kill Geran Inch?"

Sir Vinson looked from the policeman to his daughter and a tear fell. He shook his head and whispered, "I did not murder him." His voice sounded thin and raspy. "I saw a man in a ditch. I nearly stopped to see if I could help him, I spotted that medallion laying on his chest, then I recognized the wretch. He was quite dead. I saw no one. I hated that man. I remounted and had Asif trample him. My poor Asif did not like that at all." He showed more sympathy for the horse than the man. "I rode on home. I can't help you Ferguson. I don't know who killed him." The man coughed, winced in pain.

Ferguson said, "Last chance, Sir Vinson. You don't have long to clear your soul. That Christmas, years ago. did you kill Jenna and your grandson?"

"Of course not."

The terrible moan they experienced before, began again as a whine, and quickly became a howl, sounding as if the rafters might rip apart. It filled the hallway with a thick, dark lament, full of anger and hatred.

Ferguson couldn't believe his luck. If this house settles any more it will fall in on us. But he would use it. Ferguson shouted over the noise. "There is a terrible, vengeful ghost that haunts this place, Sir Vinson, and it thinks you did kill them."

A mask of terror froze Sir Vinson's face, as he stared up the stairway gaping at some horror, only visible to himself. The house quieted as instantly as it had started.

A sharp intake of breath from Sir Vincent, then he became very calm, resigned. "I did," he said. "I killed him. That child had polluted blood, son of a goddammed gypsy. I had to. He could never become lord of Tredwen. Never!" Lady Edra drew back in horror, shaking her head in disbelief. "I planned the Christmas holiday carefully, so no one would be around. I hadn't worked out the details. I thought I would grab the boy while the maid slept and he would just disappear. She saw me so I sent her to check on her mother." He imagined the scene as he spoke. "I tried to separate her from the bastard child of Geran Inch. I couldn't get him to be quiet so I smashed the lad's head against that little copper bathtub. You can see I had to do that? When she came back, unfortunately she had to die too." As God is my witness, I would have killed that bedeviled child of hers, Keyan, except she took him with her, and left him with her mother. She returned to her own death." He paused a moment. "I strangled her. I planned to bury both damned gypsies under the Tredwen oak quickly." His voice shook. "No one saw any of this. Not a soul stirred. It was quite early Christmas morning. I didn't have much time. Mary Inch would show up soon to find out why Keyan had been left with her at the shop." He coughed again. His voice seemed weaker. "But digging was terribly difficult. The ground was nearly frozen, so I stuck the boy in and covered him up. I had to drag her all the way to the cliff's edge and dump her over. I figured she would take the blame. The plan worked so beautifully." His voice quickened, as if he needed to get it all out before he died. "Yes, I paid Geran handsomely to abandon Edra. It took little to persuade him. He jumped at the cash and the freedom. And yes, he periodically blackmailed me for more, to stay gone. Worth every penny."

Lady Edra could not believe it. She dropped to her knees and one heartbreaking moan escaped her lips, small and quiet. Her voice, barely above a whisper, she asked, "My beautiful Caden?" She shook her head in disbelief. Her voice grew stronger as she became disgusted. "You murdered two people, Father? Jenna and Caden—because they embarrassed you?" Tears poured from her eyes. She shook with anger, her fists balled up. She became quiet again. "You knew all this time how to contact Geran? I could have been married to Jory long ago."

Sir Vinson said, "What if Geran Inch chose to return and claim what he should never have had a claim on? You and Tredwen. He needed to remain gone." That sickened her and she stood up and stepped back from him. Jory put his arm around her.

The glass transom over the front door exploded suddenly with a deafening crash that hurled down shimmering red, green and blue shards. Everyone scrambled away, shocked, as colored shards of many sizes furiously shot through Sir Vinson's clothing, repeatedly lancing his body. One large, deep blue shard pierced his neck. Blood flowed out, killing him. They stood stunned and speechless by the spectacle. Taking their eyes from the bleeding body, and brushing tiny bits of multicolored, broken glass from their clothes, they discovered no one else had even been nicked by the glass. Lady Edra bent as if to touch him, but her hand became a fist and she stopped before touching him. She stood up again, looking blankly at Jory.

Without warning, a raging gust thundered down the stairway, with such force the doors and windows shook. Pictures on the walls rattled, and it blew hair and clothes, as it drove over and through them out the front door, leaving a surprising quiet. A lightness wound through with palpable peace settled over the scene, overshadowing the tragedy. As they looked around, the rooms, the entire house appeared brighter, as if sunshine shone directly into the house. Abby knew the truth of it. She could feel it. "The haunting is over. Jenna is finally at peace."

Outside, Geever, Sir William and Stark stood, mesmerized, while the drama inside unfolded. Geever still held Stark's arm. "Hicca Stark," he began hesitantly and cleared his throat. "I'm arresting you for the murder," he looked back at the body, "or the attempted murder of Sir Vinson Bandry." Geever's brother stood frozen exactly as he had been when the astonishing scene started. Sir William eyed his little brother—impressed.

Anne Stark rode up to them and slid off her horse screaming, "God, no! You haven't shot him, have you?" She ran to her husband.

"I killed the bastard, Annie. What did you think? You let that man touch you."

"You idiot! You fool! Of course, I never let him touch me. I swore that, and you know I never lie to you."

Ferguson came outside, still dazed from Sir Vinson's death, while Anne continued. "I told you! If only you would listen. You were in Truro for the night on business last Sunday night. The wind howled and it poured rain. I looked out at the storm, and Sir Vinson and his horse were standing just under the eaves of the barn, out of the rain. I yelled for him to come inside until it stopped. I made some tea, and we chatted until the rain quit. He was a polite, perfect gentleman. I told you nothing at all happened. Hicca, you've destroyed our lives. You fool, you murdered a man!"

Doc Abby heard them and stepped outside. "Hicca Stark didn't murder Sir Vinson. He probably would have recovered from his wound. The bullet passed through his side. He died when the transom glass sliced his carotid artery." She wanted to make sure they knew Stark needn't hang for the death. She went back inside, stepping past the body and the blood, crunching through the broken glass under her feet. She glanced at Jory holding tightly to Edra, while she continued to sob. The blood from her father's body nearly touched Edra's feet. Abby knew she would need her help through all this trauma. For now, the whole thing seemed surreal. She stepped away into her surgery to clear her head. She took a deep breath, then washed the blood off her hands in her new sink, with her newly acquired running water.

The servants stood at the back of the hallway near the kitchen door, drawn by the commotion. Dobbs sent Sukie upstairs for a sheet, and they covered the man's body.

Geever led Stark toward the police car and informed Ferguson, "I'll put him in the cell, and call Pengilley from the station to pick up another body." Ferguson nodded.

Geever's brother, Sir William, stepped forward and asked politely, "Could I give you a ride? They might need the police car for something else." Geever looked unsure. Sir William shrugged, as if to say, whatever you decide. Geever chose to go with his brother. They squeezed the silent Stark between them and roared off in William's runabout.

Back inside, Ferguson spoke to Jory, "Get Lady Edra out of here." Jory nodded and led her back to the manor. Ferguson turned to Alan. "Find Marrak. The two of you need to patch the hole in the transom, Alan. Do that now. Then, get shovels. We'll need them shortly." Alan rushed out, carefully avoiding the pooling blood.

Abby leaned against the doorway into her surgery, arms crossed. "Should I measure wound sizes or anything before Pengilley moves the body?"

"I don't think so," Ferguson answered. "You are willing to testify that the gunshot wound would not have been fatal?"

"I am. It went through his side. It didn't hit anything vital."

He nodded. "You're sure his carotid artery being sliced is the cause of death?"

"Absolutely. The rapid exsanguination and rapid death make it obvious."

"Would you go with Pengilley and verify all this—or I could give you a ride to the station now."

She shook her head. "I'll be fine. I'll go with Pengilley. You go." He gazed around the rooms. It knew it to be an allusion, of course, but it did seem to be a different place. Same house, only brighter, and for some reason, it seemed more in focus.

Dobbs and Sukie stared at Ferguson. "Once the body—once Sir Vinson is taken away, please see that this is cleaned up."

"Absolutely, sir," Dobbs said.

Anne Stark stood holding the reins of her horse, right outside the front door. Ferguson couldn't deal with her right now. He needed to deal with Stark. "Go home Mrs. Stark." He left in the police car, watching her stand, as if turned to stone, in the rearview mirror.

Hicca Stark sat on the cot in the cell, straight as the proud, honorable man he was—the proud, honorable attempted murderer that he was. Ferguson shook his head. Stark waited quietly for whatever would happen next. Geever stood, arms crossed, looking into the cell. His brother, Sir William, stood quietly by the door to the station, watching. Geever looked from Stark to Ferguson, and gave him a look as if to say "can you believe this?" Ferguson nodded his agreement that seeing Hicca Stark in a jail cell seemed difficult to believe. Without turning his head, he said, "Sir William, I need you to leave the station while we do our job. I'd appreciate it if you gave Anne Stark a ride home." He stopped, then added, "Perhaps get her a cup of tea. She's in shock." At first Sir William looked surprised to be spoken to in such a manner, then answered, "Of course. Of course. I'll see to it," and he left just as Constable Sam entered.

"I've talked to everyone who lives close to the train station. No one saw or heard anything."

"That's fine, Sam. We'll deal with that later. Right now, I need to know if you can write up a charge of attempted murder for Hicca Stark?" The questioning look from the constable convinced Ferguson that 'no' was his answer. "I'll ask Inspector Geever to do that." Geever nodded and moved to find the paperwork. Ferguson noticed the wallet and riding pants sitting beside the medallion and the handkerchief on the constable's desk. "Sam, take notes about everything that happened this morning. Every bit of what you did, and who you spoke to, while it is all very fresh in your mind. Then list everything we brought in that's on your desk. Mark it as evidence and lock it up, please." Sam sorted a charge sheet for Geever, and took out his own notebook to record the crime scene, including with Wherry's body and the Bentley. Ferguson went into Jory's office.

He slumped into Jory's chair behind the desk. The murder from seven years ago had apparently been solved. The astonishing confession seemed real enough. He believed Sir Vinson when he said he didn't kill Geran Inch. But he wasn't any closer to whoever had killed him—the job he had been sent to solve, or Howel Wherry's murder. He thought about what to tell his boss. Alistair Howell would not be sitting at his desk in Scotland Yard on Sunday morning. He could send a telegram. What could it possibly say?

ANOTHER MURDER THIS MORNING—STOP CLUELESS AS TO MOTIVE OR SUSPECTS—STOP LAST SUNDAY'S MURDER—STILL CLUELESS—STOP ATTEMPTED MURDER THIS MORNING—STOP CULPRIT BRAVELY APPREHENDED IMMEDIATELY—STOP.

Ferguson thought it rather lucky that he had no idea where Howell lived, so he couldn't possibly send a telegram. He sighed. I think I'll wait until tomorrow morning to disappoint him. I can't abandon last Sunday's vicious murder to work on this Sunday's vicious murder.

Jory walked into his office interrupting Ferguson's ruminating and sat in the chair facing Ferguson and waited for him to speak.

"Jory, I need to ask you some questions. Yesterday, did you and Lady Edra visit a doctor by chance?" He studied Jory's face, as he answered.

"How did you know? We needed the doctor to confirm our baby was fine. From her accident last Sunday, she's had…some issues."

"And you feared Abby might not be comfortable with Lady Edra being pregnant?"

"Edra thought she might lose respect for her. So, we went to a stranger in Truro. Everything's fine. How did you know?"

"Probably the rushed wedding in three weeks made me think. You certainly wasted no time, once you found out about Geran's death."

"We had posted all the paperwork to have him declared dead weeks ago. It's officially seven years since the bastard's been gone. Ferguson, I truly love Edra. It has nothing to do with her title or her money. I've loved her since before she even met Geran. I'm the luckiest man in the world."

"And would you do anything in the world for her?"

"Not that. I wouldn't murder anyone. He could have shown up here. I would have gotten him to give her a divorce, whether he chose to or not— somehow. Look, Ferguson, we waited all this time for our love to be proper, to be legal. I didn't hunt him down. I guess I can't prove it to you. I wouldn't murder anyone." He stared at Ferguson, hopefully.

"I'm going to have to look into your claims, your doctor in Truro, and your bank account, et cetera." He slowly let out his breath, exasperated. "Right now, Penrose is my prime suspect in Geran's murder. I need to try and rattle him, and get him to make a mistake. He has quite a temper. His wife is one of Inch's many conquests. Maybe we can upset him enough to get him to blurt out something he shouldn't."

"And Penrose has a dark-haired son," Jory finished, "who looks more like an Inch than a Penrose."

"Exactly. A boy who he regularly beats, according to Abby. I don't think he'll cop to the murder, but I'd like to bring in his anxious little wife. She won't say anything with him hovering and threatening her. I'd like to pressure her. Bring her to the station, put her in the cell, and try to scare her, and get her to expose him some way." Ferguson had stopped being accusatory, and chose to treat Jory as a colleague, because he still couldn't see Jory as a devious murderer.

Jory looked irritated. "Are you sure you can trust me not to tell my criminal mob?" Ferguson's expression didn't change; he merely shrugged. Jory shook his head. "Okay, once Stark is charged, I'll let him go home. He's not going to run."

Ferguson knew Hicca Stark to be a man who would stand and hold fast to his beliefs, even if it meant the rope. "I agree."

Geever stepped into the office. "I charged Hicca Stark formally with attempted murder. Ferguson, did you get hold of anyone at the Yard and give them an update?"

Ferguson mumbled, "No one around. We'll report tomorrow—early. We need Stark released and taken home. We need the cell. Geever, I need you and Sam to drive him home. We certainly could use an extra vehicle. Wait, does Stark have a phone at home, with all his businesses?"

"Yes, he does,"

"Sam call the Stark house. Geever, your brother probably has Mrs. Stark home by now. Tell him we need his help. We need to use his car."

Jory said, "I spotted him driving her very slowly, with her horse tied on behind the car. They're there by now"

Ferguson said, "Good. If he agrees to let us use his car, that frees us to use the police car for the rest of the plan."

Jory stepped out and told Sam to call Stark's house and what to ask.

"Jory, I think it best if you bring her in, possibly handcuffed—or would it scare Penrose more if Geever, the Scotland Yard man, does that?"

Jory said, "He sees me as the law. I think I ought to do that."

"Good," Ferguson nodded. "While we question her, Geever and Sam will go and search Penrose's house, his outbuildings, everywhere, for the spade or anything remotely suspicious."

Geever said, "He'd be a fool to have kept the bloody spade without carefully washing away any evidence."

"Probably. He won't want you looking around his domain anyway. He won't want us questioning his wife, and this will be one more way to rile him. After we question her, we release her, and imply she told us everything. Maybe she'll drop some bit we can use to get him to talk. Are they still harvesting? I saw truckloads of grain being hauled yesterday. Were men harvesting his fields?"

Jory said, "Don't know who yesterday's grain belongs to, but doesn't it seem strange Penrose chose a fishing weekend with the kids, when he was desperate to harvest while the weather held?"

"That's primarily why he's my top suspect," Ferguson answered.

"Sir William agreed," Sam announced. "He's on his way."

When Sir William came in minutes later, he looked excited to be included. He escorted the still silent Stark to his car and roared off.

Jory took the police car to Penroses' and he and Sam and Geever piled out. Jory knocked on the door with Sam and Geever standing behind him. When he answered, Jory said, "Penrose, I brought Constable Colley and DI Geever here to search your property for evidence of the murder of Geran Inch last Sunday night. While they do that, I need to take Eva to the station and ask her some questions. She'll be back shortly." Jory pulled his handcuffs ready to force the issue. Penrose stood, stunned and anxious, but he knew it would happen whatever he did, so he kept his head down, and gave in without arguing.

He nodded saying, "You don't need the handcuffs. Eva, don't worry. You don't need to tell them anything."

Eva, eyes wide, stood shaking. Her mouth opened and shut silently, then she cried, "Arthur!" She stepped next to him and grabbed his sleeve.

Penrose said in a quiet voice, "Listen, Eva. It'll be fine. Don't worry." He pushed her hand away and nodded to Jory, with a look of pure fury on his face. Jory walked her out and placed her in the car, knowing Penrose watched every step.

Ferguson waited in Jory's office until he returned, and sat Eva in the chair opposite. Ferguson said, "You, Eva Penrose, are being questioned in connection with Geran Inch's murder. We have reason to believe you have knowledge of who killed Geran Inch." Jory leaned against the wall as Ferguson spoke, waiting to see her reaction.

"I don't know anything," she whined, barely above a whisper.

"You certainly knew Geran quite well before he disappeared, didn't you?"

She said nothing but squirmed in her chair.

"Eva, Tommy is Geran's son, isn't he? Everybody can see that. Your husband certainly knows that the lad isn't his? That's why he hits Tommy, isn't it?"

"Tommy is careless and clumsy. He needs discipline." She shook her head.

Once Jory left with Eva, Geever and Sam entered the Penrose house. "Good afternoon, Mr. Penrose. We have reason to believe that you might have evidence on your property of a grievous crime."

Penrose stood up and came near them. "Such rot! Get off my property. Now!"

"I'm afraid that we will not be leaving. The law allows us to search everywhere on this property. Please, step aside." Penrose stood belligerently, legs wide, arms crossed.

"Constable, please arrest Mr. Penrose, and handcuff him." Sam grinned slightly and stepped up. "Yes, sir."

After another moment of bristling, Penrose screamed, "This beggers belief!" Shaking his head, he moved out of their way.

Geever marveled. Penrose complied with his order. It worked. Geever quite liked this. "Upstairs to the bedrooms first, Officer Colley." The two men started rifling through drawers, turning mattresses and probing for hidden recesses. They searched the ground floor with the same cursory job. "Now we'll search the various barns for a spade."

"A spade?" Penrose cried. "Of course we have spades…"

"We're looking for one with blood on it."

"What? Anyone would have to be crazy to stash the spade that killed Inch, with his blood still on it."

"Exactly," and the two policemen marched toward the barns.

Sir William spotted them while driving back from the Starks, and stopped on the road. Geever walked to the car. "Why don't you park in front of the dower? They might need the use of your car again, but they don't want you in the station. If you don't mind." Sir William readily agreed and roared off, as Geever rejoined Sam to pretend to search for the murder weapon.

"Eva, I'm going to have to put you in the cell. I know you're lying. I need you to tell me the truth. Now!"

She started shaking now and glanced up at Ferguson. He could see fear beginning around her eyes. "My husband didn't hurt Tommy. He didn't hurt anyone," she said in her whiny voice, shaking her head.

"Come with me." He came around the desk, took her by the arm, stood her up and marched her out of the office. Jory stayed quiet, and moved out of the way, following.

Ferguson hoped Geever was having luck bullying Penrose. They probably had less than an hour to be able to hold her without a shred of evidence. He would badger and goad her, as she sat forlornly in the cell. He hoped she would get upset enough to give him something. They had absolutely no legal reason to hold her. If this doesn't work, and they don't miraculously find a bloody spade, we haven't gotten anywhere.

Eva stopped so suddenly as he marched her to the cell that he nearly bumped into her. He saw why. The constable hadn't had time to catalogue their pathetic trove of evidence, and it still lay on his desk. Eva stared at it.

"Geran's wallet." Her voice had become dreamy, and she looked off in the distance. "It can't be here. We buried it. We buried it!" Her voice rose. "He told me no one would ever find it. It can't be here. It's some kind of trick." She turned on Ferguson. Her eyes. She was far away. He didn't know whether he should touch her or not. She was obviously in a state, but he knew nothing of how to deal with this. Her eyes changed and focused on his face. Suddenly she lunged at him, trying to scratch his face, screeching, "You! This is a trick!"

He ducked out of the way and held her arms. "Into the cell, Eva!" Ferguson practically yelled. She started twisting and squirming. He had to hold her tight, until he locked her in. He didn't want to break the spell. He grabbed the blood-stained wallet off the desk and held it up. "Where did you get this? We found it. You and Wherry buried it." Had she been the second person Keyan saw burying it? "Why would you do that? Whose blood is this? Is it Geran Inch's blood? Did you help your husband kill him? Did you help Wherry kill him? Or did you only help to hide their crime?"

She returned to cowering, shaking her head, eyes down, mumbling. Abruptly, she stood and came near the bars. The last step, she charged forward, thrusting her arms through the bars, attempting again to scratch his face, screaming, "You know nothing!" He stepped back. She kept shouting, her face red with fury, tears streaming down her face. "Men!" she shrieked. "They hurt you! They lie!" She kicked at the bars with her shoe. "Howel wanted what they all want. He lied too. He said he would take me away from Arthur, away from it all. I thought he understood. I couldn't take any more from Arthur. Always needing." Her voice became guttural, disgusted. "And those wicked children. I have to discipline them all the time. Especially Tommy. He was born wicked. He never should have been. Neither of them mind me at all. They do whatever they want. They whisper and laugh. Always there. Always needing. They are sucking the very life from me." She seemed unaware of what she was telling them. Ferguson glanced at Jory, who looked as astonished as him.

Ferguson nodded to her, encouraging her to continue, and asked. "Wherry, Howel Wherry, promised to take you away from all the needing? Is that right?"

She nodded forcefully, then craned her head, not really focusing on anything.

"He lied to you, didn't he? Just like Arthur." He decided to add, "Just like Geran did all those years ago."

"Geran abandoned me." It sounded like she just remembered that. "I told Geran about the pregnancy. He didn't care. He married Lady Edra. My father forced me to marry Arthur Penrose." She practically spit out his name. "To give a name to Geran's bastard son and protect my virtue." That came out with a snort.

Ferguson glanced at Jory before saying to her, "When you saw that horrible man, Geran, come walking back that night, you had to do something."

"Exactly. I recognized him walking down the road just past Menadue Woods. The rain poured and the wind howled as if his evil caused it. My whole life came rushing past. He had destroyed me. He smiled." She looked at each policeman. "He actually smiled at me. I stood at the edge of our drive with a spade cleaning off some of the grain spillage from the trucks, bringing load after load all day. A spade was the only shovel left for me. The men harvesting were using all the other shovels. I didn't think about it. He came right up to me with that nasty little grin—smirking. Laughing! At! Me! I bashed him. I didn't even realize it. Over and over. Once I knew, I grabbed his wallet so nobody would know he came back."

She stopped abruptly. The hatred became fear. "Don't tell Arthur. He would start yelling at me. I never do anything right. He wants the kids to be good, and he yells at me if they aren't. Tommy is way too much like his real father. I try to beat it out of him. He's still a terror. Arthur tells me I must stop. But really, Tommy is evil. The evil is what must stop."

Ferguson wondered if he could possibly be hearing this correctly? "You…you are the one who hurts the lad? You are the one who needs Doc Abby to fix Tommy up?"

She nodded. "I have to be strict, or he won't listen. He is bad. I can't get it out of him."

She looked from Ferguson to Jory. "You must understand now why I left with Howel. It was all too much. We were to drive off and never come back. He would save me. It would be all right. We were taking the car, the beautiful Tredwen Bentley. Howel and I hid the bloody pants, so Sir Vinson couldn't stop us. Howel said he'd tell the coppers what Sir Vinson did if he tried to stop us. I sure didn't tell him it wasn't Sir Vinson killed him. I dropped the wallet in as we wrapped the pants. Then he said to me, 'we need to take the kids'. Just like that. He's no different from all of you. He would force me to have them two still hanging on me, needing me. He lied. I said no. I shouted it. NO! I tried to force him to go. He wouldn't budge unless I brought my kids. I had worked it out, so they were with Arthur, and we could escape. Just the two of us." Her voice became a sing song mockery. "He said, 'You're their mother. I never had a mum. They need you. They need to be away from their abusive father. We have to take them.'"

She looked from Ferguson to Jory, pleading. "You must understand, don't you? He lied. He wouldn't go without them. We would have to go grab them from Arthur at the fishing camp. I saw the lie now. I would still be stuck with evil children. I had to stop him. He wouldn't stop talking about how happy we'd all be together. I had a knife in my pocket from working in the garden. I took it out, and he just kept saying we had to take them.

He tried to grab me and take my knife, but I made him quit talking." Her voice seemed rational now. "Finally, he got quiet. I had to push him over, so I could hide the car behind the train station. I hid it so it would take time before you found it. I never drove a car before. It was hard to park. I moved Howel's body back into the driver's seat. She envisioned the scene as she told them about it. "I walked home. Arthur wasn't there. No one was. I burned my clothes in the fireplace, just like after Geran. I took a bath, and washed my hair, and fell asleep in my bed. I got up right before you lot brought Arthur home. You must understand why those men had to die, don't you?" She looked at Ferguson and then at Jory. She shrugged when neither man answered. She sat down on the cot quietly, and seemed rather satisfied, now that she had explained everything.

Both men were speechless for a moment. Then Jory stepped in front of her and said, "Eva Penrose, I'm charging you with the murders of Geran Inch and Howel Wherry." He stopped and looked at Ferguson puzzled, and asked him, "We did just solve both murders, didn't we?"

As amazed as Jory, Ferguson nodded his head. "Absolutely, if we believe everything she said." He looked at Eva, who curled up on the cot with her back to them. "Her story seems to match what we know to be fact."

Jory asked, "Could she be protecting Penrose and taking the blame?"

"I'll go talk to him now." Neither spoke for a moment and they simply stared at her back.

Ferguson drove to the farm, while Jory stayed with Eva. Ferguson parked next to a horse-drawn wagon, with camping gear and fishing poles in the back. He assumed Crocker had returned with the children. Ferguson got out and breathed in the clean cool air. He needed a few minutes. This day just kept spiraling. Dark clouds were building overhead. He took a couple of deep breaths before approaching the house. Sam stood nearest the door and opened it. Ferguson told him, "You can walk to the station, Constable." Sam could tell that now was not the time to ask questions, and left Ferguson standing at the threshold. Inside he found happy chatter and laughter. Crocker and the children were regaling Penrose with tales of the fishing trip. Penrose sat stone-faced, staring past them at Ferguson, while the others talked around him.

The little girl asked, "Where's Mummy? I want to show her what I found." She held out a round rock. Crocker noticed Ferguson standing there and stopped talking. Geever turned and went to meet him. Without speaking, Ferguson motioned Penrose and Geever to follow him onto the porch. Only bird song could be heard far off. Black clouds raced to obscure the sun. The cool air smelled like rain. Penrose met Ferguson's eyes and he knew something serious had happened.

Ferguson said, "Eva has admitted to murdering Geran as he came to Woodcomb last Sunday." Geever looked surprised. Penrose sat down on the step dazed, and placed both hands on top of his head. "Did you know that, Penrose?" Ferguson asked him.

He shook his head. "No. What makes you sure she's not making it up? She's hated him for all these years. Maybe she wishes she killed him?" He asked hopefully.

"She described how she had a spade when she saw him. She described taking his wallet, hoping he remained unidentified. Unless she was burying it, so no one would find out you killed him. We know she helped Wherry bury the wallet last night. They buried it before they stole Sir Vinson's car, to run away together."

When that registered, Penrose crumpled, holding his hands together in front of his face shaking his head. He jumped up, "What are you talking about? She didn't run away. She was here, in the house, when you let me out this morning."

"She was leaving you. Running away with Howel Wherry. She wanted to be free of you. Mostly she wanted free of the children."

Penrose looked incredulous. "Wherry? The valet? She hardly knew the man." He admitted, "The children. She was abandoning Tommy and Claire? They do make her very nervous. Sometimes she explodes and…hits them. Especially Tommy. She imagines everyone in this village knows he really came from Geran. Tommy disgusts her. She believed I must hate raising another man's son. But he's not. He's not another man's son. He's my son. I try to make him see that. Even if I could never make her believe it."

"According to her, she and Wherry were stealing the Bentley and disappearing forever. Except Wherry decided she would eventually miss her kids, and he tried to convince her they needed to take them. She flew into a rage and killed him, before she realized what she was doing. Apparently, she walked home last night to wait for your return."

Penrose sobbed. "What do you mean, she killed him? What happened to him?"

"We found Wherry's body this morning. She described how she stabbed him and tried to hide the car, but she really couldn't drive it. I believe her. She described both murders exactly as our evidence suggests. Unless you know otherwise."

Penrose said, "What a goddamned mess. Lately she's been getting more out of control. Her rages. She scares Claire and Tommy. They hide from her. She terrifies me, but I thought I could keep everything under control." Penrose stared out toward the granary and the other out buildings, without really seeing anything. The tranquil, orderly farm spread in front of them, in contrast to the hidden chaos in the house. "What happens now, Inspector?"

"She'll be tried for the murders."

"She'll hang for them?" Penrose became very agitated, his voice broke, and his eyes filled with tears.

"I doubt that will happen. I think she'll be put into mental care."

"An asylum? God, how awful!"

"There's always hope she might recover," Geever said.

Penrose just nodded, unbelieving.

"Can I see her now?"

"Not now. Later." Ferguson thought about saying he was sorry how everything turned out, but didn't. They drove off, leaving Penrose still sitting on his porch, staring at nothing. Neither spoke until they reached the Tredwen columns, and Ferguson asked Geever to stop the car. "Tell Jory to charge Eva and deal with that. We have more to do. If Sir Vinson told the truth, we need to dig around the oak. See if there truly is a body." Geever nodded, letting Ferguson out to walk up to the manor, and returned to the police station.

The Tinks pulled in ahead of Ferguson, back from the weekend at Chough Hall. Mitch drove the truck. Kitto rode Asif, who pranced around, as if he knew what a beauty he was. Ferguson realized the Tinks don't know all that's happened. Sir Vinson will never ride Asif again. His valet, Howel, has been murdered. The groundskeeper's wife has been arrested for murder. One of the most respected men in the county, Stark, has been arrested for attempted murder. They still believe that all is as it always has been. At least for a little while longer. Ferguson continued to watch, until they stopped at the stables.

Turning back to the dower, Ferguson saw that a board had been nailed to the transom over the door, very clumsily. It would do for now. Inside he called, "Alan, did you and Marrak round up a couple of shovels?"

Alan and Marrak came from the kitchen. "Yes, sir." They held two shovels. Ferguson glanced into the surgery and didn't see Abby. Alan said, "She went to the manor to stay with Lady Edra." Ferguson nodded, very glad Lady Edra wouldn't see what they were doing. The three men walked up the drive, onto the manicured lawns, and up to the huge oak tree. "Alan, did you hear what Sir Vinson said? Do you know what…"

"Yes sir, I heard. Best Lady Edra and Doc Abby aren't here."

"So, now we dig. Probably not very deep. We'll try several places."

Dobbs and Sukie stood next to Sir William beside his car and watched from the front step of the dower. Lady Edra sat in the conservatory with her grandmother, mostly silent. Abby rose to look out at the oak. She had been thinking about what Sir Vinson claimed, and spotted Ferguson and the two servants begin to dig. If he had truly buried a little child, she knew it would be gruesome. If, Sir Vinson had been telling the truth. Lady Edra must have had the same thought because she stepped up behind her. Doc Abby faced Lady Edra, and placed her hands on her shoulders, and said, "We need to wait here. If it's true, you don't…"

"Absolutely not! I will not wait in here. Could my own father be this depraved?" She marched to the oak. Abby followed and looked at Ferguson, shaking her head, as if to say I couldn't stop her.

Geever drove up with Jory, who went to Lady Edra, and they spoke quietly. Geever joined the other men standing under the umbrella of the huge oak. Alan and Marrak dug through the leaves and grass, down nearly two feet. Each chose another spot and dug, while the tree gently showered them with its dying, blood-red leaves. Ferguson reached for one shovel and surprisingly Geever took the other. Lady Edra said, "We need more men and shovels. This is taking too…"

Keyan stepped up and pointed. "Dig here." Oscar and Blue started to sniff. "Back!" Keyan ordered. The dogs sat and whined. Ferguson noted that Keyan must have been given permission, so soon, to again roam wherever he chose. He dug where Keyan pointed. Ferguson stopped and turned, "Keyan, go home. We'll tell you whatever we find."

Keyan looked at Lady Edra and said, very quietly, "It'll be the boy. He'll be glad you found him." Keyan knew they wouldn't let him stay. He turned toward the stables to talk to the Tinks and greet Asif.

Once the lad left them, Ferguson looked at Lady Edra, who stood her ground. "Finish digging." Ferguson dug gingerly where Keyan had pointed. Very soon the shovel hit something. He brushed the dirt away and touched some pieces of dirty, rotting cloth. He picked one up and set it aside. Lady Edra picked it up and held it to her chest, expectantly. Ferguson gently pushed aside more dirt, and a skull materialized slowly. A very small skull. Lady Edra fell to her knees, and an animal, guttural howl tore from her throat that rose to a primal scream. The crows flew overhead, silently.

It started to rain.

Chapter 15

The Monday morning train sent a thick Cornwall fog swirling away as it sliced its way toward London. Ferguson and Geever silently sat side by side with their own thoughts. Alistair Howell, back at Scotland Yard, had been informed of their success and sounded properly delighted. No supernatural Green Man murdered by the horned Cernunnos riding a fiery horse from hell or whatever they called him in Cornwall.

Ferguson thought of all the strange happenings in the dower. Although he never figured out how they happened, and he had no qualms about using a man's fears to get Sir Vinson's confession, he knew nothing supernatural had been going on—because the supernatural doesn't exist. All things bad or good happen by what living people do. John thought of all that had happened in a week, and how many people had been touched. Eva Penrose and Hicca Stark arrested. And all the death: Sir Vinson, Howel Wherry, Geran Inch, even the old murders of little Caden and Jenna. Then there were the good people of Woodcomb. When any murder gets cleared up there's always good people left who have to somehow carry on. What will become of Arthur Penrose and his two children?

Lady Edra decided Mary Inch and Keyan would share the dower house with Abby, and Keyan would become Lady Edra's ward. How could he even think about Lady Edra. So much horror. Could she be happy getting married in three weeks and having another baby? She would need Doc Abby's help for some time.

Jory Moon's future looked dazzling. Ferguson knew, the new life he was stepping into made it easy for Jory to forgive him for considering him a murder suspect. He could picture Jory as a gentleman running the Tredwen estate. Or maybe he would become a gentleman policeman running Tredwen. Maybe. Maybe they would all be happy eventually.

Abby. John couldn't stop thinking about her and about last night. Abby had been very upset and had gone to her room. When he went to check on her, he quietly opened the door and found her weeping in the darkened bedroom. When she turned to him and said, "John, don't leave me here alone tonight. Stay. Please." He had laid down beside her to calm her, so overwhelmed, she was babbling. He lightly kissed her lips to quiet her which turned into a rather desperate passion that made them cling for some solace to each other. Later, they lay in each other's arms for awhile before he returned to his room. It felt as if they were the last two sane people left on earth. He found it nearly impossible to leave her this morning. He had never met anyone like her, and he wanted to be with her. The only bright spot in his leaving became her impending visit to London in four weeks for a conference at a hospital with a wing for children with mental problems. They had agreed to spend time together. He didn't know for sure how she felt, but he anticipated a torrid weekend.

Geever interrupted his musing. "Do you think Arthur Penrose will still be charged for assaulting Doc Abby?"

"Abby said she would be dropping the charges first thing this morning—if the charge actually got written up with all the other excitement." They both seemed to be wondering about Eva Penrose's future, but neither voiced an opinion.

"What do you think will happen to Hicca Stark?" Geever asked.

"Jory said he didn't believe much would happen. Stark is very well respected for his integrity, and he's the agent for many powerful men in Cornwall. Sir Vinson was not well respected. Jory thought it will be explained to a jury as merely an attempt to frighten the man and the old gun had misfired—something like that." Geever nodded and smiled. Ferguson also hoped that was truly what would happen.

Geever took a deep breath before saying, "This has been an eye-opening experience for me, Ferguson. I find I quite enjoy solving murders, and I'll be sure to mention to Howell what a help you were to me in solving these murders." He smiled slyly, watching for Ferguson's response out of the corner of his eye. Ferguson said nothing. His expression gave nothing away.

"Ferguson, of course, I'll tell them you, in fact, solved the whole thing."

Ferguson looked at him as if this surprised him a bit and added sarcastically, "That's good of you." He looked at the man he previously had always called Dickie and knew he had earned some respect. No more Dickie, but Richard didn't work for Ferguson either, so Geever it would be from now on. Ferguson relented his sarcastic remark and said, "You did help with the investigation. You could become a fine detective."

"Thank you. That means a lot to me. Of course, when we get back to Scotland Yard, I'll still be a toff, you understand, but perhaps I'll be less of a wanker, eh?"

Ferguson smiled broadly. "Yes, you're definitely less of a wanker. And you have the beginnings of a real detective, if you choose to be."

"Oh, I choose to be. And remember, Ferguson, it is always good to be the second son of an earl."

About the Author

Vicki Kinzie is an American novelist, an experienced traveler, an avid mystery reader, and history devotee and teacher of twenty years. Vicki puts her knowledge and passions together to take her readers on adventures through murder and mazes across ancient streets and times. She loves to travel and spent several summers sailing around northern Europe, including much of England with her husband. Vicki lives in Colorado with her husband and dogs.